First you cry, then you get mad

# SHELL GAME

## A BLACK CAT NOVEL

A.B. Funkhauser

Solstice Publishing - www.solsticepublishing.com

# Shell Game

## A.B. Funkhauser

*For all those seeking safe harbor*

# Foreword

I've always been a "cat person." Their aloof, self-sufficient nature matches my own, and I enjoy a good meow. As a child, I would spend hours spooning the family cat in some quiet corner of the house, whispering secrets and insecurities into his twitching ear, as if he were a best friend or a diary. Skin to fur, heart to heart. We had other pets, but it was the cat I sought out for this ritual: something in his jewel eyes told me he was really listening.

My mother once told me that on Christmas Eve the cats could speak. Though I never witnessed these conversations, I did not doubt their reality; the cats were capable of magic because they were *cats*. It seemed silly not to believe.

My belief was strengthened when I met Kobe. Even as I wrote these words, he appeared at the kitchen door, as if summoned by my thoughts of him. We started as roommates in a windowless basement apartment, where Kobe focused his energy on squeezing into holes in the drywall or escaping out the side door between the legs of the pizza man. Without a word, he was sending me a message: Let me go.

We moved Kobe into the suburbs, to my family home. There, his territory grew like the muscles beneath his fur, and he transformed from house cat to panther, watching over the sleeping streets and feasting on the season's rabbits. The neighbors quickly got to know him, and he needed no collar to bare his identity (mostly because there wasn't a collar he couldn't slip). A graceful, savvy creature with a mind as sharp as his claws and a love for human attention made him the talk of the neighborhood. Our own local celebrity, if you will.

Kobe met A.B. before I did, though her home is closer than our mailbox. A writer who, at the time, did not consider herself a cat lover, she fell hard for the feline (tall, dark, and handsome works for cats too). Kobe changed both of our lives, inspiring Funkhauser's writing, and gifting me a mentor and dear friend.

Kobe haunts our neighborhood like a friendly ghost, lingering long enough to be missed. He shows up when he is least expected, but most needed, providing comfort in the touch of his fur and a silence that says: Lay it all on me. At times Kobe is stingy with his affection, but he is just guarding his truth, keeping we humans guessing. We must remember that a cat's trust has to be earned, like a blue ribbon pinned on the wall.

*Shell Game* was born because of a cat. The muscular, onyx beast who is undeniably something more. He will keep you waiting longer than the guy who hasn't called, but love you for all of his nine lives. Kobe, or "Carlos the Wonder Cat," as you'll come to know him, is as unique and complex as any human character you'll read. He is the magic. He is our friend.

*Bri Volinz*
*June 27, 2017*
*Pickering, Ontario*
*Canada*

# Cast of Characters

### BRONAGH CALEY
A predator

### POONAM KHANZADA RAJPUT
A victim

### ZOLTAN KÁRPÁTY
A gardener

### MUMMYY JI
A pundit

### CARLOS THE WONDER CAT
A hero

### BILL CALEY
A philosopher

### RUDOLF FISCHER
A nemesis

### IRME FISCHER
A missing person

### ZOEY FISCHER
A cat lover

### GODDESS MOONBOW
A spiritual leader

### SILS BANKS
A feminist icon

JACK FREWER
A love interest

CAMPAIGN BOB
A fool

THE BEAUTIFUL BOY POLITICIAN
A magician

LECH BOBIENSKI
An advocate

GUS THE PILOT
A swinger

PILSON GÜDDERAMMERÜNG
A visionary

THE YOYO MAN / CONTROLLER
An allegorical figure

*The year 2016*
*In a liberal democracy*

# Chapter One
## On the Cusp of Hell

On September 6, 2016, a letter was received. In it were a set of instructions and a veiled threat. *"Dear Home Owner: It has come to our attention that residents have not been cleaning up after their pets. This is particularly true of Saffron Drive where cats have been roaming freely without proper banding and/or licensing."*

The homeowner frowned.

*"City bylaws are explicit. Failure to comply shall result in seizure and a fine of up to and including $5,000. All pets seized by the municipality shall be considered forfeit, property to be retained pending appeal or adoption by an appropriate third party."*

Bronagh Caley scowled. It was barely past sunrise, the morning air still carrying on it that vaporous layer of moisture from a cool night mixing with above average daytime highs. The missive in her hand wrinkled with the wet of it. Plain stock, Helvetica lettered and bearing the stamp of the nascent city's newly minted coat of arms, it was not franked, but hand delivered. Her tax dollars at work.

She crumpled the paper in disgust. The assessors would be out soon to see if they could raise the levy on her building renovation. Meantime, she could recycle the plain stock paper. What else could she do with it? She didn't own a goddamned cat.

"Good morning!" a voice called out across the shared lawn with its overgrown wheat grass and scrubby clover patches. Bronagh's neighbor Poonam Khanzada Rajput was up early.

"Good morning, neighbor," Bronagh replied, happy to have one friend on the street. "Looks like we're in for a nice day after all." She stuffed the paper into her pocket, making a mental note to place it in her blue box bin next to yesterday's newspaper.

Poonam, short, svelte and unbelievably gorgeous, read her thoughts with aquamarine green eyes. "They say he's going to win." She crossed her arms, a gesture that in one so fine and small appeared uncharacteristically aggressive. The 'he' she referred to was a fine young man of impressive stock, with wealth and family achievements dating back to the founding of the country. Rarely a day went by when his beautiful face and boyish head of hair didn't cover the front page of every newspaper. He had been anointed to succeed the current administration, which had bogged down in a morass of negativity and self defeat.

"It's what the polls say," Bronagh shrugged, her Limerick accent creeping out from under a consciousness not yet fully awakened owing to a lack of caffeine. "But the polls have been wildly wrong before, so I won't believe it until I see it."

Poonam nodded, though she seemed unconvinced.

What the Beautiful Boy Politician lacked in credentials, he made up for in lineage. A prince among mortals, his paternal grandfather was elected to lead the nation sometime after the First Nations had left, while the other, on his mom's side, commanded the high bench well into his nineties, incontinence taking him away before his diminishing faculties could.

Poonam shifted from slippered foot to slippered foot, her rapid eye movements betraying a great weight. "Your renovations almost done?"

There it was: a hardened segue into shaky territory.

Poonam's parents came over from Madhya Pradesh, India after the war with Pakistan in '65. Raised on PacMan, MuchMusic and Madonna videos, Poonie was progressive in her politics, but intransigent where home improvement was concerned. The dust coming off the concrete pour for the Caley's new basement, combined with the mounds of earth from the excavation that dappled the front garden, killed off a lot of the new grass growth both women had worked so hard to cultivate. The loss of green drove Poonie crazy.

Bronagh didn't blame her neighbor for hating the dirt piles. She hated them too. But what she really hated was the extra-large campaign sign erected on her neighbor's patch of earth just days after the first shovel hit the ground. For Bronagh Caley, politics was like religion—best left in the chapel where it cured among the policy wonks and crisis junkies who eked out poor livings writing about it. There was no place for grandstanding among the rank and file—certainly not here on the Caley/Khanzada Rajput shared front lawn. Poonie's sign called her out, demanding that she declare herself. The older woman would have none of it.

"Not yet," Bronagh muttered. "We've hit a snag, and that's going to delay us, no doubt."

The Free Range Party—Poonam's party—pushed hard for legal dope and higher taxes while placing a moratorium on public holiday celebrations and culturally sensitive Hallowe'en costumes. Free Ranger's opposed anything that made anyone feel 'bad,' including things offensive and dangerous, like wearing kimonos in October when one wasn't Japanese, or allowing kids to play baseball on the now grassed-over city diamonds where they might hurt themselves. There was a lot of support behind these prohibitions: community action groups pooh-poohed the wearing of costumes because they mocked the unsuspecting, while insurance companies condemned balling in any form because the exposure was simply too great.

Poonie batted her long eyelashes for several seconds, announcing very clearly her complicity in the plot to topple Bronagh's renovation dreams. A letter from the Department of City Works, also hand delivered to the Caley's front door, this time on August 10, bore the news like a bad omen. A cursory sidewalk inspection had been performed, confirming that Bronagh and her husband Bill had violated several ordinances despite all the paperwork done and dutifully filed well in advance of all deadlines. They had dug too deep and the water table was compromised. They weren't complying. If they didn't fall into line, they would be fined.

"That's too bad," Poonie sighed. "The dust must be driving you crazy." She took a pull on her oversized coffee mug. "My Uncle Jin had similar difficulties years ago when he tried to install a sauna in his basement. The carpet rotted and the mold crept out to the street."

Bronagh, fingering the crumpled paper in the right pocket of her chenille bathrobe, felt the heat rise through the follicles in her scalp.

"If only he had hired a proper contractor in the first place. You know? You should always hire a contractor. But I suppose it's different for you with your Bill being so handy and all. But you know the wiring, if it isn't done properly, can lead to smoke and then fire."

Poonie's effort at covering her tracks with vapid blather sort of worked, distracting Bronagh long enough to provoke a smile. But the facts were clear: someone had ratted them out to the city, and that someone had revealed herself over an oversized mug of coffee and a pair of fluffy slippers.

"Someone complained," Bronagh said, her attention veering off to something across the street on another neighbor's lawn. Under a pile of crayon colored leaves, something moved, something dark, sleek, and too clever to be caught up in the absurdities that plagued the humankind of Saffron Drive.

Bronagh watched the black cat zigzag across Zoltan the Gardener's lawn onto the street and across, cutting a precise path directly to *her*. She looked down at him. Ragged, innocent and falsely accused, he steeled her resolve.

"Someone has ratted us out," she said, fingering the crushed letter in her pocket. "And that is not right."

# Chapter Two
## The Cat From Cavan

The black cat, much maligned and adored throughout history, is little more than a tabby with a recessive gene. Put into the light, his stripes and spots appear only briefly before disappearing beneath a fine sheath of cinnamon. The effect, quite startling, is called 'rusting' by feline aficionados. For the untutored, it is an unqualified confirmation that black cats are slippery, conniving little shapeshifters that will snuff out sleeping infants and flatulent hounds if given half a chance.

Such was the mantle conferred upon Carlos the Wonder Cat. Even before he had a name, even before he was rescued by gentle Rudolf and Irme Fischer, this unassuming house cat was blighted by a label that threatened him daily.

Carlos' life began inauspiciously enough in cottage country, where kitties were allowed to free range without malice under the umbrella of relaxed bylaws and few, if any, animal control officers willing to make a career out of chasing them. At nearly fifty centimetres in length (head and body) with an additional thirty centimetres of tail, Carlos was an impressive beast with an all-black coat and chalcedony green eyes that evoked something almost mystical in those humans who exchanged glances with him. Perhaps it was his trusting nature that got him into trouble in the first place? He had a habit of wandering carefree up to the back doors of complete strangers seeking a pat and a snack in exchange for varmint control services.

Carlos' exploits were legendary. A killer of the first grade, he once wiped out in a single spring, three complete

Robin families that nested in the backyard of K.H. Banford and Sons, Contractors. That the Banfords were all He-Men and accomplished hunters accounted for the story gaining currency in the small town where the cat's life began. They thought the slaughter was funny.

From birdies, Carlos went through the usual mice and rats, even taking down a wayward mink—vicious beast—at great cost to his appearance. For his effort, he nearly lost an eye and earned a scar across his left cheek that, some said, only added to his mystique.

Men and women, boys and girls, took him in without worry of fleas or ticks. A beast so fine had to belong to someone with insect powder they reasoned, as they spoiled him with tummy rubs, fancy kibble and binge television sessions congenially provided by the latest streaming service.

The idyll, made spectacular for its many touching moments, could not last. Things changed when Carlos took down a little girl's bunny rabbit, a fat, domestic, over-fed thing, that left the cat to moan and groan and fart for three days until the fur and grease passed.

No one could say for sure if Carlos was the culprit as his direct whereabouts could not be confirmed by direct witness. But his run of the town, the fact that he managed to gain entry to so many homes, charming the occupants out of their goodies and their love, sent up red flag comments like: "I don't know a cat that behaves the way that cat does. He's feral and not...like a man."

Maybe the townspeople were right about him being more than just a common tabby cat with a recessive gene. Because as soon as the people made up their minds that Carlos had to be picked up, he disappeared from the town, leaving no trace other than a cotton tail and a ragged foot on the Reeve's front lawn.

His story was just beginning. After a weeklong journey that took him through fields and barns, a big box department store that left a back door open, and, finally, a brand new pre-fabricated bedroom community with six different types of mansions to choose from, Carlos met a girl outside Cavan.

Zoey was just passing through en route to her first semester in Early Childhood Ed at the community college. Kind hearted, she took the cat up immediately, wanting to save him from the hardships independence brings. When the cooped-up feline clawed through her drywall, trapping himself between the main room of her tiny bachelor and a two-piece bathroom no bigger than a broom closet, her grandparents, Rudolf and Irme Fischer, were dispatched, and the rest was history.

Bronagh Caley had never met the elderly couple prior to the hate letter from Animal Control, so it was with great hesitancy that she scooped up the cat at her feet in preparation for a long walk up the street.

"He's beautiful," Poonie chimed, her coffee cup now empty. "Is he yours?"

This comment, Bronagh thought, said a great deal about how clueless her politically challenged friend was. On a grand scale, she was dialectically bound to a public policy position that championed the latest bafflegab. And that was okay, a lot of people did that—even Bronagh, once upon a time. But in a microcosm, there should have been more to her: a random act of kindness every now and then, or a nod to a neighbor that involved more than an exchange of extemporaneous views about weather from the front porch. Poonie was unobservant in her own front yard, her immediate surroundings no more than window dressing to a life preoccupied with mush.

"No," Bronagh said, gripping the squirming beast tighter. "But I'll keep you posted on the reno when I have news to tell."

She did not look back as she walked down her front steps, now cracked from the jackhammer Bill used to break up the concrete in the too deep basement. Irrespective of the fact that she was still in her bathrobe and Zoltan the Gardener was staring queerly at her from behind his one-ton pickup truck, she convinced herself that what she was about to do was the right thing.

The Fischer house at the end of the street needed a good coat of paint despite the owner's efforts to conceal the wear and tear with brightly colored faerie lights that sparkled year-round after dark. "Perhaps it's a German thing?" Bill, her husband of twenty-two years, commented whenever she complained about the brownish evergreen and saggy birch that added nothing to the fake jollity of the place. "They don't go out much. I don't think they're well."

The cat, twisting in her arms, seemed to confirm what they had suspected, and at once she felt protective. "What is your name, my beauty, and why aren't you wearing a collar?"

On closer observation, the two-storey brick and parge home showed all the marks of tremendous age: creeping vines, canting fences, a rusting roadside mailbox. Yet it was the same age as Bronagh Caley's home. Crossing the threshold on to the front yard, she nearly tripped as the collarless cat broke free of her grasp, making a beeline to the front door where he sat stock still, full of expectations. From his stance, there could be no doubt: This was his home.

Bronagh reached for what she thought was the doorbell, her fancy Italian monochrome bifocals absent and of no use to her on the nightstand where she had left them. Instead, her hand grazed something dry, wrinkled and plant-like; a token to ward off evil spirits, perhaps?

Before she could knock, the door opened and an elderly man no more than five-foot three inches in height greeted her with a very foreign "Guten Morgen."

Bronagh recoiled, not because the man was offensive looking in any major way, but because he advanced toward her as if to shoo her off. "I beg your pardon," she said, suddenly feeling like the intrusive kind of busy body she despised, "but I think this is yours." She pointed to the cat.

The old man looked down at the animal which had assumed a position between them.

"Ja," he replied, clearly unaware that he was going on in a foreign language.

Bronagh cleared her throat, already regretting the long walk over. Her mind, still sludgy for lack of coffee, betrayed her in the small talk department. The old man in front of her was clear eyed but dishevelled—like his home—and now that she thought about it, had a voice so gravelly in quality as to suggest that he might not have used it for quite a while. She turned out the right pocket of her chenille bathrobe, unfurling the soggy paper from Animal Control.

"I don't know if you've seen this yet," she stammered, her long dormant brogue re-emerging, "Mr. Fischer, is it?"

"Ja." He stepped closer, this time violating the arms length rule between two bodies that defined personal space.

Bronagh stepped back as the cat, making perfunctory overtures, wrapped himself around her calves and ankles. She grasped the paper. "It's from Animal Control—" she faltered.

Something smelled funny, like boiling fat of witches' brew. The odor, and indeed that's what it was, at first went unnoticed. But the early fall wind that blew gently past her face suddenly dropped, as if it, too, wished to make a point. In the stillness, the offensive parfum wafted somewhere from inside the house, a place that harbored interior features obscured by aid of curtained windows.

"Mr. Fischer?"

"Ja?"

He stepped nearer, his body, close enough to expel the subtle, yet self-conscious bouquet of garlic, onion and paprika as it exited his pores.

She drew back, repulsed. The cat meowed and the old man froze. She had gone too far, too fast. Gravity interceded and in a second that would become a moment that would change everything, Bronagh Caley lost her footing, falling backward off the Fischer porch and into the rest of her life.

# Chapter Three
## The Widow Rajput

Like so many widows before her, Poonam Khanzada Rajput went through the motions after her husband's funeral. She woke, washed, fed and then minded her neighbor's business with a phone call to city officials. Begun just after her husband's death, the irritating renovation next door—Poonam now knew—had nothing to do with her loss. She only saw it that way. Having set the inspection in motion, she was hard pressed to stop it for fear of drawing unwanted negative attention. That said, it probably didn't help when she put a lawn sign up announcing her voting intentions. Bronagh, reasonably warm towards her, began to withdraw in what was, clearly, a flagrant effort to dismiss her right to exercise her opinion. Poonie's therapist felt otherwise: "For a time, you will feel that everything around you is connected; every word, action and slight. That is not the case. It is merely an exaggerated sense of false reality heightened by the loss you have endured."

That same sentiment was voiced before she had been sent home from work days after Sikander's passing. "Too soon after the death," her boss intoned, like a degree in pharmacy somehow gave him insights superseding that of her psychotherapist's.

Intended or not, Poonam's actions got a rise from her neighbors. "I see you have a sign," Bill Caley said, just hours after her electoral choice went public. A tall man with kind eyes and a head of hair and beard reminiscent of old Papa Hemingway, he seemed an odd choice of mate for her often shrill and opinionated neighbor.

"Yes," she remembered saying, faltering in the presence of the large man. "My Sikander was not big on advertising personal beliefs."

As she watched her neighbor tumble ass over heel onto the Fischer lawn, she wondered if that moment with the woman's husband triggered what she was about to do. She thought of *her* husband: average height, with gray hair waving attractively at the temples in contrast to eyes as black as her thoughts. His name was an old one, claimed by Greeks, Hindus, Punjabis and Sikhs: Sikander, "man's protector," "protector of man."

"Forgive me, Sikander, if I take my time."

It had become her habit of late to speak to him, as if he were in the room, or, in this case, on the stoop right next to her. Her therapist assured her that this was normal. He even suggested that she communicate with her husband through a journal.

That wouldn't be necessary. The time for dialogue had long passed. Emptying her coffee grinds into the flower bed, she advanced in the direction of her fallen neighbor. Slowly. Very slowly.

\*\*\*

Bronagh Caley regained consciousness determined to ignore everything she'd ever learned from St. John's Ambulance. When she tried to stand up on her own, she failed miserably, lurching from side to side in a dance that alarmed the onlookers. Trying to assist, Poonam Khanzada Rajput and Zoltan the Gardener were brushed aside by hand gestures signifying a mute assurance that she was fine. She wasn't. Bronagh was back on the ground covered in sheep manure.

*Where did all this shit come from?* she wanted to ask, but the words wouldn't come. Her thoughts, numbed by the ringing in her ears, had trouble gelling.

Poonam Rajput and Zoltan Kárpáty, Saffron's go-to gardener of choice, exchanged glances, and in that moment Bronagh thought she'd caught a trace of something esoteric. They raised her to a sitting position, looking frantically this way and that for the 'who' or 'what' that had precipitated the fall. But there was no one there. The old bastard Rudolf Fischer had taken cover, along with the over-friendly cat, whose motivations in choosing her had become suspect. She would have words with them later on; the cat's owner, most certainly, across a high gloss boardroom table in the lushly appointed offices of an experienced slip and fall lawyer.

But for now, the matter at hand:

Her foot had distended, gnarling garishly over two pronounced hematomas that were purpling as her acquaintances chattered. A lumpy protuberance just below her ankle bone suggested that something had given way and would not return to its proper place without aid of some hack from Emergency.

She shuddered at the thought of having to go to the hospital, in part, because of the condescension she would encounter from staff. But there was also a worry that she'd run into one person, in particular.

*I'm mature*, she thought, *and I still look okay.*

"I still look okay." She said this every day to make it real, yet something in the back of her mind began to treble loud and mean after her fiftieth birthday. She wasn't a kid anymore, and all the foolish things she'd done, past and near present, were no longer available to her given her age. This made her incredibly sad.

*Are you all right? Did you hit your head?* Poonam and Zoltan seemed to be saying, though she did not hear them through ears that wouldn't stop ringing. How old were they? Were they past it too?

"Why am I covered in sheep shit?" she hollered. "And where'd that old sonofabitch go? He was muscling into my space."

She was averse to crowding, like a claustrophobe in the extreme. Even in a crowd of one or two, she felt the oppressiveness of the air around her.

*"Try to stand, if you can,"* Zoltan, a largish man with meaty hands and bushy eyebrows, mouthed. His words, obscured in an imperfect vacuum—not totally silent, but lined, as if with malleable tin sheets banged upon by a gaggle of monkeys—quivered a peculiar, yet compelling music.

"I think so," she mumbled, reading bowed lips framed by a woolly thatch of man whisker.

Her neighbor blushed at the sight of the man wool, and in the craziness of the moment, Bronagh Caley resolved to put aside her prejudices about politics and plumbing to get closer to Poonam Khanzada Rajput.

# Chapter Four
## The Curious Fischer People

Carlos' original owner, Zoey Fischer, did the right thing when she handed him over to her grandparents. What could she have been thinking, anyway? A single girl, away from home for the first time, basking in the student life, far away from prying eyes...

It was precisely for lack of prying eyes that she became a serial adventurist, bringing home anything that said 'yes.' For Carlos, it wasn't a problem, the boyfriends providing a great excuse for Miss Zoey to order pizza and wings.

Feral kitties, as a rule, exist on a diet of fast-cooling rodent easily dispatched with a single bite from powerful jaws. Hard to catch, and a bit on the chewy side, the rewards of predation kept him sleek. Cooped-up in Zoey's apartment noshing on trans fats, on the other hand, left him farty and distempered.

"What on earth were you thinking?" was the first thing out of Rudolf Fischer's mouth on Liberation Day, as Carlos' change of address came to be known. "Cats belong outdoors."

Zoey offered no protest as her kind, but stern, granddad reamed her out while pulling her drywall down. Instead, she took comfort in the fiction that wanderlust had taken hold of her beloved Carlos, so named after Santana, the greatest guitarist of all time. In fact, it was her penchant for playing Santana's version of Tito Puente's *Oye Como Va* over and over again that got him digging with both paws into the drywall in the first place.

Like the Count of Monte Cristo, Carlos' confinement could, in reality, only be a temporary one, because he had a very specific agenda to pursue and no one, no matter how well-intentioned, would obstruct his progress.

Herr Fischer was old school. A eugenist of the first order, he believed, as many of his generation did, that dogs and cats were animals and should to be treated as such. Stuffing a cat with fast food and giving him a spot on the master bed next to the master was unthinkable, and he said so to his long-suffering wife Irme on the ride home in their impeccably restored '65 Pontiac Parisienne.

For Rudolf, putting the cat out at the side of the road made more sense and would probably be better for everybody in the long run. But Irme would have none of it, citing her Austrian roots as a basis for offering the cat above average accommodations and the occasional pat on the head. "I come from a long line of breeders, so I know what I'm talking about when I say an animal is better off with a little human intervention. Not even PETA can argue with that."

Carlos certainly didn't, delighting in the outdoor diversions offered up by Saffron Drive. The Greek guy at the bottom of the street had a seemingly endless supply of pepperoni, which he generously shared with the 'visitor' as the cat came to be known over time. The swingers two streets over were very affectionate, while the Hungarian gentleman and his many wives opened up to him whenever he appeared at their back door. Like the Fischers, they all gave him different names: Rudolf called him Panzer after his favorite WWII vehicle of choice, while the Greek man called him Kosta. Gus, a pilot and one of the aforementioned swingers, called him Yuri and one lady, a bit slow on the uptake, called him Clara.

He didn't mind the monikers; Carlos answered to them all, making him something of a wonder to the people of Saffron Drive and its environs. That he had all these crazy names in the first place came from his new owners' dedication to sticking it to authority. Their granddaughter's suggestion that he be licensed after a routine visit to the vet, for example, was deliberately ignored.

"We pay enough in taxes," Rudolf assured Irme over Pilsner beers in front of the T.V. "I'm not paying twenty-five dollars for a goddamned cat."

Frau Fischer, differing vastly in countenance and taste, did not agree. Whereas Rudolf was short and slight, she was tall and plucky, standing at an impressive 1.74 metres, to use the unit of measurement employed in her country of origin. "I can see, Rudolf, that you might not want to pay the government, but we cannot fall down on our responsibilities to care for another living thing."

A gentrified-loving Austrian, Irme's attitude towards animals was logical. Her great grandfather, Egon, was the junior game keeper assigned to one of Emperor Franz Jozef's northern estates before the First World War, his primary responsibility to curate the red deer population. Ensuring a steady supply of German Short Haired Pointer hunting dogs through an ambitious breeding program was another. Photos of Egon and prize-winning dogs dotted the Fischer mantelpiece. Clearly, this was a history in which to be immensely proud.

"And the cat will be good for us," she continued, "since we both come from dog people."

Carlos came and went at regular intervals in the early years, departing each morning between five thirty and six a.m., and returning at precisely half past eleven p.m. as the Fischers watched the evening news. That his meow was loud but never annoying was a plus, his call alerting his owners to get off the couch and open the door. He was never feted, nor was he taken to the vet, the Fischer's relying on his overall spectacular appearance and diet of high end dry kibble over the road kill he was accustomed to being the indicator that fussing was not needed.

Then something changed. Carlos came home one night at the customary half past eleven to find the house dark and the door closed against him. For the first time in the three years he had lived with the Fischers, he found himself out of doors. The lock out dragged on for nearly two weeks until a kind hearted old biddy with his best interests in mind intercepted him and surrendered him to Animal Control.

***

"You have fractured the fifth metatarsal on your right foot and quite possibly the ninth rib on your left side, but we don't bother with ribs," Dr. Fingle explained to Bronagh in the large, impersonal examination room just off Emerg. Since the $50 million expansion, the hospital had gone from twelfth place in the country to fourth, necessitating a cutback in services, including living, breathing parking attendants. In the time it took Bill to figure out the mechanized parking procedures, Bronagh managed to clear Triage.

Dr. Fingle, tall, pale, cold and soft skinned, fingered the enormous flat screen monitor, whooshing through many screens with a sleight of hand before landing on her foot. "As you see here from the X-ray," he pointed for emphasis with a pricey Monteblanc pen, "you are very lucky. It's a fine fracture—well removed from the tuberosity." He paused, clearly weighing his words. "Verrrrry lucky. Probably six to eight weeks in a soft cast, give or take."

Bronagh wondered if her luck stemmed from landing in a pile of sheep shit that had not been spread on the Fischer lawn prior to the frost. If it had been a few degrees colder, she could have cracked a few more flat bones, possibly upping her future statement of claim.

"And the rib?" Bronagh asked, fighting back a desire to say something smart-alecky.

"We don't bother with that."

Bill had gone off for coffee, so Dr. Fingle was spared the detailed kind of questioning her husband specialized in. When Bill Caley worked the mines up north, he was especially fearsome in matters of worker's compensation.

A man appeared at the door of her examination room.

"I believe you know Jaan?" Dr. Fingle said jovially.

Bronagh waved to the nice middle-aged man with the hairnet. Yes, she knew Jaan.

"Jaan put casts on all my kids."

"I see you have an avulsion fracture of the proximal fifth metatarsal. How the hell you manage that?" Jaan's familiarity was enough to send Dr. Fingle off in hot pursuit of a Code Blue announced with great import over the sound system. "Someone went down in Psychiatric. I'll hear about it later, for sure. What happened to you?"

Bronagh hadn't seen Jaan in about five years and before that, at least ten when the last cast went on the last Caley kid before she grew up and moved away. With Jaan, Bronagh had experienced a slip and fall of quite another kind; the kind born out of a fear of death and/or old age. It was a stupid thing to do, and she regretted it. Looking at him, she might have shrunk at his presence, but the sickly fluorescent light calling attention to every physical flaw they shared had emboldened her. To hell with buccal fat removal, she didn't need it. Her ex-sweetheart was grayer, and his middle was thicker in the way mature animals get when they've been clipped. This thought, delighting her, strengthened her resolve to show him how much she did not care about seeing him again.

"I fell stalking wild turkeys in the wood off my property," Bronagh lied, teasing the man she once 'could not get on without' with the notion that she hunted.

"Wild Turkey?" he smirked. "Try going to the liquor store next time."

She breathed a sigh of relief as the man wrapped her foot in plaster-soaked linen. Clearly, Jaan didn't know the first thing about hunting, wild turkeys coming into season in May, not September.

"I thought I was getting a soft cast," she said, ignoring his joke. Jaan could never tell jokes, and when he tried, it was always at the wrong time.

"You are," he said, producing a strap-on Franken boot of such ugliness that it made her wince. "It's better than the alternative. You can take this one off if you need to drive somewhere."

The smug bastard winked.

Bronagh wondered if he still had trouble with his hip flexors, but decided against asking. Let the jerk do his job. There was nothing to be gained from being bitchy.

# Chapter Five
## Bronagh Caley's Weird Society

There is a belief out there that a lot goes on behind a whole lot of nothing, much like still waters running deep. In many instances, this is nothing but bunk. Still waters, like strong silent types, are boring, because they fail to leave an impression and have nothing to say.

This wasn't to say that sleepy Pictontown on the Downs was a boring place. Far from it. 'Pics,' as the residents were affectionately referred to by kith and kin, had an above average Lion's Club and a fantastic soccer dome. Add to that, an equestrian centre opened the previous year to provide entertainment for the genetically superior, and a recipe for a perfect storm of social tumult became a practical 'given.'

If the blind and the stubborn doubted that things were changing, the wilful and observant could point to the preponderance of shiny new McMansions constructed for the captains of industry. Seeking Pic charm and discretion, they encroached like Mongol hoards bent on destruction. It was no longer unusual to see a Maserati or Lamborghini tooling around the subdivisions. Gold plated spouses, likewise, came and went with new model years.

But if Pictontown on the Downs wasn't boring, it wasn't lighting any fires either. Not a single politician elected in the boroughs had been to rehab, nor had any of their spouses been embarrassed by a badly lit low-res sex tape.

As a fifty year old woman on the brink, Bronagh Caley found this hard to digest, her ability to suspend disbelief having been lost along with her first edition

Tolkein's. "If one is very lucky and looks deeply enough," a wise sage once told her, "a germ of a thing is bound to show up. Observed over time, that germ can grow without aid of petri dish just large enough for everyone to see without aid of microscope."

Bronagh Caley was not a scientist, merely a woman on the lookout for a cause. Growing up around politics, this should have been easy. But the changing landscape, clouded by her own prejudices, forced her to negate the memories of the once promising legislative career she abandoned. The horse she backed had decided to shy, retire to pasture, and seed a few more politicians-in-waiting with not one, but two girlfriends.

Without connections, she should have left right away, but a flexible moral compass had prevented her from doing so. A massive debark of brain power from the ranks changed her mind. "I got no sway, no reason to stay," she moaned to her boss and mentor, who reminded her, rather indelicately, that trench politics was for the young. "You need shallow roots and a wanderer's fearlessness, my dear." Bronagh Caley had deep roots: two kids in post secondary and a home paid in full.

And she wasn't hot anymore.

And so, it went that in tremulous retirement, another type of diversion emerged, this one a little risky, but extremely rewarding if one got something out of peeping through other people's windows. "There's laws against that," her beloved Bill cautioned the first time he came upon her, prone and on the floor with binoculars, peering into Zoltan Kárpáty's bedroom window.

"I can't believe how many people he's got in there with him," she replied breathlessly. "I can't even confirm that they're all female."

"Don't say?" Bill replied. "Maybe he's one of those swingers we keep hearing about."

Pictontown on the Downs had a bit of a reputation, thanks to a flinty little article penned by one Goddess Moonbow. On special assignment for *The Downsview*, a local rag that normally ran stories on the latest teacher work-to-rule alongside recipes for safe, "offensive-free" gender neutral costumes for Hallowe'en, she captured the hearts and slavering drool of a population seeking thrall.

The article titled *Come Knock on My Door. Come. Please!* was a sensation on its own, relying on a bawdy homograph in the headline to tease and draw the reader in. According to Ms. Moonbow, Pics made a habit of picking on one another for a little coitus integrum on secretly appointed Friday's. Revellers were pre-screened before joining the party to ensure good character and quality motives above the mere prurient. Singles were prohibited from participating as was anyone under the age of twenty-five years. People didn't necessarily have to be good looking, but they did have to be clean-smelling without aid of allergy causing deodorants.

There were, of course, subdivisions within the Swinging Pics. Although they'd never swap rides, some shared classic car interests in common, while others wrote short stories, or entered their pets in competitions for ribbons and cash prizes.

"It's possible he's a swinger, I guess," Bronagh quipped, as she refocused on Zoltan. "But I don't see any keys, and the couples aren't evenly matched. Besides, don't swingers fly stars on their barn doors to let people know that they do what they do?"

"I hadn't heard of that," Bill laughed, "though the Pennsylvania Dutch had a thing going with pentacles."

Back home with a broken foot and greatly reduced mobility, Saffron Drive's resident lady without a cause busied herself with two things: linking Poonam Rajput's obvious fascination with Zoltan the Gardener to something unsavory, and finding a good attorney to screw the Kraut that wrecked her foot hard to the wall.

# Chapter Six
## The White Cat

Coffee cups coated with day's old grinds rattled across the console as the van came to rest like a cliché out of a stakeout movie. The officers inside felt it most acutely. Saffron Drive had been on their radar for a very long time. Now, it appeared to be on fire. A plume of gray smoke rising above the trees was their first clue that something was wrong.

"My first instinct is to call it in," Animal Control Officer Sils Banks said between mouthfuls of pumpkin cruller. "But then, we're not supposed to be here, are we?"

Banks' companion, Jack Frewer, concurred. Looking over the steering wheel of the large utility vehicle, his demeanor super cool, he seemed to care less about the source of the smoke than he did about rifling through his pockets.

Banks stifled a burp. As animal control specialists for the municipality, it was incumbent upon them to follow orders precisely and without question. And they had done so up until this point. Saffron Drive, one of the older pockets in a block of Pic subdivisions under their purview, had been singled out for special treatment, owing to conflagrating facts dealing with census and school tithes. It had, in fact, been reallocated to a different jurisdiction just in time for election day. This meant they had no business being there.

"Why are we here?" Banks asked, her eyes zeroing in on the large gash over Frewer's left eye. She had only known him for a short time, they both having come up from the basement at around the same time but from different departments. Water cooler gossip was sketchy: Jack was single, tall enough, and he owned his own place. As far as anyone knew, he didn't swing any particular way, and he was open to 'openness.' Banks grinned at the notion.

"We had a complaint," he said, sighing, his large head bobbing back and forth with the effort to liberate something of great importance from his front trouser pocket. "And we're in the neighborhood. No one's gonna give a damn if we cross the line."

At that he winked, opening the scab over his brow. The resultant puss, oozing at its distal margins, made for a startling side effect.

Banks gagged. Suddenly, Jack wasn't so fetching.

"Yeah, well, I suppose it's inevitable," she said, recovering. "I mean, redrawing the boundaries. It's change, ya know?"

The decision to redraw municipal boundary lines, born out of a multi-jurisdictional brouhaha that put one councillor in hospital with heart murmurs and another on a Form 1 psychological lock down, had to be made. Saffron, among other unique little pockets in the Downs, was left inadequately represented after the last federal election. To redress the democratic imbalance, the community and its environs had been electorally redistributed—moved across the train tracks figuratively speaking—placing it with a voting bloc guaranteed to favor the Free Range Party.

Banks had a big problem with that—her girlfriend having sucked her into committee room work for the opposing political party in direct contravention of the public servant's act that prohibited partisan alliances. Like many her age, she wanted cheap, legal marijuana, but the vote gerrymandering meant to achieve that end also triggered the loss of Saffron, and with it, the preponderance of wandering beasties that padded Animal Control pockets with fat bonuses at Christmastime.

"It's not officially official," Jack Frewer grunted, finally retrieving the much sought after stick of waxy chewing gum from the front side pocket of his sensible uniform. "I mean, there's so much confusion over where the boundaries begin and end." He unwrapped the gum deliberately, appearing thoughtful. "So as long as *we* stay confused—"

"—we continue to make quota." Banks smiled, liking how she could finish Frewer's sentence before he could.

He popped the gum into his mouth. "And this street is the place to make it. Look."

Just over the dashboard and a mere fifteen feet from their vehicle, a white cat crossed in front of them. Appearing nervous and furtive, the creature looked over its shoulder several times before coming to rest directly in front of the animal control officers.

"Is that the one?" Banks asked, her growing excitement evident with the heat rising in her face. Phone calls from a single Saffron Drive resident who wished to remain anonymous told harrowing tales of a wayward puss that butchered everything that moved—rats, bats, small dogs and possibly even a sloe-eyed coyote. Abnormally large for its breed, the cat was described as sinewy and vile, gaining unlawful and unwelcomed entry through the complainant's home by way of a screen door.

"No," Frewer answered. "The one we're looking for is a black."

Banks chewed her doughnut thoughtfully. While some might have questioned a grown man's obsession over one black cat, others, like Sils Banks, accepted the facts such as they were. Cats belonged indoors. Period. She and Frewer were paid to hunt, and hunt they would, even if they had strayed into a competitor's territory.

The white cat, its mustard colored eyes darting between the vehicle's occupants, seemed to be weighing its options, if one could believe a tatty *Felis catus* capable of such sentience.

"I don't believe for one minute that a common house cat could take down a coyote. The caller's a loon."

"Complaint's a complaint," Frewer said, pushing the box of crullers to one side. "It don't much matter what the color is. Hand me the loop."

Banks was already ahead of him, shimmying over the console that separated the bucket seats and into the back of the vehicle where the intercept devices were arranged neatly on swing hooks above four transport cages large enough to house Mastiffs and German Shepherds.

"Hey," Banks called out, fumbling with an assemblage of ropes and lock levers that had wrapped themselves around her Doc Martens. "Remember the time Fogler got the call for the bear. He nearly shit himself." She laughed, not realizing that her colleague had exited the vehicle. Freeing herself, Sils Banks called out annoyed: "Hey, asshole, I was telling a story."

Frewer didn't answer. Outside the vehicle, he stood, head hung low over a figure in motion, its tremors disturbing even to the most insensitive of thinking species.

Banks took her place next to him, gaping.

"Forget about the snare," he whispered, his voice so low as to be otherworldly. "I don't think we'll be needing it."

The white cat, bleeding prodigiously from the right ear, had risen on hind quarters before lurching, listing and then coming to rest at Frewer's feet.

Banks, eyes wide, questioned him wordlessly. The answer was clear.

"There's nothing we can do. She's been poisoned."

\*\*\*

Across the street, behind a copse of trees, denuded, with dense interlocking branches that provided ideal coverage for spying, Poonam Rajput watched the unfolding drama with growing interest. The city staff, previously cavorting over doughnuts, made a lukewarm attempt at action, scratching their backsides while an innocent thrashed and twisted to a heart wrenching end. Something about the scene reminded Poonie of old history of the kind that one must not visit; certainly, not on account of a silly cat. But the dying beast before her eyes tugged, reminding her of her recent loss and her guilt over her frustrating lack of power to change things.

Poonie's mom, a sweet old gal who had come to live with her after the funeral barged her way into the scene almost on cue. Draped from head to toe in fine linen, her white hair slicked back into a tight, aristocratic chignon, she joined her daughter at the window, waving her cane at the scene playing out before them.

"What is going on then?" the old lady said, squinting through round, golden eye glasses brought back from her recent trip to the old country. "I can hardly make out a thing."

"It's the trees that hide us, Mummy Ji, and they are very frustrating, but they give us the illusion of minding our own business even when we don't."

"What are they doing?" Mummy Ji asked, with reference to the animal control officers who stood apparently helpless over the prone, quivering figure of a hapless pussy cat. "They look like they don't know their business. Have they never seen a dying thing before?"

The two animal control officers, now decked out in elbow length rubber gauntlet gloves and smocks, were poking at the fallen animal with great care. Their efforts, no doubt sensitive, seemed ludicrous to the two widows observing from their second storey window.

Thinking more about the smoke rising above the trees in pretty, gray ribbons, Poonam turned her back to the window. The thing she sought had not come out, and it had left her sad.

"Come away from the window Mummy Ji and have some tea and sweet cake. There is much to do before I go to the committee room."

The old lady shot her daughter a glance, the disapproval burning holes into the wall behind Poonie's head. Mummy Ji was old school, not keen on mixing with the natives. Given her way, she'd fetch a nice man for her Poonie, who was much too young to sit alone. *"We may be Hindu, but we don't sit purdah."*

*Exactly,* Poonam thought, recalling that conversation as she reached for the black cat that had jumped down from its place on the settee. Mummy Ji wanted her to find a man. For now, all she needed was the kitty purring in her lap: so handsome, so charming, with his big chalcedony green eyes.

"What do you think, my love?" she whispered, as the tabby with the recessive gene tapped his forehead against hers in a welcomed gesture of reassurance.

*I think you know what needs to be done, but before you can act, you must fall,* Carlos purred.

He licked the tip of her nose with his rough, sandpaper tongue.

*Most certainly, you must have something done to you first.*

# Chapter Seven
## A Cat's Life in Purgatory

*Three weeks ago*

Before settling in with Poonam Khanzada Rajput, Carlos the Wonder Cat trod alone, wandering in inhospitable territory. Worse, he faced life behind bars.

It began immediately and without trial. For that, he could thank the Fischers—for abandoning him—and the silly old cow that found him, and couldn't leave well enough alone.

"I'd like to surrender this cat," she said solemnly, handing him across the counter at City Hall.

For a moment, he thought he might escape the hammer. The official behind the console, fidgety and desperate, handed him back with a despondent "down there," dismissing the older woman with the point of a stubby finger.

A marvel of modern architecture, the new city hall was designed to impress and subdue, transforming, magically, a once rural boon into a burgeoning metropolis over night. So far, the illusion of grandeur held, not just because of all the Maserati's and Lambo's boogying about, but also because of the attention city status drew from power brokers with larger designs. Rumor became fact when council unveiled utopian plans for an airport that could accommodate jet aircraft, as well as a casino and hotel complex geared (presumably) toward transient business traffic and, many hinted, 'leisure' tourism.

The city official behind the counter waved her thick wrist again, coaxing woman and cat in the direction of a long corridor, its terminus bathed in peaked, pale sunlight.

Of indeterminate length, the glowy hall with many doors conveyed to the cat and his human transport an unearthly quality of the type found in Sci-Fi movies and speculative fiction. Each windowless door, couched in hues of battleship gray, played tricks on the viewer, suggesting, in the absence of name plates, that the people working behind them did so without accountability or transparency.

The old woman shivered, and Carlos, picking up her unease, tried to soothe her with a comforting purr. This act, a simple conscious gesture of vibrating vocals against compressed feline epiglottis, meant to convey tranquility, had an opposite effect on the do-gooder interfering with his life's progress. She turned on her stumpy heels, prepping for a dash to the front door. Carlos purred louder to spur her along, lest she change her mind. In typical human fashion, she faltered, half-witted, succumbing to the overtures of a jerk wearing corduroy.

"Can I help ma'am," the goof offered, insinuating himself a little too closely for everyone's comfort.

Carlos immediately ceased to purr.

His transport, too old to have the kinds of feelings her quickened heart suggested, spread her lips in bacchanal pleasure, reconfirming for the cat, at least, that the neighborhood was indeed going to hell.

"I *was* looking for the authority that accepts abandoned cats," she burbled, staring slyly into the younger man's slate blue eyes.

Carlos licked his paw, unimpressed. Though he lacked sufficient optical cones to perceive color intensity so taken for granted by humans, he had a synesthete's intuition of what he was dealing with. Eyes without depth smacked of deception nine times out of ten. This joker, with his corduroy pants and Lycra mohair combo V-necked top, looked innocuous enough, but inside, something bubbled.

Was it possible that the cat was caught in a thriller playing out in real time? Was kitty walking the mile?

Do-gooder number two might have been twenty-five if he was a day, in which case, his choice of dress was more distressing than Carlos first thought. No one dressed this way in 2016, no one who left the basement and interacted with humans, anyway.

"You seem distressed," the man oozed. "I can take it from here, if that would help." He extended his arms, long and spidery, to accept Carlos, who struggled fulsomely against the handover. The cat was not an "it," but a sentient being every bit as much, and maybe even more so, than the two clownish humans who condescended to decide his fate.

The old lady, perspiring heavily under the weight of change of life issues, liked the man's suggestion very much. She'd been having a lot of trouble with her ankles, the edema surrounding them having moved from the tops of her feet clean through the joints to continue its journey to the summit of her knees. She was only trying to do the right thing: rescue a lost pet. Maybe the city had a website where pictures could be posted? Maybe the cat's owners were looking for him?

"Now, now, little dude," the man cooed, as if the cat were insensate and incapable of resisting dominance. "I promise that you are going to a better place."

Carlos hissed, an act rarely employed by him since humans with overactive imaginations associated the gesture with things Satanical.

"You won't hurt him, will you?"

"Of course, we won't," the young man smiled. "We don't euthanize here."

Carlos wanted to fight the man—scratch his eyes out, or bite his nuts—but the stranger grasped him by the scruff, waving do-gooder lady and her edematous ankles away, before disappearing behind one of the gray windowless doors.

# Chapter Eight
## The Scourge of City Works

Things weren't looking good for Bronagh Caley.

First, there was the matter of her fractured rib and busted metatarsal, which threatened her, as yet, unrevealed plans to return to public life.

An early morning call from the district organizer some weeks back had outlined the tenuous position of the Frettinger Party.[1] A merger with Western refusniks had gone south, having the undesirable effect of tilting the party five degrees off axis. Self-serving Frets looking to grow had taken the party in a progressive direction, allowing free speech, full disclosure and a transparency that brought Kumbaya's over the mountains and into the fold. Self determination in gender, religion and advocacy was endorsed at a full meeting of the faithful, along with the right to ignore all of the above when necessary. This could not stand.

Then came the Department of City Works with its small army of sweaty inspectors keen to ferret out problems faster than could be corrected.

"If they don't fine us one way, they'll fine us another," Bronagh huffed, ignoring the plume of gray smoke rising above the tree tops. Her immediate concern—the one that would dominate her thoughts in the coming weeks—centered on one thing, and he wasn't even human.

"Is that smoke, I smell?" Bill Caley asked over his morning coffee and crumpets.

---

[1] Current party in power and staunch opponent of the Free Range.

She had not seen the cat since her fall, and while she was less apt to blame the creature for her mishap now than before, she felt herself drawn to dark questions like: Why him? Why now? A lapsed Catholic, she had little use for universal questions. Still, the cat nagged at her. What did the Existentialists posit? Hopelessness in lock step with connectedness?

"Bullshit," she said aloud.

"I disagree," Bill said. "It's definitely smoke." He waved the broadsheet tabloid he was reading in her face. This act, on its own, was a great insult, given that Bill, a prodigious internet and social media snob, never touched printed materials.

With more than sixty per cent of its cover surface dedicated to a single cheesy photograph, *The Downsview* leapt out at her with equal affront. The Beautiful Boy Politician with the fantastic head of hair was all over it, taunting her with youth and vigor and unrestrained potential.

This vexed the shit out of her. It wasn't so much that she objected to his right to exist: he had a nice family, worked hard despite lavish inherited wealth, and he took care of his mother, a widow held in high esteem in country club circles. No, it wasn't the man that irked her at all. It was the *idea* of him: the power, how he was seizing it, and how he presumed to keep it—so effortlessly—without a shot being fired.

"It's definitely a fire," Bill sniffed, dunking a lady finger into a fresh cup of java newly poured from the pot on the stove. "I don't think it's our house—"

Bronagh's lips tightened as her fingers, clawed around the broadsheet, shredded it with uncompromising emotion. She had lost so much in recent months: her looks, her hopes, and now her physical vitality. Fighting a good fight, dirty or otherwise, was the best way to dig herself out of a hole. The question was how to achieve her aims. She looked at her Franken foot. Bound by gauze, rubber and polyurethane supports, the thing disgusted her.

Bill, at the window, adjusted his thick, dark sunglasses, which he insisted on wearing long after the side effects of corrective laser eye surgery had passed. "There's definitely smoke. It's coming from the front."

"There's a Town Hall next month," Bronagh muttered, ignoring him, "and I'm gonna be there if I have to take a cane and a cab to do it." She punched what remained of the pretty face decorating her paper. "We shouldn't just give it to him. D'ya hear?"

A knock at the front door brought the Caley's together, their eyes locking over crumpets and shredded newsmakers in the idyllic kitchen Bill built. Well to the back of the house, it overlooked a forested lot that had somehow managed to escape the developers.

"I hear what I need to hear," he smiled, patting his broken wife on the shoulder. "The rest I ignore."

A second knock, this one louder, challenged Bill's assertion. It could not be smudged over. Brash and tinny, it had too much anger behind it to be a Jehovah's Witness or even a gas contract flunky. Bronagh knew in an instant that it was the wizened inspector and his skinny rube assistant from City Works returned for another pound of flesh.

"You get the door, my dear," she instructed. "I'll get a shovel and bury our savings. The rest we'll move offshore before the politicians have us eating out of garbage cans."

Bill Caley made his way to the front door, relieved that someone other than Bronagh would avail themselves of his time and conversation. While he loved his wife to a fault, her increasingly strident attitude since the injury had begun to grate. Though her fractures were deemed "superficial resulting from an accidental fall," her maniacal insistence that the little old Fischer man had meant her harm concerned him. These concerns grew dramatically when she announced her intention to exact redress.

Calling the lawyer was out of the question, Bill had insisted, citing several on-line articles detailing the fallout from frivolous litigation. The notion that one could pursue a lawsuit to scare and then call it off with impunity was one of the greatest urban revenge myths out there. He simply could not afford to salve her rage.

He peered through the front door cut-out. As anticipated, the view of the street was obscured by a hawkish little man with a tablet and a smallish, fine-boned woman who couldn't weigh more than eighty pounds. Both wore uniforms.

Bill, feigning non-recognition behind the opened door, suppressed a half grin. "Are you here about the smoke?"

The little man's lips thinned. "City Works, Mr. Caley. We have an appointment."

"Ahhhh. The inspection." Bill pulled his mottled bathrobe shut. "I forgot. Come in."

Bronagh, clearly recognizing the bowed figure of Inspector Kirsch and his nubile assistant, Arthurs, hollered comments from the kitchen that receded as the small group advanced to a narrow door and the relative safety of a poorly lit staircase going down.

"Maybe City Council could do something about the sex offender across the street," Bill Caley whispered in a lame ass play at levity while on descent.

Arthurs clamped a hand over her pink mouth.

Though not old by any reasonable measure, the Caley house had an attitude of sober solicitude like a rock that never moves, regardless of weather, and, in so doing, is reassuring on its own. This overall impression ran contrary to its dishevelled occupants—the Caley's—and their even worse excuse for home improvement.

Maybe Poonam Khanzada Rajput had a point in ratting them out, Bill thought, as the little party weaved its way through a series of boxes arranged without pretension in a zigzagging pattern. These gave way to a dampish room clothed in drop sheets to conceal the obvious catastrophe that was the Caley renovation.

Kirsch cleared his throat.

"I have complied with every list item on the work order," Bill explained. "As you see, the floor is almost dry." Bill raised his bushy eyebrows over the tops of his glasses for emphasis. It had taken him well over a week to bust up the concrete, back fill and re-pour. The six-inch loss of ceiling height was a drawback of sorts, but if he factored in the new space's intended use, a low ceiling really didn't matter.

"I can't stand upright," Arthurs noted, scratching it all down on her palm thingy device with a nifty stylus. "Are you making a crawl space?"

Bill frowned at the inference. She knew full well that he wanted a rec room to accommodate a snooker table he had planned for eons.

"No," he answered a little too harshly. "But I assure you that the intended future use is well within acceptable definitions." He gestured to her work order which clearly stated: 'recreational use space.' "And I trust there have been no further complaints." This last bit was said more as an afterthought, for while Bronagh was convinced that Poonie Rajput was behind the tell all to City Works, he could not bring himself to believe Sikander's widow capable of such mischief. "We have done everything cited in the initial report. As you see, everything has been corrected."

He gestured again with the full expanse of his long arms.

Inspector Kirsch "hmmmm'd" and "uh huh'd" over his tablet, checking boxes before photographing the floor.

"If you measure floor to ceiling with that pointer of yours, you will see that the depth is correct. Also, the floor is dry. Almost."

The inspector pulled a fine silver tube from his bag of tricks, releasing a thin red stream of funky laser light that confirmed everything Bill Caley said.

"Hmmmmm. And the wiring?"

"To Code. I have the book, see?" He waved a thick yellow paperback retrieved from a dust covered shelf in the man's face.

"Uh, huh."

Sensing trouble, Bill changed tack. "Paper says the city's shoddy finances don't come from a lack of revenue, but from overspending..."

"Eh?"

Bill had barely caught the inspector's attention. While it was unlike him to engage a stranger, or anyone for that matter, in the deceitful practice of politicking, he could not block out what Bronagh read from the paper each morning. The new council, elected just six months ago to replace the old town council, was comprised principally of lifers; those career politicians that ran thirty years ago and then re-ran, never leaving. Things never changed: The debate over four-laning the highway had lasted for over forty years, along with promises of subway extensions and better-quality housing for the borough's fixed incomes.

Becoming a city was supposed to challenge all of that.

"The housing authority dumped three quarters of a million into renos for its headquarters."

The inspector, plunging his hand into a dry bag of all purpose ready mix cement had about as much interest in current events than he did in looking a fellow human being in the eye.

Trying to maintain control, Bill tugged at his long sea captain's beard. "You almost done?"

Kirsch's colleague Arthurs suppressed a smile from behind a cup of strong brew brought along, he noted, from The Skinny Pic downtown. Kirsch, communicating something to her with eyes dark and deadly, didn't crack a smile. She responded appropriately, depositing her soggy cup on top of the water heater before disappearing behind the furnace.

Bill took his heart into his mouth.

"What's this?" Arthurs queried from behind the furnace where she insinuated herself with great dexterity. Bending in the sheltering darkness, she shimmied comically in an effort to ground herself as she tugged on a large oblong object, the weight of it apparent from the bulging temple veins road-mapping across her head.

Bill cringed. Arthurs found the contraband.

"It's not mine," he lied, throwing in a weak aside about the convict all over Gooblie News who spent his days making lousy art and reading about the Third Reich.

The scrawny inspector, nonplussed, replied with a previously unrevealed air of self-satisfaction. "Even if it isn't yours, sir, you are in possession of non-approved herbicide, which, by the label, appears to have been imported illegally from across the border. There are severe consequences attached to unlawful storage, and, of course, there is a fine."

# Chapter Nine
## Showdown

The next day, Bronagh caught her neighbor outside on the lawn staring longingly at Zoltan Kárpáty's house. Dressed gorgeously in saffron colored silk, her sari dotted with what appeared to be seed pearls, and hemmed with real silver thread, she looked otherworldly and entirely undeserving of her neighbor's pique. But piqued she was after Bill broke the news of the additional $1,500 tagged on to a growing list of offences that now included unlawful possession of controlled herbicides. They didn't have the resources to pay, plain and simple; not unless she hawked some jewellery, which she would never do. That left revenge as a logical course in restoring some balance to The Force, but even that seemed harsh, given the Widow Rajput's current standing. Loveless, longing and living alone with her mother, she was clearly a victim of cruel circumstance, deserving better from a fellow sister in humankind.

Bronagh tried to bend her cardboard heart. "Good afternoon, neighbor."

The sky, rocking high above their heads, answered with a rumble and many vascular bolts. Poonam, jolted, landed hard. "Good afternoon."

Bronagh, eyeing her neighbor's campaign sign, now flaccid in the damp breeze, made the most of a philosophical moment. "It's like the cosmos is reminding us that it's still here."

"I don't doubt it." Poonam rewarded her with a weak smile. "What I do doubt are the idiots who presume to control us."

Bronagh smoothed the pleats on her heavy twill skirt.

"I mean, don't you find things more suffocating than ever before?" Poonam took three steps toward the Caley stoop.

"I don't know," the older lady responded, taking a mean pull off her oversized Frettinger Party coffee mug. "People 'round here don't hesitate to raise the alarm when they see something they don't like." She took the three steps down onto the lawn, coming to rest alongside Poonam's Free Range Party lawn sign, which had for company, a tight knot of dried out knee-high sneeze weeds winding round its wooden base. Bill should have used the herbicide when he had the chance. If he had, they wouldn't be in the mess they were in, and she wouldn't be so goddamned furious with her goddamned neighbor.

Poonam's lips thinned as she pointed at the sign with the candidate's smiling face, which appeared next to the party logo: a field of tall grasses dotted by a trinity of windmills. Ludicrous!

"Are you saying, dear Bronagh, that people oughtn't speak?"

*Oughtn't speak?* Bronagh fumed at the 'oughtn't.' This wasn't the first time Poonie Rajput had traipsed out the Oxford English to challenge her Limerick vowels. "What's speech gotta do with keepin' the peace?"

Back home, action spoke, and when everything was done and there was nothing left, that's when everyone knew what the real agenda was.

The heavens cracked, greening over with a keenness that seemed to say: *"back away."*

"Speech has everything to do with peace." She looked again at Zoltan's house. "I have been quiet for far too long."

Bronagh swallowed her spit. Either her neighbor was firing spears at her, or she was alluding to something to do with the gardener. It was a decisive moment: Bronagh Caley could be nice, or she could not be nice.

She opted for both.

"The inspectors came 'round yesterday. Fined our behinds off. Jus' like them to rob us in an election year...'specially when they're *not* up for election."

Poonam remained mute.

"They have no compunction at Council about building monuments to themselves. Have you seen it? The city hall? Like the bloody Duomo in Florence—half moon ceiling and everything."

"I have not," Poonam said, her eyes scanning the lawn in search of something else.

"But the new city hall isn't the issue, is it?" Bronagh demanded. "Someone set the dogs on me and Bill and I think the one with the goddamned leash is YOU!"

There! She had said it out loud, and it felt pretty fucking good!

Poonam did not engage. Didn't even look her in the face. Instead, she knelt down, extending her arms in the direction of the fabulous blue spruce tree her husband Sikander planted the first year they lived there. A mere spindle at the time, it had grown to over twenty-five feet. Rich and verdant in summer, it looked like something out of *White Christmas* just before Yuletide. Bronagh appreciated it most at that time of year and never tired of telling Sikander Rajput how grateful she was to him for planting it.

"You have a great deal of nerve, neighbor." Poonam, her profile sleek and adjunct, looked impressive and controlled.

Bronagh, her skirt creeping up over her padded hips, couldn't even get in her face. The woman, still kneeling, was gesturing towards the black cat hiding beneath the prickly bows. Its eyes, clear, crisp and cunning, responded; the irises widening in a single evocative motion that was almost romantic. Poonam spoke to it in her native tongue, the kind of language, like German, that could sound awful if it weren't endemic to the speaker.

Bronagh suddenly felt like an asshole. "I don't understand this weather. It's fall and it's raining like springtime."

"It's raining like hope," Poonam said, rising to her feet. The cat in hand, it nestled into her neck, purring loudly like a lover, warm and satisfied. "That is why the earth is warming. The beating heart grows larger, moves faster. It's telling us something."

"Why did you call City Works on us, Poonam? Why? We never did anything to you."

Poonam smiled, taking two steps back and away. "That's just the thing, you see. You have never done anything for me."

# Chapter Ten
## Zoltan's Fire

Mummy Ji must have read Poonam's mind because when she came in out of the weather with the cat in her arms, she made no comment, opting instead to dither around in the kitchen.

After a long while, Poonam broke the silence. "I've had a run in with our neighbor. She is growing worse."

Mummy Ji clucked out an old home song about a woman washing clothes in the river. It was her custom to do this whenever she needed to muster her thoughts to buy time. Finally, she said: "And are you going to that place today?" She gestured at the green sky outside. "It is not a day fit for man or beast. Surely, you see that."

By 'that place,' Mummy meant the campaign office of Free Range Party candidate Errol Deutscher, whose poll numbers were climbing in no small part because of the party leader's focus on their electoral district. Pictontown on the Downs was a jewel in the electoral crown because it spoke to rapid change and the good that comes with it. Jobs. Immigration. Diversity. Growth. Love. Understanding. The Works! Policy wonks loved it and so did Poonam Rajput, especially since it flew in the face of Mummy's old way of thinking. Her reference to 'man' and 'beast' was a clear and deliberate reference aimed to strike at the political landscape.

Poonam chuckled at Mummy's omission. "I agree that it is neither fit for things furry or tumescent. I am, therefore, free to go, am I not?" She placed the cat on the divan in the hall adjacent the closet which contained many sensible pairs of Wellies with raincoats to match. The need to prepare for weather, a dear holdover from their time spent in England before migrating west, was ingrained.

"You'll catch a bolt," Mummy chastised, as the black cat, rising to his mistress's defense, ran up the hall to wind his sleek body around Mummy's ankles. The old lady chuckled.

"I'll be fine," Poonam assured, conferring on cat an obligatory nod of thanks. She wasn't heading for the campaign office, but somewhere else.

*You smell fire,* the cat said with eyes greener than normal.

Mummy struggled to free herself of him, but he held fast, as if to endorse Poonam's decision to seek out the source.

*Yes, I do smell fire,* she thought. *At the very least, smoke. And what harm is there in that?*

\*\*\*

Two streets over, in a remarkably conceived clearing, ringed only by oak and maple trees, Zoltan Kárpáty burned leaves. That he did this without apparent care spoke to his flagrant disregard for the bylaws that tried to steal his retirement money.

A tall man, broad shouldered, and rather dashing if one got past all the body hair, the newly single gardener and all-around decent guy on Saffron Drive commanded a lot of attention. Poonam Rajput knew all about him, having picked up the details at a Hatha yoga class she signed up for after her husband's death.

Never one for Lehenga Choli[2], she easily donned yoga skins and sweated out her pain with the others who, between no-fat sour cream smoothies touched with mint and cucumber, talked about 'who was doing whom' in their not so quiet neighborhood.

---

[2] Casual skirt and blouse worn in India.

"This was way before you Poonie," her new friend from Hatha yoga said one day over drinks, "but that street north of yours used to be a hotbed for swinging."

"Swinging?" Poonie's eyebrows vaulted with interest. She had read Gay Talese's *Thy Neighbor's Wife* clandestinely in her neighbor's basement growing up. Presented as a studious effort into the psychology of multiple attraction, the thick volume was widely celebrated as a major and honest breakthrough. Well ahead of her peers intellectually, Poonie took it in, and rejected it quickly; the idea of partner swapping, even then, unappealing.

Poonie was a square back then, and she knew it, ignoring school friends' hints at Kama Sutra and their questioning looks when she said she knew nothing about it. "Kama Sutra," her mother told her, "was devil's work, perpetuated by devils and taken up by the hippies in San Francisco when they weren't doing the hashish."

Poonie accepted this. She was neither from San Francisco, nor was she a hippie. While she enjoyed night-time soaps like *Dallas* and *Dynasty*, her prurient interests were sublimated into English literature and, later, pharmacological studies.

But things were different now. Her beloved Sikander, imported for her from Bangalore after her eighteenth birthday, had been a steady and dutiful companion throughout their marriage. Like she, he had little interest in Kama Sutra, and in that, she could explain—if she wanted to—their lack of progeny after two decades of marriage. That was then. Siki was dead. At thirty-eight, she still had a chance. But not from swingers two streets over, or from anyone in hot yoga class.

Why then had she put the cat down in favor of an autumnal walk instead of hopping into her sensible Volvo and heading over to the campaign office?

Zoltan the Gardener provided the answer.

"Hello," she offered shyly, trespassing onto his property.

"Hello to you" he responded, without so much as a backward glance. It was like he didn't need to capture her image because it was already there, digitized and stored, inside his large head.

Poonam's heart picked up speed.

"I was looking for my cat—" she lied, "—and I saw your smoke. I thought maybe he would follow it." She wiped her hands on her sari.

Zoltan poked at the mass of smoldering leaves that fought heroically against his ministrations. Damp from overnight, they refused to go quietly.

"Not here," he said, turning, this time, to face her. "Not likely to ever be. Cats, like all animals, know to avoid fire."

"Oh?" Poonie mumbled, taking in his awesomeness. She delighted in seeing the big Hungarian up close again.

"How's your friend?"

"Who?" Poonie couldn't stop thinking about smoke and fire.

"The lady in the housecoat. She broke her foot, didn't she?"

Poonie resented the insertion of Bronagh Caley into their moment. She shrugged, switching back to wildlife. "Animals are a lot smarter than we give them credit for."

Zoltan nodded in agreement. "It's in their genes. That's why I never smoke when I go hunting."

He reached into his woolly Mackinaw, which sported a multitude of pockets, each with its own assigned utility. At face value, it was a dangerous article of clothing for a dangerous man; the kind of man who navigated by compass, walked the woods in the dark, and stuffed his pockets with shotgun shells and a Bowie knife.

Poonam Rajput was not put off. While the coat's function aided in the slaughter of innocent animals, its pattern was, strangely enough, compelling, suggesting an attitude quite opposite to the sinister one intended. Brown, black, yellow and red, with geometric bars intersecting to create fantastic squares, the pattern on his coat seemed comical, as if wooing animals to come tither, when they ought to turn tail and flee, was a joke they should all be in on.

Zoltan was quite tall—much taller than Sikander—and, even better, somewhat darker in the epidermis. His hair, black, his eyes, occipital in their wolfish yellow-gray, sent thoughts of lycanthropy through her synapses that made her shift in her rubber boots. She stuffed her hands into the pockets of her raincoat to still their fidgeting, an affectation that hounded her from youth, and was a dead giveaway to anyone searching for flaws.

His hands, large, veined, scarred and brown, like oiled walnuts, produced a crumpled pack of Marlboro Golds, which he pried apart to produce two perfectly unsullied filter-tipped cigarettes.

Suddenly, he grinned.

"Would you like one?"

Poonam wanted to demur in spite of a strong desire to accept the offering. Reaching for the smoke would enable her to touch his hand, if only for a brief moment, then and only then, would she know if her feelings were real. But then her upbringing and education weighed in with the full force of an animated angel sitting on her shoulder, just like the ones she saw in the cartoons she watched as a kid.

*"What are you doing?'* the angel commanded. *"Smoking is bad. Say 'no' and leave at once."*

*"That's well and good, and oh so fine for you to say, moron,"* the little devil on the other shoulder burst in, as all little devil's do. *"You haven't walked in her shoes. Our lady's not going to curl up and die!"* He nudged her in Zoltan's direction. *"Go for it, little sister."*

"Thank you," she said, reaching for the cigarette and the hand that held it.

Solid and sturdy, Zoltan felt amazing on first brush; even better when she clamped both hands around his to receive his light.

"Thank you," she repeated, unselfconsciously blowing out the flame through the ciggie clamped between her lips.

"*Stultus est sicut stultus facit,*"[3] said the angel on her shoulder.

"*Adversus solem ne loquitor,*"[4] said the devil in her corner.

Zoltan gallantly flipped the top of the old butane lighter shut with a clack that sounded final. Clearly, he had done this many times before—lit cigarettes for women in rubber boots in the middle of the forest. But he never smoked when he hunted—he said that earlier. He wasn't hunting now...

The realization sank in when he turned his back to her. Poonie swallowed her heart.

"Well, I guess I should move along—" She took a few steps back and away from the fire that had drawn her there. Under the circumstances, flight made a great deal of sense.

"You live across the street from me," he said, not inviting her to stay, but not telling her to leave either. "I see you on the lawn with your mother."

Poonie's emotions flat-lined. If there was any moment to be had, it would not be today, and it wouldn't be with him.

"Yes," she said, matter-of-factly. "Mother came to live with me after my husband died."

---

[3] Latin. "Stupid is as stupid does."

[4] Latin. "Don't speak against the sun." Idiom. In this you are completely wrong.

"I'm very sorry," he said, straightening, the Mackinaw flexing across his wide shoulders.

Poonie stopped breathing.

*Vescere bracis meis.*[5]

"I just lost my wife to a fancy divorce lawyer with a Porsche."

Poonie feigned seriousness, not knowing if the split was a blessing or a disappointment.

Zoltan shrugged. "I always knew she'd throw me out. Just my luck. She's his problem now."

He looked at her.

A hint of a grin passing for a knowing smirk crossed her face. She ached with the desire to let go.

"Ahhhhh," he exhaled a plume of smoke, igniting the air around them. "I think I came *this close* to making you laugh." He pinched his thumb and forefinger together, making a perfect zero.

Poonie bowed her head. She had not only studied him, but his history as well. What he was, where he came from; all the things he could and should be...for her.

The gardener was slick, mysterious, and splendidly Hungarian, from a place of Danube cruises and soaring violins; where crowned heads, long dead, had started wars, and gypsy fires lit the night! Paprika and pálinka, lecsó and czardas, cigányok and flame set her world alight like a Bollywood story without the angst and tree hugging. And it could all be hers if she'd only allow it!

Poonie took one last draw before grinding the Marley out under her boot.

"Thank you for the smoke."

"Thank you."

At home, asleep on her bed, in front of the fireplace channel, the black cat was waiting, his love perceptible over Zoltan's fire. Calling, calling, with reassurance and a

---

[5] Latin. "Eat my shorts."

promise, he had given her a means to leave the house and with it, first contact with the one she now compulsively loved! Poonam Khanzada Rajput smiled.

She owed that cat a lot.

# Chapter Eleven
## The Fetishists

*One week ago*

Carlos didn't see their faces because they wore black hooded capes lined with shiny red fabric. Skulking and shadowed, they whispered, moving listlessly, like keyed automatons in a bloodless universe. He remembered dank air and wall coverings—old and new—arranged to dapple irregular surfaced walls of cork and exposed fiberglass pink: the stuff of monster movies, minus the chainsaws and plastic sheeting.

The black cat shuddered. For fourteen days and fourteen nights he had waited, along with the others, in flimsy plexiglass cages for an end that could not be good. Two cats—a Persian and a Burmese—had been removed from this place, never to return. Carlos, fearing the worst, resolved never to give them a chance to do to him what had, so clearly and finally, been done to the others.

He had enough to cope with, given his observations to date. Human beings, unlike any other creatures on the planet, assumed the high ground where bad behavior was concerned. They weren't harming anybody, they reasoned. They were merely 'trying things on,' 'exploring,' and 'being curious,' all under constant cover of 'consent' with a capital C. What they were doing was 'private,' 'adult-themed,' and felt 'pretty damned good.' Best of all, it was legal.

Carlos mewled softly to the full moon after the first party. After that, he assuaged insult with cat nip, promising that if he was ever free again, he would exact his revenge against the jerk with the corduroy pants.

"There, there, my beautiful boy," Corduroy cooed, once he had Carlos safely hidden away behind the big gray door. "I'm going to introduce you to some very appreciative people, people who understand what you are and what you mean."

Carlos flashed wide crazy-eyed saucer pupils at the pervert, but these had no measurable effect as Corduroy turned to the human seated behind a large, ugly metal desk.

"They'll like him. Don't you think?"

The human behind the desk, older, thicker, and red in the cheeks, shuffled through trouser pockets searching for something of great importance—greater than what Corduroy was saying, because the question was ignored.

"I mean, I can't take my hands off him," he continued, over-stroking the hissing beastie that would not calm. Addled by his own appetites, the fawning human failed to comprehend that his master was in no mood to stroke him with platitudes or words of thanks: he was busy, playing with a bright blue YoYo.

Corduroy frowned, his features giving way to a petulant snarl more common to small children, whose contempt for those who minded them could not be easily masked. "Cuz we have to keep doing this. It's the only way."

Carlos hoped not, inferring from the one-sided conversation that his captors did not enjoy equal status. A tinkly desk clock of antiquated design gonged, marking the passage of time as the YoYo Man, lost in dense contemplation over a plate of honey crullers, punched his companion's mindless patter with primordial grunts to accompany burps and farts from a squat water cooler. The only animated object in the room other than the clock and YoYo that swung precariously from foreshortened fingers, the water cooler represented life-giving refreshment; something Carlos refused as the hours torqued by.

They were waiting for something, these humans. But what?

As the light outside receded and visitors' knocks were rebuffed by curt "Not now's," the cat sensed the answer: They were waiting for the cover of night, at which point to remove him for their dark purposes.

Like all living things, Carlos could forego food for extended periods, but he could not live without water, so when it was finally offered to him again, he took it, succumbing very shortly thereafter to whatever Corduroy and the YoYo Man had put into it.

An indeterminate time later, he woke to the sweet visage of a comely Siamese who licked the plexiglass walls that separated them in a kind of tender greeting. Eyes clear, fur unmatted, the female appeared to be well-treated, but this did little to calm the cornered kitty. Siamese did not answer back when he tried to communicate, indicating that something other than food and fresh litter had been done to her.

Carlos paced off the four corners of his cell that first night, his thoughts obscured by the stench of kitty toilette, something he'd never had to deal with before. Among his many charms, it was said, was his dog-like attitude with respect to going to the bathroom. Much to Zoey and her grandparents' delight, he ignored the litter box provided in favor of meowing at the back door when he wanted out. It was a good thing Zoey's flat was a three step walk up from the street; were it not for those easy outings, however brief, he would have died in that little apartment.

As time passed, compulsive grooming and a study of his surroundings for possible breaches gave way to thoughts of the Fischer's and what might have become of them. The old man, he knew, could take him or leave him—he very nearly did at the side of the road. But the woman surprised him. Distant, but kind, he never figured her for a pick up and leaver.

The door opened, and Carlos' thoughts of the Fischer's evaporated at the sight of the hooded humans, returned and in deep discussion.

"I'll quote it again for you, if you're having trouble," a familiar, but sexless voice offered to the quavering frame on high heels trailing not far behind.

"It will take more than film festivals to convince me," the respondent female replied with a candor uncharacteristic for such heuristic surroundings. "'The most exhilarating aspect of our existence is the fabric, much of which is esoteric and, therefore, demanding of further inspection.' Did I get it right, honey?"

Though not big on the arts, the cat had a certain fondness for T.V., watching and liking a good deal of what previous keepers selected for him. He recognized the quote from Pilsen Güdderammerüng's *Blod av Däggdjur* immediately. While the scenes with the mopey red-haired woman dragged, the colorful characters her squat little husband played with were something to note. They were, in fact, a foretaste of what he was soon to meet, as well as a reminder that real life seldom mimicked fantasy no matter how hard the humans tried to hide behind it.

Escorted with force up creaky wooden stairs into a passageway straight out of Kafka, the cat squirmed as the space opened into a large windowless room. There, light from tall lamps shot white hot from floor to ceiling, their beams reminiscent of Nuremburg on its worst day. These, uniform in design, were placed with deliberate care every six feet or so, like the stations of the cross in a Catholic cathedral. The lack of adornments on the walls and in the cornices, however, made this place anything but holy, the ecclesiastical taking a back seat to amateur theatrical.

Kitty growled a thousand growls, all unheard.

Unlike their hooded counterparts from down below, the humans upstairs concealed their identities not with comic book capes, but with papier mâché masks, obscuring what were probably facial features of little worth. Their bodies, once unshrouded, offered an array of tattoos and piercings. Many were on the heavy side, their adipose jiggling with the multitudes that tried to copulate in interesting ways. Nothing at all like Güdderammerüng's *Blod av Däggdjur*, which supported an aesthete both elegant and worshipful, this sexy orgy party tried way too hard to be what it clearly was not.

Large cat statues in the Egyptian fashion added to the absurdity of the occasion. Eight feet tall, the polystyrene golden statues came by way of a prop wrangler and his girlfriend, who had purloined them from a storage locker after a film wrap in Vancouver. Under red-pink lights, the cat sentinels were positioned in equal numbers on either side of a large altar, marked by numerous fetish objects and eschatological symbols. In line with the forced revelry that abounded, their uses gained currency with the rather strange choice of Seventies-era rock music that assaulted the senses.

Working up a large hairball, Carlos barely caught his breath for all the hookah vapors filling the room. Humans of all genders did what they did together, separately and severally. Many appeared older, their sagging midsections reminding him of the old Tom's that lived out their lives in the Banford barn outside Cavan.

Claiming to want something more, something more in line with Güdderammerüng's vision, their attempts at consciousness raising from the "darkness to the light" fell flat. These humans, for all their writhing and hookah smoking, fundamentally lacked what the cats had: that state of grace that comes with knowing who you are and what you're here for.

"Over here," sexless voice yelled through the cacophony that was the tinny sound of old King Biscuit Flower Hour radio shows, rebroadcast from a reel-to-reel over a sub-par sound system. The Siamese female, held aloft by a large goatish male, cast a beseeching look his way, as she was lowered with loving reverence onto the back of a hairy homo sap that mated his female vigorously face to face.

In the melee, Carlos made out other shapes—the American shorthair, Maine Coon, Scottish Rag Doll, Sphinx and Peterbald, along with a Common, like himself, though snipped at the tail to look like a Manx—all employed in the service of the kooky humans.

"Gimme a Himalayan," a throaty female with a smoker's rasp gasped, as the sweet Munchkin dragged across her back gave out, exhausted from its efforts.

"Blood letting is essential to our beliefs," a hooded freak with a blue YoYo explained to a quivering couple. Clearly "new," Carlos could not discern if they were excited or fearful.

"We don't force religious beliefs on anyone, per se," YoYo continued, as he rocked the cradle with the spinning orb, "but it helps if you have a healthy appreciation for the beauty that is cat."

\*\*\*

When muffled voices, signifying meal-time, bled under the door, Carlos made ready. He had no compunction about dying from exposure after a life outdoors. Heck, he'd even go gracefully under the wheels of a careless driver if given a choice. What he would not do was succumb to this perverse charade.

He was tired of being a loofa.

Maybe it was the darkness of the windowless hole he'd been placed in that gave him the advantage, or maybe it was human arrogance that presupposed the feline's reluctance to fight back. But fight back he did. With a snap of his powerful hind legs, he vaulted at the hooded figure that removed the top of his cage, catching the fool on his left eye with claws grown too long in captivity.

The idiot responded with a prolonged howl that did not bring friends to assist, but a large ladder and a pair of two by fours propped against the wall instead. Freeing themselves from their pitiless moorings, the second-grade planks gave way, bringing the ladder along with it, each falling with enough force to set the cages on edge like dominoes in a free fall.

If his compatriots could have talked, they would have sung his praises. If they could have voted, they would have elected him to office. They were free!

Carlos the Wonder Cat had done a great thing. He was just getting started.

# Chapter Twelve
## On the Campaign Trail

Poonam Rajput said nothing when her neighbor put a campaign sign right up next to hers on their shared front lawn. This disappointed Bronagh terribly. Even as she limped into the committee room, where the party faithful assembled awaiting orders on how best to slay the bright young man with the amazing head of hair, all she could think about was her neighbor's sudden lack of interest in politics.

"Maybe she's in love," the young campaign staffer assigned to Bronagh and her automobile contended, as they drove off with a trunk full of signs and wooden stakes. Not yet ready to knock on doors owing to her injury, sign crew was the next best thing Bronagh could come up with to aid in the fight against legal dope and fiscal irresponsibility.

"I don't know that it could be that. She's a widow. It would be too soon, I think."

"You'd be surprised," the young woman replied. "It's not how it used to be—you know—like in my mom's time. People move on faster now. It's allowed."

Bronagh wondered how she'd react if she was in Poonam's shoes, but disavowed all thoughts as quickly as they had appeared. It was bad luck to speculate on such things, and she would not invite anything in that didn't belong. Bill was a gem, anyway, and could never be replaced, so speculating on such notions was not just counter intuitive, but a wholesale waste of time.

Shaking off waves of heat, she wiped her hand on her coat. She was hot flashing again, something that she wished she could control better, but could not without aid of drugs she didn't trust. Lately, Bill had taken to sleeping in the family room, assuring her that it compromised in no way the high esteem in which he always held her. "You're hot stuff, is all," he said easily. "When it passes, I'll come back."

"We have the funniest little cat on our street," Bronagh said, changing the subject. "A real curiosity. Acts more like a dog than a cat."

The young woman, deep into her ear buds, didn't answer. This suited Bronagh just fine. In addition to sweating like a teenager, she had taken to engaging in heartfelt chats with herself, an activity that was unacceptable in her mother's time.

"He runs to me like a puma when he sees me. Full on and with great speed, like he knows me." She swallowed back the lump forming in her throat, the first of many she'd have in a day, her emotions gaining ground like a disease she couldn't treat. "I'm sorry," she sniffed. "I've been having a lot of trouble with City Works and now they're after my cat. The neighbor complained."

"I have a neighbor who stares at me through the fence," the younger woman said, pulling out her earbuds. "I used to think he was just an old perv, but the neighbor says he's a war criminal of some sort."

"War criminal?" Her interest piqued, Bronagh quickly got hold of herself.

"That's what they say. But ya know, I don't know what war he'd be a criminal from. I mean, we're always at war, right?"

Bronagh's eyes filled for maybe the hundredth time that day, and with that, she weighed the pluses and minuses of confiding in the stranger next to her. "Do you have a cat?" she asked.

The woman shrugged. "I used to. Long time ago. But my grandma let him out and I never saw him again."

"Really? That's unusual for a house cat, isn't it?"

"No. Not if he was feral to begin with. My dad brought him home from the food terminal where he worked. Beautiful cat. An all-black Persian. Called him Eight Ball. We had no business trying to keep him. Once something's free, it's free forever."

They pulled into Dunkin' Donuts. "I have to pee," Bronagh's new friend announced. "You need anything?"

Bronagh thought of her constricting waist band, and of how it had tightened since her injury. Her throat spasmed in a sob. Everything was going to hell fast.

"No thank you, darlin.' I'm set for now."

\*\*\*

"Baby steps," Poonam chanted as her Volvo pulled into the campaign office parking lot. Never one to be political— Mummy Ji cited wrinkles and a lousy disposition as a major side effect of civic activism—she was driven more by the promises a change in leadership would bring than an adherence to a specific ideology.

"Liar," Jujaka, the little devil on her shoulder whispered.

"Well, okay, I'll concede that the party leader is pretty cute."

At just forty years, he stood a good chance of becoming the second youngest leader ever of a G7 country. This didn't make her especially proud as much as it would show the world how brave they were if they actually voted him in.

Her heart suddenly quickened. Thoughts of Zoltan Kárpáty and their flinty cigarette smoking exchange crept into her consciousness yet again.

*"Ambaji, Maha Kali, Parvati, I beg thee..."*

"For what?" Jujaka asked, making himself overly at home on her shoulder. "The gods are busy."

"For strength, of course," she replied, conscious that she was speaking out loud and alone in one of the safest automobiles in the world.

Immediately in front of her, crowds thronged. This was unexpected. She had merely been asked by a stranger on the telephone if the local candidate, Errol Deutscher, could count on her support on election day. *"Yes."* Would she like a lawn sign? *"Yes."* Would she like to come in and volunteer? *"Sure."* If it got her out of the house, 'why not?' If she got to meet the amazing man with the fantastic hair, even better.

Zoltan Kárpáty disappeared into the mists of the unimportant. Something big was happening. The throng, pulsing with fervid excitement, swayed to and fro in a sea of tri-color ribbons, the colors of the party redolent, as hatted campaign staffers passed out plastic pom-poms on long wooden dowels to be waved above their heads.

Poonam, uncertain, threw the car into reverse, as if commanded by forces unseen to get out of the way. A sharp rap across the roof of the car brought her to earth as she jammed the brake pedal with enough force to make her foot burn.

A young man with slate blue eyes appeared at the driver's side, rotating his right hand in clockwise motion. She rolled her window down.

"You're fine where you are," the young man— 'Bob,' as indicated by his 'Hello My Name Is' sticker— breezed, as he flipped through his iPhone with steady determination. "If you'd been a minute later, you'd have never got in here. Dr. Pepper?" Still iPhoning, he pushed a fizzy pop through her window, the familiar white and maroon aluminum can jimmied up with campaign stickers that read *Vote Errol Deutscher* and *All Things Are Equal Now*.

"All things are equal now," a beautifully suited woman in a foam hat with tri-colored foam finger roared into a set mic from a fixed riser barely visible to Poonam from behind the crowd.

"Is that Errol Deutscher?" Poonam asked Bob, who looked at her like she was insane.

"Uhhhhhhhh," he said, punctuating his impressive eloquence with a long pause.

Poonam scanned the front windows of the storefront campaign office, which confirmed her mistake in spectacular fashion. Errol Deutscher was their amazing woman candidate, but not the woman currently hogging the riser.

"That's her honor, Mayor Lagerqvist," Bob sniffed, suddenly unfriendly.

Of course it was, Poonam reddened, patting the steering wheel of her sensible Swedish auto. Mummy Ji had voted for Freja Lagerqvist, citing the politician's strength against those bullies at city hall who would "turn Pictontown on the Downs into another Babylon."

"I know who it is, Bob," Poonam said, squaring her shoulders in haughty recovery. "She fought the airport, and the sewage treatment plant." (No one wanted waste pumped in from neighboring Blenkinskane, not even the Frettinger's.)

The entire front of the committee room, papered over with near to life size renderings of the candidate, showed a woman determined. Whether suited in Calvin Klein or North Face, Errol Deutscher would take on the old ideas, just like her colleague Freja Lagerqvist had in the fight against stupidity.

"Do you support the legalization of cannabis?" Poonam asked Bob. But he was already gone.

A large, sparkly new bus of the kind used by musicians and motocross racing teams pulled into the lot, sending the crowd into peels of delighted screams. Men, women, boys and girls opened their hearts and minds to the bus's occupant. The vehicle came to rest at an angle perpendicular to Poonam's Volvo.

She gasped. Not only had she had torrid thoughts about Zoltan the Gardener this day, but now the leader of her chosen political party as well. With his bus mere steps from her front bumper, she daren't think what the hell she'd do if he walked off it and straight into her arms. Another bus marked "Media" pulled in immediately behind the first one, which had been wrapped with a gigantic image of the wondrous young man and his beautiful family.

Poonam popped a Tic Tac.

She had expected to be stuck behind a cheap desk rented from Office Plus making phone calls. Instead, she'd get to meet her idol.

The crowd pressed forward, ignoring the stanchions set up to keep the faithful back. Press, spilling from the media bus, scrambled to catch all the drama. Poonam, her Dr. Pepper in hand, exited her Volvo to join the fray. Maybe she could touch his shoulder, or even better, shake his hand? Dreams of swapping stories with him at a kaffee klatsch fundraiser over sweet rasmalai and kaju barfi rushed her brain, making it swell, making it sing.

Rounding the front of the bus, she navigated her diminutive body through the mass of humanity, searching for him. But the door to the bus, now open, revealed only a couple of tired looking suits in need of a shave.

"Where is he? Where is he?" she pleaded, not feeling the least bit stupid about it.

A woman next to her dropped a pom pom at her feet, her free hand rifling through an oversized Fossil bag for a single limp tissue. She dabbed her cheek as a wedge of supporters blocked them off.

"He's inside," the stranger whimpered, swallowing vast gasps of air that vibrated against her vocal chords to produce a strange, almost feral sound. "And we can't get in. Fire Code." She turned to Poonam. "But I'm okay. He's near. And I'm content."

# Chapter Thirteen
## Mummy Ji Loses the Cat

*Later that same day...*

To be near is to be content. A novel idea. But what if contentment is the last thing a person needs? At this juncture in Poonam Rajput's life, contentment was nothing more than an excuse to hide. Her friend Ronnie had done this for years, declining into baking and Bolly chat rooms as a replacement for real life with real people. It wasn't for her. Poonie even toyed with the idea of returning to work sooner rather than later.

Baldev "Bull Dave" Gurjar, her boss and owner of Mahaan MediPharm Drugstores, begged her at the beginning of flu season to, at least, start back part-time. "For shots." He did it again over the phone as she drove away from the chaos at Deutscher campaign H.Q. "It's just crazy here, and the people are so damn rude."

Mahaan MediPharm, once the site of a long gone video store, was ideally set to attract traffic. With two condos situated within walking distance and an above average middle-income subdivision along the northern border, it cleared rent, utilities, salaries and taxes with plenty to spare. Add on a dollar store, an in-and-out Hakka noodle place, and a big box bargain grocery anchor in the same plaza with plenty of free parking, and Bull Dave had the cost conscious and devil may care spenders all within reach.

Poonam, hanging on her cell phone, hesitated. There was nothing in their belief system that prevented her from returning insofar as mourning rituals were concerned.

But Mummy Ji's words still rang in her ears: "If you'd lived in Bapu's time, you'd have been expected to commit suttee, or at the least, disappear yourself in all piety to an ashram." Poonam, shaking after Sikander's cremation, could only think of suttee in terms of social policy and the health care savings realized if whole couples disappeared in one sweep. As for ashram—hooey—leave that to the yogi's and The Beatles worshippers that followed them.

"Are you listening to me," Bull Dave interrupted. "Where'd you go?"

Bull Dave was a great boss: young, careless, with a penthouse and an Audi, which he kept shrouded and safe in an underground garage space downtown that he paid $12,000 annually to keep. Building his store chain with seed money from the old country, he relied on her level headedness to spread the word that Mahaan MediPharm was more than an immigrant business bought and paid for by wealthy relatives. Bull Dave and his staff had heart, even when the customers got impatient and huffy.

"Hello?" Bull Dave yelled through the phone, his voice edgy like the customers that so drove him crazy.

She threw the car into 'park.' Somehow, the Volvo had brought her home. "I'm here, I'm here." She just didn't want to admit to him that she liked the time off, didn't need the career to validate herself, and could get much more from some time alone, with a little adventure thrown in for good measure.

"Let me think on it, okay?" She shut her phone off before he could reply.

What to do now? The day hadn't been a total loss— she had come *this close* to her idol.

Mummy Ji appeared at the upstairs window waving frantically. Her hair askew, her Chanderi lopsided, something was clearly amiss. Poonie, not expecting this, sprang from her car, worried that the old lady was under siege. The front door was open, just slightly, just enough for her to wish that she was armed.

"Mummy?" she called out from the foyer, cautious to take stock of her surroundings. The murtis,[6] undisturbed, kept watch over the prashad arranged with great care on the altar in the front room; flowers, incense and fruit, likewise, remained upright. The only thing *off* appeared to be the Agra Petha, made from the jack-o'-lantern pumpkins, that sat unfinished on the kitchen table.

"Mummy?" she called out, louder this time. "Why are you making Agra Petha with orange pumpkins?" There was plenty of white.

Mummy Ji's voice rang out strong and clear. Bearing no signs of strain, it deflated Poonie's alarm, but inflamed her inner unrest. "What is she playing at?" she said to the murtis, which smiled their understanding back: *Don't be so impatient, daughter.*

"You're just in time," Mummy Ji hollered, as Poonam, vaulting the stair treads by two's, came to a standstill in the family room doorway.

Her hearing aid clearly turned off, Mummy Ji swayed side to side as the T.V. sing-songed full blast.

Poonie covered her ears.

"Sanjay is on the Omni Television Network. There is going to be a marathon."

Poonie, smiling sweetly at her mother, turned the television down several decibels. Sanjay was her mother's favorite actor. Dividing his time between Bangalore and these shores, there was nothing he couldn't play that she didn't love. But Poonie was tired from her busy day and wanted to retire to her room with a book and her new friend, Carlos the Wonder Cat.

---

[6] A statue of a deity or person in Indian culture.

"Put your hearing aid in Mummy," she said, kissing Mummy Ji's forehead. "I'll go deaf before I go lame if you keep this up."

Poonam looked around the room. Cozy, inviting, draped in lush lime, yellow, and fuchsia tones, it had become her mother's preferred space. Yet, something, on closer examination, appeared off. The day had been perfect, save for a few hiccups, and now she wanted to retire to replay the movie in her head, analyse it, chew on it, enjoy it. But something was indeed missing.

"Mummy," she said slowly.

Mummy Ji didn't answer: Sanjay was back on the screen hugging a tree, singing softly of a love lost, never to be replaced.

"Oh, Mummy," Poonie said. Amidst the sound and color and the promise of joy, her dark shadow was nowhere to be seen. She immediately thought of the front door.

"Where is the cat?"

# Chapter Fourteen
## Freedom

*One week ago*

The black cat's journey from captivity was a relatively happy one given the extent of his injuries. While the fetishists, at no time, struck him, or used unwonted implements on any part of his body, he was routinely used as a living loofa, dragged across the backs of the strange humans.

Not unfamiliar with human sexual practice, Carlos found their idea of pleasure to be far removed from anything he'd ever seen or experienced in the animal kingdom. In defense, the cat did what came naturally to all felines: he hissed, nipped, bit and scratched. To his great surprise, this was exactly what the humans wanted. Blood letting by feline was central to their beliefs, their euphoria with it suggesting that the marks left behind brought them closer, united in their own strange Nirvana.

Once escaped, he ran far and fast such that he took little notice of the bald patches that dotted his chest and abdomen. The fur would grow back; a restored faith in the human race would take longer.

"Is that you?" a familiar and frightening voice called out, its shrill bringing back to him thoughts of Corduroy and the asshole with the YoYo. "I'm glad they didn't put you down."

The old pain in the ass who'd started this ill-conceived odyssey by turning him over to Animal Control spied him crossing a major artery en route to Saffron Drive.

Carlos picked up the pace, knowing that the concerned citizen with the fatted ankles hadn't a prayer of catching him this time.

The outdoors found him badly out of practice. There were no barns to take shelter in, no farmer's wives with warm, welcoming kitchens, only fields of scrub dotted by City Development Site signs earmarking the parcels for airport, casino and hotel. Free again, he should have kept going, past the McMansions, strip malls, strip clubs, and petit bourgeois consignment shops, but somehow, and not entirely consciously, his paws took him back to the Fischers.

That he was returning to the old neighborhood was divined more by instinct than by any love he might have harbored for Zoey's grandparents. What he needed now was down time, a time to heal, rest and plot next moves. He paused, scratching an itch under his jaw, noting the scar over his left cheek to be especially irksome this day. Stiff and unremitting, his mark of passage was usually celebrated with coo's of sympathy, followed by treats and invitations to heavy petting. Today, it was an invitation to a renewed friendship, his pause giving Fate enough time to place a fresh and better opportunity in his wake. As he crossed onto Saffron, a snappy looking chap in a fine blue and white uniform hailed him with calls of "Yuri! Yuri!"

Officious in appearance, this human bore the unmistakable stamp of power and influence. Epaulets on his shoulders indicated authority, but the smile crossing his lips, together with the uniformed females poised at either shoulder, told the cat instantly that he was among friendlies.

He responded in kind. Without looking both ways, Carlos bolted across the street and into the welcoming arms of Gus, commercial pilot and swinger.

"Where've ya been old friend?" he asked, scooping the tattered black cat up in easy moves. "I haven't seen you in weeks."

"He looks like he's been through a storm or two," the uniformed female named Soraya said, as she stroked him tenderly with long, vermillion fingernails.

Carlos began to purr.

The scar on his left cheek was an immediate identifier to the pilot that this was indeed his old friend, but the other marks puzzled. Gus' features creased as he rolled Carlos over onto his back, revealing the patches of white skin. The patches, together with the cat's offer of no resistance, confounded the human.

"Yuri's not usually so friendly, and his coat..." His voice trailed off, as Carlos, righting himself, bore deeper into the pilot's shoulder.

The threesome took him indoors where he was treated to Tasty Tenders cat hors d'oeuvre, a speciality of the house which, the cat noted, had undergone extensive renovations since his last visit. Gone were the plush carpets and circular spinning human-sized ottoman favored by the swingers on party nights. Richly colored wide-planked flooring dominated the main room, topped by a huge sixteen-man sectional. Marked by strategically placed blue white LED lights, the impressive piece resembled the kind of detached, free-floating interstellar objects favored on cable network T.V., the sparkly lights clearly intended to represent constellations on a midsummer night.

A combination of shredded chicken and beef neatly arranged in an attractive oblong dish placed in front of him disappeared in under thirty seconds as did the second and third.

"He hasn't eaten in days," Dakota, their busty, warm-blooded companion exclaimed, her slender arms criss-crossing her chest with tremendous authority.

In that, she was right. After weeks of dining on Juicy Vittles, a shitty B grade cat food picked up for cheap from the Thrift Mart, Carlos found himself incapable of processing wild game without getting the runs. In response, he had taken to chewing on moist, wheat-colored grasses and little else.

"You can eat as much as you want, old friend," Gus soothed, stroking the cat's back in sombre reassurance. "Whatever's been done to you stops here and now."

That night, Carlos slept like he hadn't slept in weeks nestled among warm bodies that loved generously and without pain.

***

As much as he adored Gus and his free loving companions, Carlos could not bend his pointy ears around the name 'Yuri.' Culled from the much-loved film *Doctor Zhivago*, which the pilot made a point of screening bi-annually, it was a dead giveaway that the cool pilot wasn't really cool at all. Hand feeding his companions in bed the next morning, the man had let his tender sentiments slip, reaffirming that he was a romantic slob, pretty much like everyone else in the room.

Dakota frowned over her custard tart. A clod of dull matted fur came away in her hands as she stroked the kitty, still exhausted from his travels. "We should take him to the vet. Whoever did this should be shot."

"How do you know anyone did anything?" Soraya asked, running her long fingers along the length of Dakota's spine. "He's an outside cat. Right, Gustavo?"

Gus, yawning, stretched his full length, much to the delight of his companions, who straddled him then and there. The cat, forgotten, escaped the confines of too many fluffy pillows on a down filled duvet. Soraya, of course, was right. He was an outside cat, and it was to the wild he would return. But not yet. For while it was true that the feline was governed, first and always, by instinct, something like Yuri Zhivago's desire to return to his Lara spurred Carlos in a direction contrary to common cat sense. Down the stairs, past the zebra-striped divan—a favorite vantage point from which to watch the swingers in action—through the mirror-lined hall—another feature that added oomph to the parties—into the kitchen and through a screen door left ajar, as if his companions had already anticipated his need to press on, Carlos headed for Saffron Drive.

Zoey Fischer had seen to his medical needs in his first months of life, beginning with a pair of snips that took away his desire to love females of his species. Too young at the time to understand anything beyond the pain and discomfort inflicted, he later learned that the act was intended to keep him in his place, where his energies could, absurdly enough, be devoted exclusively to creatures of a different species.

Humans were odd things, too preoccupied at times to see to their own good. And so, it was with this in mind that Carlos passed by the house of the dear lady who called him 'Clara' and the home of George, the Greek guy who fed him pepperoni. Upright, present and uncomplicated, they did not need him.

He pressed on.

A pile of leaves, multicolored and variegated with blackened veins and lacy cut outs left by insects now off the job, caught his attention as he mounted Zoltan Kárpáty's lawn. A breeze grown frosty picked up speed hinting, perhaps, at an early snowfall. The gust—nature's air kiss—caused a stir beneath the leaves, revealing black eyes and bristle brush fur, quivering, to betray the owner: a hapless vole. The cat's paw, raised and ready to strike, stopped mid-air when a piercing shriek from a location he knew well interrupted him.

Quite unlike everything he knew about the Fischers—neat, orderly, Teutonic—their loud, creaky garage door had been pulled open to reveal the back end of Rudolf's Pontiac Parisienne. Bobbing and weaving, the car appeared to be self-animated, until two sets of feet—bipeds—came into view.

Carlos drew closer, his senses overtaken by something alluring. The car heaved a great heave on its wide tires in what looked like a reaction to a great load being placed inside of it. There was an odor too. Not rank, not unpleasant, but rich and tangy like animal protein curing in fresh, vapid oxygenated air.

Women's voices to his rear tickled his back, and he turned to look at them. On their porches, still in sleeping clothes and with coffee cups in hand, the females focused on him with unsettling interest.

Choices beckoned—as always—pulling the object of niggling questions in opposite directions. What was Rudolf Fischer getting up to in his garage? And why was the woman in the pink bathrobe eyeing him like one of the freaks across town?

Carlos asked himself these questions as he crossed the road to meet Bronagh Caley for the first time.

### END OF ACT 1

# Chapter Fifteen
## The Tale of Shashthi and Her Vahana[7]

The door, ajar, taunted Poonie, along with the freshening sky that seemed to say: 'don't worry, all's well.' The cat was gone. She clasped her hands with so much force that she might have drawn blood were it not for the large jade ring that slowed her grip.

Mummy Ji had let the cat out, and in so doing managed to unfold and scatter the emotional laundry Poonie had so cleverly starched and concealed these many months. She thought of Sikander and Zoltan, each appearing in rapid motion behind her eyes, and then quaked with the pale sun, its UV a warning of things sinister to come.

The cat was gone.

She bowed her head to stave off reverberating sobs along with a very real desire to do murder.

"Let me tell you the story of Shashthi and her vahana who is cat."

Poonam turned to face her mother who, incredibly, had managed to tear herself away from Sanjay and the Bolly TV marathon. "She is a most beautiful goddess, and very fair. When a selfish young woman blames cat for stealing food meant for Shashthi, the cat is beaten. That cat is Shashthi's; the young woman, the thief."

Poonie smoothed her hair, which had somehow managed to stand on end. "Mummy—"

"Let me finish!" The old woman hobbled to the door, shutting it in plain sight of the murtis, which offered

---

[7] An animal entity that transports a Hindu deity; a "mount."

knowing grins. "When Shashthi learned of the cat's mistreatment, she divined to have the liar punished. Cat stole each and every one of her children, and ate them all, except for one. This one was spared after Shashthi demanded and got for cat, an apology from the young woman who so offended him."

Poonie's eyes narrowed incredulously. "You turned my cat out because Shashthi's vahana ate babies?"

Mummy Ji waggled her cane. "No, silly one. I let cat go because to keep him is to offend him, and heaven alone knows what that would cost in apologies if we don't heed God."

Poonie scratched her tapered locks, wondering if she shouldn't cut them all off and go to ashram after all. "Thank you Mummy and thank you for your story."

Life was not a Bollywood movie; there were no quick fixes with a sing-song and a big dish of jalebi.

"You are welcome, dear one. Don't look for happiness in cat. Look for happiness in one like...Sanjay!" Her face brightened, stripping the years away. Somehow Mummy Ji could always channel joy in a crisis, as with the loss of a husband which—if she was to be believed—was not a tragedy, but a thing to be celebrated.

Mummy withdrew, leaving Poonie to consider these great insights. The murtis, on the other hand, plotted their mischief, smiling as their mistress struggled with larger questions. Did she ever love Sikander? Why was she obsessing over politics? And *what*, specifically, would she do to Zoltan if she ever got him alone?

Poonie's heart blackened. It was wrong to deny God—yes—but it was worse to deny truth; worse, still, to misread the signs.

The cat was gone, just like Sikander, and she wondered if it mattered.

She placed her hands together, seeking out the little altar in her living room. Lighting incense, she recited Shiv Prarthana, in hopes of finding her center:

*"Om Sarva Mangal Manglaye Shivay Sarvaarth Sadhike; Sharanye Trayambake Gauri Narayaani Namostu Te."*

She bit back the wash of emotions that sought to cripple her, undo her, keep her in her place. No! No more! She would focus on her well-being, prosperity, and enlightenment.

And get back a bit of her own!

Her mind turned to her lumpy neighbor and their first encounter with the magnificent black cat—*her* vahana. "Is he yours?" she asked. Bronagh hadn't answered directly, aiming instead for some deflective bullshit about her crappy reno and how she'd keep her neighbor informed as to its progress. More bullshit. The Caley's did as the Caley's saw fit. They didn't even have the decency to attend Sikander's cremation.

*"Oh, Lord Ganesha…"*

A quick breath brought hints of crayon colored leaves and the man who tended them. Their flames, snuffed out by weather, carried sultry smoke, both renewing and dangerous.

She smiled at Ganesha the Elephant. Seated next to Shiva, his purpose, to remove life hindering obstacles, was just the thing she needed.

*"Let me read the signs so that I may take the path…"*

She would find her balance. She would find her way. If not with cat, then with man.

\*\*\*

In the days following Poonam Rajput's revelation that man, not beast, would put a cap on widowhood, she deigned to find a way to run into Zoltan Kárpáty. The grocery store bearing the telltale logo of unripen tomatoes on the shopping bags he carried in from his truck was as good a place as any to begin. And she tried many times, often overlooking the green fuzzy spots on the cheese in a dairy case that shared overhead shelves with $1 shampoo and scrubby brushes.

Mummy Ji, of course, protested. The stink of halogen bleach used in generous amounts around the blood-spattered—and very stinky—butcher's case, made it less than 'kosher' in Mummy's words, and no place for decent people to park their money. "It is a bargain mart," she sniffed. "You'd do better shopping at the Big Box, although I hear their meat is quite sketchy too."

Poonie had to agree after her fourth visit. Her eyes red, her nose running, the bleach had attached to her skin, making her body an unlikely vessel for chlorine gas. After washing herself down thoroughly, she decided to troll the garden shops and larger nurseries for winter fertilizers and burlap. Any other woman, of course, would have just sidled over when he was outside working on his truck and make idle chit chat. But not her. She'd already done that in Zoltan's clearing, and nothing newsworthy had come of it.

Then one day, Bull Dave, her boss, called with an offer to get her out of the house; their destination: an interactive art expo featuring the works of eccentric German-Norwegian film auteur Pilsen Güdderammerüng.

"You won't believe it," Bull Dave gushed from behind the wheel of his Audi 8, a beautiful thing that made her Volvo look and feel like a wheelbarrow. "Güdderammerüng posits that animals and humans can enjoy satisfying interpersonal relationships over and above what society tolerates."

Poonie, freezing her ass off and dying for a drink, had an idea about what he was getting at. "Humans have been doing that for centuries, my friend. Goat herders, cattlemen in Texas, the lady one street over with the Rottweilers. It's hardly Nirvana."

Bull Dave, his long, wavy blond hair dancing *krpa*[8] against the chilly cross winds spilling over the convertible's windshield, threw his head back, as if she were a naïve school girl. "Poonie Ji. You've heard of bestiality, haven't you?"

She thought of the stories about Catherine the Great and the stallion and, of course, there were the German Bestiality Laws of 1969, which had only recently been repealed. "I've heard about it Bull Dave, but I don't fixate on it. I know it's been hinted at in *The Pic*."

"Really?" Bull Dave jammed on the brakes, avoiding a letter carrier who had no business being in front of his bumper. "I didn't think that went on around here."

"Not here," she said authoritatively. "Up north, near the mines."

Bull Dave clearly did not follow Goddess Moonbow, whose telltale hints in her *Pic* columns (a side gig, completely separate from her *Downsview* human interest pieces) were anything but subtle.

Poonie chuckled. "There was a shooting last month north of Yarker on the Cooper Road. Moonbow said it was because of the wife, but all her anonymous sources seemed to think it had more to do with the sheep."

Bull Dave clamped a heavily ringed hand over his handsome mouth. Since coming to work for him, she had come out of her shell, saying what she thought—no matter how spicy—always aware of Sikander's stern disapproval had he been there to hear.

Bull Dave wheeled the snazzy Audi into the parking lot of what had once been a pottery barn. Inside, the old kilns, long gone cold, had been restored as stand-alone art pieces, along with the thick planked rendering tables once

---

[8] 'Grace' in Hindi.

used for clay pots, now manufactured elsewhere for a kitsch-hungry world looking for its past.

It was a beautiful space.

"I don't see him—this Güdderammerüng," Poonie said, connecting the dots between the imposing mile high posters of the great man, and the mix of guests that clearly did not include him. "I thought you said he was expected."

Bull Dave barely had a chance to get a word out, choking on a glass of Veuve Clicquot offered freely on what was, clearly, an auspicious occasion. Along with the mile-high posters lining the perimeter walls were moving liquid interactive screens, assembling and reassembling at the touch of a palm to reveal outtakes from the Maestro's renaissance period.

"That's from *Wütend unter den Kirchtürme*," Bull Dave piped excitedly, drawing her across the room to a black and white feature playing out against another, set perpendicular, and at right angles. The piece, originally filmed in 70 mm Cinemascope, and in full Technicolor, featured humans, stripped naked, and wedged in cages, only to be freed by heavily sedated elephants swaying this way and that with multiple shining hoops on pierced tusks.

Bull Dave, slightly drunk and profoundly moved, pointed at the adjoining display. "This film is called *Zootrope auf Frukkasia*. In Sweden, it was called *Blod av Däggdjur.*"

Poonie Rajput downed another glass of champagne. "Why have you brought me here Bull Dave?"

The lights dimmed and the one and only Goddess Moonbow took center position on a delicately draped riser splattered in a "too red to be real" blood motif. Poonam caught her breath. Hardly one to be taken by celebrity—that was Mummy Ji's department—the sight of Pictontown's nearly famous sister in the flesh was overwhelming. Iridescent and impossibly petite, her straight, waist-length silver hair, dotted with sequins and pearls, matched, exactly, the startling luminosity of her bare feet. Fan-like, they swam instead of walked.

"She's beautiful," Poonie gasped.

"In a holistic and entirely unselfconscious kind of way," a disembodied voice from behind her replied.

Goddess Moonbow beamed. "It gives me great pleasure to introduce to you tonight, an artist of raw power, unmatched in his humanity, and unfettered in his avowed willingness to join every animal, right here, right now, on the ground."

"That's our cue to get down on the ground," the voice said, accompanied by strong, oiled hands applied to elbows to draw her down.

Poonie Rajput did not resist; did not even try to wheel about to see who'd laid hands upon her because she knew who it was. "Mr. Kárpáty?"

"Call me Zoltan. We are animals now."

# Chapter Sixteen
## The Güdderammerüng Society

The Güdderammerüng show was a smash in that it made quite clear, for once and for all, that Pics were more than witnesses in a charming backwater. Shirking off their provincial attitudes, they were ready to shake the trees with a rockin' new ethos. This was how Goddess Moonbow saw it the morning after in her gossip column.

Poonam Khanzada Rajput felt the same, at first, but after a week, when the heat and glow of the magical evening had receded, the feeling wore away. Zoltan had not called.

"It's like yoga," he assured her, as his hands ran the length of her body over top her clothes. "It's part of the whole Güdderammerüng experience."

Bull Dave was nowhere in sight, having receded into the din, along with the other squidgy, writhing bodies that followed Herr Güdderammerüng's every heady request: "Move right, now left, now bark!"

Woof! Woof!

Poonam felt ridiculous, carrying on in such a manner and in a public place too. "Aren't you worried about someone seeing you?" she asked, as the hairy Hungarian wagged his ass to and fro.

"Not at all. Here, we are all the same, and Güdderammerite's know not to talk about it outside the circle."

"This is a society?" she managed, popping an ice cube from a nearby bucket into her shocked, puckered mouth.

"A secret one, yes."

Sort of secret. Goddess Moonbow referred to the Güdderammerite's in her column as an enlightened group of intellectuals who selected Pictontown on the Downs as a place of quiet repose. Of course, the Güdderammerite's weren't named specifically, nor was the group referred to wholly as The Güdderammerüng Society. Moonbow merely framed the evening as an arts event that favored eclectic tastes from Europe:

> *"Guests were treated to hors d'oeuvres in the French fashion and sparkling champagne that gave the evening 'feathers'."*
>
> *"I've never seen anything like it,"* one overawed guest reported. *"I especially enjoyed the Mistress of Ceremonies."*

A lot of people did if Poonie's rufie-laced cocktail could be relied upon to furnish semi-accurate recollections.

The telephone rang and for a moment she allowed herself to hope:

"Hello?"

"Hello. I'm calling from Greenleaf Windows. Are you tired of being spied on? Do you feel unsafe in your skin? Our no-break one-way polymers with micro reinforced fibers like those found in our maximum security penitentiaries will—"

Click.

"If you like what I did for you, I can offer you more," the Hungarian said, when they parted. Poonam, freaked out with the new freedom he'd given her, did not answer. One week later, she was more than ready to.

\*\*\*

Animal control officers, like all public servants in the borough, existed for the rewards the system handed down in the form of bonuses for a job well-done. Frewer and Banks, each brought up from the basement, were keen to cash in, and fast.

"I have my eye on a pair of hip waders," he said, offhandedly. "You know, to go with the bass boat I wanna get."

Banks smiled. Frewer was awfully dim, his penchant for counting animals before they were caught being the surest sign of this weakness. Shifting on the van's hard bucket seat, she craned her thick neck for a better view of the copse of trees behind Saffron Drive. "I still think someone is burning leaves in contravention of article 19 sub 2."

"Huh?" Frewer didn't even meet her gaze, something that could not be excused no matter how attractive a person was.

"The smoke, over there. I think it's the trailers."

Frewer, still coming off the death of the white Persian, shifted listlessly behind the wheel of their utility van. He had never seen an animal writhe to a painful death and the scene, replaying over again in his head, made his stomach heave. "What was that thing you were trying to tell me, you know, before the cat started bleeding out and all..." He looked at his watch, timing her.

Banks reached for another cruller. "You mean the one about Fogler and the bear?"

"Yeah, that's the one. He shit himself, right?"

Banks nodded. "You'd shit yourself too if you showed up at a gun fight with a loop and a couple of darts."

Fogler, an experienced animal control officer with years as a game warden under his belt before that, grossly underestimated the size and aggressive nature of the *Ursus americanus*. Trapped under two by fours it had knocked loose when it stumbled onto a construction site, the beast was out of its element. Alert Dobermans had charged, setting the bear on a tear that took out a load bearing wall in a partially finished McMansion, burying it under several hundred pounds of debris. That, Fogler recalled, really should have been the end of the bear, which he had hoped to truss up and later have mounted with proper permission from the right authority. Somehow, the bear came to, rising up from under the debris like an avenger after Thor's mighty hammer. Fogler, armed with a piddly little .38 revolver, had barely enough time to crack off a couple of shots before the Dobermans took over. Just how badly he soiled himself that day was between Fogler and the dry cleaner who processed his uniform on a rush same day service.

"You're making that up," Frewer said, turning the key in the ignition.

"Maybe a little bit," Banks said, adjusting her belt buckle to accommodate the morning crullers. "But I'll tell you something that is true; whoever is burning leaves over there is drawing a lot of attention, almost purposefully. And if I know my water cooler gossip, it's those opt-outers that hang out in the trailers."

Frewer chewed his gum harder, his eyes narrowing in on another van, this one from City Works.

"Trailers?"

"Yeah. You're forgetting that patch that went up for sale last year. The sale fell through. Works says the owner lets people park their trailers back in the woods."

Works employees had a lot to say about what went on in the community. If ever there was a confidentiality breach, you could pretty much bet that a Works official was behind it.

Frewer narrowed his eyes at the approaching vehicle. "I think we'd better hit the road. That's a Works van, and if it belongs to that sullen bastard Kirsch, I don't want to run into him."

Banks nodded in vigorous agreement. "I don't think we need an excuse—" She pointed. "There's a reason right in front of us."

For the second time in as many weeks, a cat crossed their path on Saffron Drive. This time, the cat was black.

# Chapter Seventeen
## The Beautiful Boy Politician

Poonam Rajput needed air, but Fate stopped her before she reached the shoe closet. An astonishing downpour outside had announced itself with a rhythmic tap, tap, tap on the front windows.

"Dammit all. Why should today be any different?"

Devoid of cat, devoid of Zoltan, she found herself in Mother Nature's crosshairs. But as quickly as she found herself banging her head against the window, something amazing interceded and saved her life. Outside, plain as day, the campaign bus belonging to the one she so adored came to a stop mere steps from her front door. She gasped. Lord Shiva had heard her prayers!

The doorbell rang and Poonie smoothed her hair, not registering that she had already opened her door, and so it was not her doorbell that called out. Perplexed, she stepped outside, coming to a crestfallen halt, barefooted, on her own front stoop. It was like running into a plexiglass wall, her features flattening with the force of the imaginary impact. In her face, in the rain, the all-too familiar butt end of snarky Bob, the jerk with the Dr. Pepper, disappeared inside Bronagh Caley's house.

*** 

Bronagh had just finished a huge fight with Bill over two things: 1) his decision to take a consultancy up north right in the middle of the renovation, and 2) his abject disapproval over pursuing a lawsuit against Rudolf Fischer.

"They will smell you coming," Bill warned, while rummaging through the second closet in search of his old mining togs. "You didn't press charges, which means you intuitively felt 'safe.' The argument for assault is null. Now you want to get him for personal injury? I don't know who's more crooked, the wankers plastered all over the buses, or you for wanting to hire one."

That was kinda harsh and Bronagh, putting her soft cast forward, said so with a few well-chosen cuss words and a basket of dirty laundry, lobbed far and with conviction.

Then the doorbell rang.

"Saved!" Bill yammered, stepping into a pair of Kodiac work boots and then heading to the door.

The first thing he saw was the stoic face of Errol Deutscher, who gripped campaign literature in clenching hands to go with what looked like stage fright.

The only face Bronagh saw was that of the Beautiful Boy Politician with the amazing hair.

"Holy shit," she muttered. His suit was gorgeous— shimmery, wrinkle free and waterproof.

Bill looked at the leader of the Free Range Party. "I hope you're not a lawyer man, cuz if you are, you're about to get an earful. 'Scuse me."

Bronagh had to hand it to Bill: for all his pig-headedness, there was no one else out there who could recuse himself with greater aplomb.

Except perhaps, the beautiful boy.

"I'm not a lawyer" he said, flipping a thatch of wet hair out of his eyes. "I'm—"

"I know who you are," Bronagh said, pushing Bill out into the rain. The droplets raining down on the politician from her clogged eaves trough stripped away his laurels and made him man. "I'd be a moron if I didn't. Come out of this rain."

The beautiful boy did so, along with his campaign colleague Errol Deutscher and a soggy-eyed staffer named Bob.

"Your name tag is dripping."

"We only just hit the hustings," Bob said earnestly, "when the sky opened up. We were supposed to do some door knocking."

Bronagh eyed the big shiny bus, at once wondering why they didn't cool their heels inside it. A twist of fate, or was the universe sending her a clue? She offered them her living room with a wave of her hand. "Feel free to land, if you like—" She smirked at that moment, remembering her father's penchant for inviting in the Jehovah's and then yakking them up for sport. "But you'll find a warmer place next door, I'm sure. She has a sign." Bronagh pointed in the direction of Poonam's house.

The young man had radiant teeth—he warmed the room with them—and excellent manners, taking care not to mention her injury, which she'd grown tired of talking about.

"I'm keen on those who don't vote for me," he said moving into her foyer.

"That so?" She took a seat on the hippopotamus ottoman she bought for fun at an expo the previous summer. "You remind me of my dad then."

The beautiful boy seemed to read her mind, picking up the thread without need of further explanation. "You can always learn from people who don't believe in you. *My* father always said that."

Bronagh grabbed a tri-color mint from a candy dish, strategically placed on an attractive, but utterly useless coffee table. "Isn't that counterproductive? I mean, if the point here is to get votes, why waste your time on hostiles like me?"

Beautiful Boy had taken a seat opposite her on the elegant four-seater couch she'd had recovered at great expense. At over fifty years of age, the couch was an antique with a lot of history worth preserving, much like the grand old Frettinger Party, which she steadfastly supported.

He leaned in, significantly reducing the gap between them. "You assume that I'm a mind reader. How do I know that you're not for me?"

"My lawn sign?" She smirked.

"Could be your partner's."

That was a pretty damned good reply. The kid was clever.

"Muffin?"

She'd baked a batch of pumpkin spice first thing that morning. They had turned out plump and gorgeous. The idea that he'd want one seemed foolish once she'd offered it.

"We'd love to," Bob burbled, but we have a schedule to keep. He pointed to his watch to drive the point home that she was 'thick' and unable to take a hint without a nudge.

The politician, too new to be called a 'careerist,' dabbed the end of his aquiline nose on his sleeve, the effect totally charming. "You must excuse my colleague, Bob. He thinks I can stop the rain."

Bronagh smiled back in appreciation. "Only City Hall can do that, in case you haven't heard."

Errol Deutscher, who remained standing and silent, looked stupidly at the floor. Before seeking higher office, she had served on council for seventeen years. Her successful campaign against fixed terms of no more than four years each to a maximum of two per councillor, stuck in people's minds.

Bronagh, sensing Deutscher's discomfort, excused herself to retrieve the muffins that now served as an anchor for the strange, impromptu meeting.

"What do we have here?" Campaign Bob asked on her return. His voice, velvety and sure, rose slightly, as if responding to something wonderful, like the touch of an oversized plushie. The black cat had entered the room, pausing briefly to inspect Deutscher before padding over to the settee.

"Heee's beeeautiful," Bob gushed, dragging out his vowels. "So at ease. Like a dog, almost."

"Yes, he is," Bronagh replied, with muffins in hand. Something about Bob made her uneasy. His soggy, creased corduroy pants for one, seemed out of place, even in a campaign as free and easy-does-it as this one seemed to be. The cat, likewise, responded to the annoying human with a discordant sneeze, opening the door for Bronagh to deflect with an issue close to her heart.

"We don't want that airport, you know. No one does, though you wouldn't know it if you read *The Downsview.*" She waved a red knuckled hand at the local Pic rag. Within reach, it now fell into the care of the cat who proceeded to draw his wet ass across Goddess Moonbow's latest column on anal bleaching.

Campaign Bob coughed and there followed the kind of uncomfortable silence that only an animal could salvage. The cat, so easily the focal of everyone's attention moments earlier, stepped up to take his place at the feet of the beautiful boy.

"The airport," Bronagh repeated, noting this time, a visible dampness spoiling his once perfect suit. "We don't want it. We don't want what it will bring."

Like all Frets, she resisted change, the overriding assumption being that change conferred evil or, more correctly put, drew out the evil that was already there.

"I've heard that view expressed a few times," the leader of the Free Range Party replied, stroking the cat's wet and matted back.

At that moment, Bronagh wanted to offer him a towel. But something held her back. As a fiscal conservative, she was his natural enemy. Offering muffins was one thing, but a towel? No way. Too intimate.

The politician looked down at the cat. The cat began to purr.

Bronagh eyed Bob, whose fixed expression conveyed something queer and uncomfortable, like charity that means anything but. "And the waste treatment plant. We don't deserve that either."

The young man with the fantastic hair looked at her, his pause weighted and deliberate. Walls at once solid and intact, now inexplicably disappeared, along with irksome Bob and sour Errol Deutscher, who was barely there anyway. Now alone—just the two of them—Bronagh received the good news—*his* news—in a river song of words and, boy, were they ever good!

"I can't speak to the proposal out of Blenkinskane. That is between the jurisdictions. But air transport is another matter. I have listened. I am still listening, and I promise you that if the research bears out, there will be no jet travel into blah, blah, blah, blah, blah, blah, blah, blah…"

Bronagh didn't know what he was saying, and she didn't care. Such sweet music in her living room was uncommon lately. "And the deficit?"

"Blah, blah, blah, blah, blah," beautiful boy said.

The cat meowed.

Time, suspended, finally let go, and the room, restored, returned to them Errol Deutscher and Campaign Bob. Both equally transfixed, they appeared nonplussed, as if vote getting through transcendental out-of-body experience was normal.

Bronagh wanted to give the lad a hug, but demurred, recouping her senses enough to wish him well with a handshake and a fare thee well.

# Chapter Eighteen
## The Caravan Park

Outside, Poonam Rajput stood in her shiny green Wellies as the great man and his minions withdrew across her neighbor's lawn. Sopping wet and incensed, she would never see the Beautiful Boy Politician in the flesh again, and a good thing too. For as much as daydreams can answer an immediate need with a solid rush of endorphins, nothing could take the place of the real thing.

Zoltan appeared to her then, dressed as before in a Mackinaw and rubber boots. "You should put on something warmer if you're going to play outside," he called out.

Poonam shut her mouth tight. She hadn't seen or heard from the Hungarian gardener since the sexy art party. Waving at her from across the street like nothing had happened, he had caught her completely off guard.

Mummy told her a story once about a woman so proud that she did nothing and so died with nothing. No honors. No property. No mourners. Realizing her mistake after death, her body refused to burn. The priests, aghast, had no choice but to use benzene. She was trying to go backward and that, going against everything one knows about nature, could not be allowed.

Poonam took a step forward. "Maybe I like the rain. I'm not averse to the cold."

He laughed, throwing his big shaggy head backward. "No one likes the cold. Come with me. I have something to show you."

The big man crossed the street and taking her hand, led her on a familiar path up the road past Rudolf Fischer's house, around the bend where the big castle homes stood, and through the trees into his remarkable glade. In gray wet storm light, it appeared completely different: Not verdant because of the time of year, but flaxen and coarse—like Bull Dave's incredible hair, only better. The fire pit where Zoltan burnt leaves was located at the center of a clearing so round as to not be exactly real. Sheaves of oat grass, flattened with exposure, and coated with rain drops moved not an inch, yet reflected the light so as to draw the eye outward as the spokes of a wheel might want to do. She caught her breath with the effect of it. Zoltan took hold of her. "Look," he whispered. "Look beyond the trees. Do you see?"

Beyond the clearing ringed with oak and maple, stood a group of trailers—caravans, as he called them— each decorated with colored awnings and solar torches that glowed, he assured her, at night, regardless of cloud cover.

"I see your fire at night," she said, remembering her comments to Sikander the previous winter and his curt assurance that she must be wrong, that she'd had too much wine.

"Yet we have never been caught, our little community here." He waved to a curtained window that fluttered under the steam of an unseen occupant. "We have long attributed our success to the cat," he grinned, basalt eyes dancing in a tanned, heroic face. Poonam, wanting to faint with the wonder of it, gladly accepted his heavy Mackinaw.

"You don't really believe that?" she asked, once they'd taken cover under a big old treacly oak. "A cat is just a cat."

Zoltan lit two cigarettes, the second of which fit nicely into her mouth. She took a big satisfying pull.

"Except when he is not," Zoltan replied, expressing smoke from the mouth she knew so intimately. Her knees buckled, transporting her into one of Mummy's ridiculous movies, sans the sing-song.

"You sound like my mother," she whispered, holding his gaze. "She thinks the cat has mystical properties."

"She's a wise woman."

"You know her too?"

He kissed her. First softly. Then urgently. Just like in the movies.

"We aren't animals now," she said, floating on his energy, which moved her forward in the direction of the trees.

"We're always animals."

Coming to a stop outside one of the caravans, she didn't even think to hesitate. Zoltan opened the door. "This one's empty."

***

Sils Banks weighed the pros and cons of Jack Frewer as they wound their way through side streets abutting Saffron Drive.

"Where the fuck he go?"

Jack, she noticed, had reanimated on spying the black cat. This, she found incredibly odd, and she said so.

"Whaddaya mean, odd?" He glared, narrowly missing a lost soccer ball that worked its way into their path. "That bastard's got history."

"He's a cat, Jack."

"He's a menace. Caused thousands of dollars in property damage. And don't forget what he did to me!" He pointed to the angry wound over his eye, which had mercifully stopped oozing.

Banks, squelching thoughts of puss, had a moment of clarity. Jack Frewer was a baby with strong adolescent tendencies.

As her mind meandered back to a former college girlfriend left behind for her parents' sake, she wondered what in hell had become of her life. It was ridiculous.

"There!" Jack yelled, slamming on the brakes.

"You never told me how you got that wound," she said, her memories receding.

"Solo job. Two by fours. There! He went under the bus."

Banks sniffed. She didn't like the bus or the Beautiful Boy Politician that decorated it. "What do we do?"

Frewer, already outside their vehicle, dropped into a crouch. "I don't see anything."

"I do," she replied, forcing a smile. She waved awkwardly at the Beautiful Boy Politician who, muffin in hand, crossed the weedy lawn on the way to his awesome transport.

Banks rolled her eyes. "You better get your head out from under the bus, Jack."

It was later, after the bus rolled away and the two work colleagues gave chase for several blocks, that the cat led them to the caravan park in the woods. Now on foot, Banks could see from behind her thicket, that leaves had indeed been burnt in contravention of city by-law article 19 sub 2. That wasn't all. Water cooler gossip intimating that some of Pictontown's lustier residents got up to no good on properties bound up in escrow proved true.

The heat rising in her face and neck was unbearable. "I think someone is running a brothel off Saffron Drive."

Jack's eyes, penetrating, watched the object of his obsession weaving this way and that under cover of heady mist. "It's a Persian. A short hair."

Banks, not giving a shit about the cat, wondered what was going on in one trailer in particular, its single axel rocking in lockstep with the sombre wind and wet.

"A short hair for sure," Frewer continued, chewing his bottom lip. "Who in their right mind would let a beauty like that wander at this time of year?"

Of course, he was right to question Carlos' movements, for every superstitious person knows that autumn was probably the most dangerous time for a black cat to be out of doors.

"Lotta crazies, with Hallowe'en coming an' all" Banks murmured, inching closer to her colleague. Jack Frewer was no bargain, but the rocking trailer, gusting winds, and misty rain-fog commingling in the haunting glade created a perfect storm for her to pursue, and maybe even fulfil, her own selfish needs.

Jack looked especially awesome in profile.

"I was groped once on Hallowe'en," she whispered.

"Eh?"

"An older boy, dressed like Scooby-Doo. Thought he could grab me and get away with it."

Jack pulled the tranquilizer darts used for slobbering raccoons out of his double-down-filled vest. "It's wrong to assume that getting away with anything is even possible anymore."

Banks clenched, spying the awesome X-Calibur CO2-powered Cervid Premier high-powered rifle sheltering in the hockey bag he insisted on bringing along.

Frewer's dreamy profile, complete with aquiline nose, suddenly shrank into the background of what he was about to do.

"Is that a—"

"Shhhh. Quiet."

"What are you doing with a Cervid?"

"I need something big enough to deliver the Etorphine Hydrochloride M–99. It's okay. I'm certified."

Bullshit.

"Since when? We came up at the same time."

He didn't answer, whistling under his breath instead.

Banks swallowed her gut bile. "Cats can hear, ya know. Ultra sonically. If you're gonna shoot the poor bastard, at least shut the fuck up, why dontcha?"

Frewer laughed, a queer-sounding mix of dread-meets-euphoria.

She pinched her eyes shut, but could not mute out the unmistakable sound of ambitious fucking in the distance. Jack Frewer, though not quite rubbing shoulders with her, was proximal enough to flex his muscles with her knowing. Releasing the safety on the weapon with an elephant-sized *click*, he squeezed the trigger, releasing the dart with a *pfffffft* that hit its mark.

The cat, now a smudge, sprang off with a yowl into the nearby wood.

\*\*\*

For the first time since taking the job, Sils Banks felt like a colossal piece of shit. But not as much as Jack Frewer, or for that matter, Carlos. The feline had underestimated his assailant, the human now fumbling and panting after him, the same jerk in the black hood and cape who had confined him, and got a well-deserved claw to the face in retaliation.

As the pain in his left flank began to recede, Carlos' perceptions heightened. The gray colors he normally saw with exploded into vivid reds and oranges, yellows, greens and purples, all swirling in a welcoming universe offering protection.

He could not trust, given his history, and as tempting as his heightened sense of reality now was, he could not relent. Human voices—more than one now—were gaining on him. A distant female yelled for him, or someone else, to stop.

The woods gave way to another clearing, this one marked by a tiny river and a hulk of a vehicle, shrouded in oilskin, and distinct for its large tires.

*He picked it up cheap from the former Yugoslavia.*

Carlos stopped, shocked at what he heard—not a voice, but a vibration, coming across the field straight into his consciousness.

*What?*

Carlos' ears pricked in the direction of the unseen communication.

*You heard me.*

One of his own kind!

*Come now. There isn't much time.*

*I cannot see you. What is Yugoslavia?*

*A place that doesn't exist anymore. It doesn't matter. But you do if you'll listen to me.*

Carlos, dehydrated, panting and losing consciousness, surrendered to his helper, a comely Siamese with water eyes to float in. She licked his face.

*It's you.*

*It's me.*

*You speak.*

*I speak.*

*But how? You couldn't before.*

*I wasn't free.* She licked his face again. *Go to sleep. You'll wake again, soon. I promise you.*

# Chapter Nineteen
## The Tao of Cat

Poonam Rajput crossed on to Bronagh Caley's lawn with a number of issues on her mind, chiefly, her lover's intense grip on the animal control officers.

"Go back home," he urged. "I'll see to these and our little friend too." She worried for Carlos, of course, but the two city employees cowering like wet dogs in the rain worried her more. They were human beings after all.

The woman bearing down from her front stoop could not know this. She was still goggle-eyed over a man she did not believe in. Yet Poonie Rajput's obvious contempt for her shone through. How could the Beautiful Boy Politician spend even a moment with a woman as awful as she?

"Get inside," Bronagh commanded. "It's rainin' golf balls."

Poonam made a pivot as if to break for the safety of her own place, but then stopped, turned again, and walked to Chateau Caley. Curious—and not—Bronagh grinned. This was the moment she had been waiting for; the one where she would get to the bottom of what was really going on with her widowed neighbor.

At first, Poonam seemed to hold back, resisting her offer of pumpkin muffins and tea.

"Unless you want something stronger?"

In the year's they'd lived next to one another, she had never seen Poonam take a drinky. Today was different, evidently.

"I'll take a sherry," Poonam said, quickly accepting the towel Bronagh offered.

"How long have you been out there?" She was genuinely concerned.

"Not long," Poonam said, taking the sherry and quaffing it back with a sailor's delight. She shook the glass at Bronagh indicating a desire for seconds. "You had a visitor."

Bronagh shuffled to and from the kitchen with a plate of pumpkin muffins and a fresh bottle in hand. "I did, indeed. Kinda unexpected." She smirked.

Poonam accepted the refill, but held it in her tiny hands, refraining this time from dumping it back. "What was he like?"

"Nothing like the father which is probably a good thing. I never liked him. I think he's more like his mum. Looks a lot like her."

Poonam nodded, concealing, brilliantly, the disappointment she had to be feeling. Bronagh zeroed in for a dig. "I'm surprised he didn't knock on your door. You're the big supporter and all. Perhaps you weren't at home?"

Poonam looked down at her still full glass, the results of the first hit clearly creeping across her beautiful face. Was it the booze, or was she glowing?

"I was out looking for a cat," she stammered. "The one Animal Control seems so hot to get."

"Really? I had one here just now. Your hero was really taken with him."

Poonam slugged back the second glass as Bronagh settled herself down on the hippo ottoman.

"I really love cats, don't you?"

Poonam shrugged. "I suppose. I never had time for animals before. Seems to be a lot wandering around these days."

Bronagh wasn't sure if she meant cats, or the hairy Hungarian across the street.

"You never ask about Sikander," Poonam said, like mentioning her husband in this conversation was logical and not a non sequitur.

Bronagh cleared her throat. "No, we haven't. Bill and I aren't good at these things. We don't know what to say."

The young woman, relaxing her shoulders, freed her head from the prison of her clavicles. "Your Bill has been a wonder. Mummy Ji always comments on his courtesy and attentiveness."

Bronagh got her hackles up. Bill was anything but attentive. He was gearing up to leave her for that shitey mine. She diverted. "You were looking for a cat?"

"Yes. The black. You know him."

Indeed, she did. "He was just here."

Poonam looked puzzled. "He's outside now. I don't know if he'll be back."

"He'll be back," Bronagh said. "He's a man. They come back." She reached for another muffin, her fourth that day. "In fact, he'd better. He's responsible for my fall and I'm struggling to forgive him."

Poonam, uncomfortable, shifted in her seat, her slight figure barely eliciting a squeak from the furniture. "I don't even know his name."

"The cat? George says his name is Panzer. Typical for a Kraut to name a cat Panzer. You know George, don't you?" George was her neighbor on the other side of the fence, and was as offended by the snarky letter from Animal Control as she was.

"Only slightly," Poonam said. "Sikander was not an unfriendly man, but he preferred for us to keep to ourselves."

Bronagh nodded. She knew all about that. "Well, George says the Kraut calls him Panzer. Panther in English, which is far less offensive, I think. Typical that they'd get it wrong."

"The Fischers?" Poonam queried. "It probably never crossed their minds. We all have so little to do with one another that names hardly matter, offensive or otherwise."

Bronagh, pulling at a stray thread on her sweater, searched for perfect words.

"Well, offensive or not, that little bastard sent me ass over heel off the bloody porch, but it don't justify putting him down. That's what they'll do, you know. Animal Control. They'll put him down, and the damned Kraut won't lose any sleep over it either." She tapped her walking cast with her best bent finger, seeking a reaction from her neighbor. Any kind would do.

"Sikander, if he were alive, would weigh on the side of caution. You are angry, and nothing good comes from that."

Bronagh was far from angry. If anything, she was measured and controlled. "Is that what Sikander would do?" That sounded petulant. She reigned in. "I don't think those people are fit to raise a cat or anything else. Have another sherry?"

Poonam waived the offer of more drink away with jeweled hands, her wedding band nowhere in sight.

"Have another sherry," Bronagh, standing, insisted.

Poonam downed the third glass. Bronagh resumed her position on the hippopotamus. "I've seen animal 5-O spooking about. I'm worried they'll pick him up."

"It's a $5,000 fine," Poonie chuffed, her arms falling ragdoll-like to her sides. "I don't know anybody who'd pay that much for a cat."

Bronagh fingered the pretty enameled pendant hanging around her neck. The object, a gift, was very dear to her. "Surely *you* would pay because you love him as much as I do. I can see it in your eyes."

Poonam reached for one of Bronagh's fatty muffins. "What a queer thing to say."

"Really?" Bronagh crossed her arms. "Can you look me in the eye and tell me that my dirt pile doesn't drive you insane? Or that your hero visiting my house didn't piss you off? Can you honestly tell me that you don't feel passionate about anything?"

Poonam blanched, the weight of the sherry clearly doing its good work. "I've lost my husband, Bronagh. You remember Sikander?"

This shut her up, but only for a moment. The implication that she was heartless stabbed, because the two women were, like it or not, conjoined by land and by cat.

"Forgive me. That was thoughtless. What I meant to say was that this cat is part of our neighborhood. He belongs to everyone, not just *them*."

Her neighbor narrowed her fabulous aqua green eyes, clearly unsure about who *them* was. She didn't need to know. She only needed to fall into line.

"How's the foot?" Poonie asked, moving in the right direction. "Shouldn't you have it seen to?"

The soft cast, ugly when new, was made more so by the wear and tear that spying on people brought about. Unravelled in spots, Bronagh had quick fixed it with some duct tape over Bill's protests. The thought of seeking out Jaan the Plasterman again had made her shudder.

"I'll be fine. We'll all be." She was nodding, behaving cryptically, just as she had planned. Poonam, fanning herself with *The Downsview,* clearly felt the heat.

Bronagh lowered her voice. "I've been watching out for Zoltan, you know. He was there too, just like you."

Poonam shifted on the settee, her desire to depart taking over.

"Oh, don't worry, my dear," Bronagh reassured. "I saw nothing untoward. Just two people staring into each other's eyes over the body of a broken old woman." She patted her cast, noting her friend's hurried exhalation. Clearly, she had been thinking of something other than the accident. "I was just thinking—" Bronagh paused to pull on her pendant, an affectation she worked when driving a point home "—we could all take turns looking out for this beautiful boy, our cat. I mean, if his owners won't." She fanned herself, feeling a hot flash coming on.

"Hide and seek?" Poonie asked.

"I hadn't quite thought of it that way, but 'yes' to put a point on it. I've tried to keep him indoors, but he won't stay. Clawed clean through my back screen. Bill had a fit."

Poonie nodded. "He got away from Mummy Ji. Too busy watching Sanjay."

Bronagh fixed her steely old eyes on her neighbor searching for cracks. There weren't any. Yet.

"Then it's settled. The cat is ours."

# Chapter Twenty
## Garage Politics

Bill Caley loved his wife, but her obsession with Zoltan Kárpáty was getting out of hand. Night after night, prone on the master bed like a hunter waiting for a shot, she peered through her Hi Res zoom lens at the gardener and his party. "What are you looking for," he'd ask, at first amused.

The Hungarian was a swinger—there was no doubt about it—but spying on the guy was no way to get at the man's truth. Bill preferred more direct means: waving "hello," nattering about the weather at the mailbox, crossing the street on the pretext of borrowing an extension ladder. That's how people got to the bottom of things.

And cross the street he did, just days before leaving for the mine.

Zoltan Kárpáty's garage was utterly incredible with a heated floor, block and tackle, and a first-class hydraulic rotisserie used to work on the underside of automobiles.

"May I touch?" he asked.

The man, working away on a battered '62 Corvair, replied with an easy, "Sure, man. Mi casa es tu casa."

It had taken years for Bill to get a handle on English spoken outside of Armagh, but once he did, conversation was a piece of cake—even in Spanish.

"You are from across the street," the Hungarian said, matter-of-factly, as if it were a prison sentence.

Guilt washed over Bill. He wanted to confess everything: Bronagh's spying, her judging,—the fact that he admired his neighbor.

"I am. Where'd you get the ride?"

The Corvair's genesis was well known to Bill: Zoltan's flatmate, Lou, had told him all about it on a previous visit the gardener knew nothing about.

The Hungarian straightened to his full height, dwarfing the snappy two-door and him. "You know Polish Stan up the street? He runs the free pig roast outta his shop every summer."

"I do," Bill jumped in. "He restores the old VW's."

"And more!" Zoltan said, suddenly animated. "He knows about this barn off the highway. It's been abandoned for years. Full of treasure." He winked.

Bill was impressed. "You just pulled it out of there in broad daylight?"

"No, no." He lit a cigarette. "It takes a little more finesse than that." He offered Bill his pack, a distinct blue and white box of Gitanes. French cigarettes. Bill looked over his shoulder, forgetting that Bronagh wasn't home.

"It's okay, man," Zoltan said, like he knew what he was thinking. "No eyes today." He winked again.

Bill swallowed his shame and accepted the smoke. "I—I thought it was time to come over and say, um, 'hello,'" he began, tripping over his words. "I spend way too much time inside—"

"God damned renovations. Those fuckers are killers, man."

Bill took a long draw on the Gitane, the brune tobacco taking him back to a time before Bronagh. "Isn't it! And the inspectors! Put me in an arsey state that I can't get out of."

Both men laughed, fully aware of the creature slinking above them in the open rafters. Green eyes, glowing, the black cat took in the camaraderie until the Rottweiler interjected with a snarl.

"Pálinka!" Zoltan shouted, startling the smoke out of Bill's hand. "A kurva anyad!" He grabbed the mutt by the muzzle. "I apologize, friend, but the dog is a son of a whore. Won't get along with the cat." He gestured with a broad hand above Bill's head.

Bill leaned up against Zoltan's red and white tool chest, a beautiful multi-drawered thing that vaulted a good two feet above the top of his head. Noting the make and model number, he instinctively wanted one of his own.

"I was wondering if I could borrow your extension ladder. That is, if you have one."

Zoltan, not answering the question, released the dog and pointed at Bill's dark Ray-Ban sunglasses. "I had a pair of those once. Wife took 'em when she left."

Bill understood what he was getting at. Zoltan's flatmate told him all about that too. Bill had been married most of his adult life and was genuinely curious when he asked his neighbor if he missed his wife.

"Sharon?" he shrugged. "Of course. Yes. But she was right to leave me. My girlfriend kept calling at all hours—you know how it is—they get possessive, want more than is their right. Then once they have it, they run like rabbits." He chuckled at his simile. "It was a lot for Sharon to take in. I was an asshole."

Bill nodded, fully aware of how possessiveness worked. "So, the dancer's gone too?"

In addition to having a wife and a girlfriend who danced at the Acres out on Pontespointe, Zoltan could also boast the swinger two streets over, as well as her sister and the lady who groomed Pálinka, the Kárpáty family Rottweiler.

Zoltan paused next to the truck-sized tool chest that abutted the rotisserie. "Lou?"

"Who?"

"Lou. She's a dancer. Have you met her?"

Bill cursed his carelessness. The only reason he knew about 'Lou' was through Bronagh's spy glass. But he didn't learn her name, or even guess at her profession, until he met her face to face. That day, Lou opened the door wearing only an apron and a pair of jumper cables.

"Um, yes. I think I saw her by the mailbox once."

Zoltan smiled, pulling up his baggy drawers, as if mentioning Lou somehow demanded a more revered position north of the ass crack.

Bill cursed his carelessness a second time. "I was looking for a ladder…"

"You came to the right place," Zoltan grinned, shifting his attention back to the Corvair, which continued to hang vulnerable and expecting on her back on the rotisserie. "Lou told me all about it."

The bounce in her step as well as certain other body parts elicited the unfortunate kind of reaction that men prefer to keep private. She dismissed Bill's misbehaving appendage with a chuckle and a suggestion that he was a "DIY." He didn't know what that was, but should have, given his long-standing love affair with social media.

"You don't need a ladder, friend." Zoltan interrupted. "You need a beer and a place to rest."

They passed the remainder of the afternoon together: Bill on a stool, quaffing ales; Zoltan massaging the Corvair to life with genuine Gray tools to die for. Nothing was left unsaid: the change of the seasons, their mounting tax bills, the preponderance of ineffectual windmill power wrecking the landscape. And Bronagh's pending lawsuit.

Zoltan gestured to the animal control van idling at the curb. "They mean to fine the Fischer's $5,000. Baromarcú faszfej!" He shook his fist at Sils Banks and a man he did not recognize. "Old people do not deserve that." He looked at Bill. "I beg your pardon, friend. I just called them cattle-faced dickheads."

Carlos, descending from the rafters, wound himself around Bill's shoulders, effecting a purr that gutted his heart. His wife was blaming her injury on a cat and an old man who smelled bad.

"You cannot punish a man for smelling like onions and garlic," Zoltan offered.

"We have grown sillier," Bill shrugged.

"Not everybody." Zoltan wiped his hands on an oily rag. "They are some kind of royalty, you know? The Fischers. That is to say, the wife has ties to the old Austrian Royal Family."

Carlos purred.

It was then that both men realized they hadn't seen Mrs. Fischer out and about for quite a while.

# Chapter Twenty-One
## Sils Banks Steps Out

About a week after the run-in with Zoltan Kárpáty, Animal Control Officer Sils Banks found herself in a colossal funk. Unable to speak with her companion after the incident, she had arrived at the vexing conclusion that Jack Frewer had no animal interest in her whatsoever.

"I even gave up wine for him," she burbled, patting her fatted pillow gut over low fat chai with her friend, the political scientist.

For days since the unfortunate incident in the woods, she had watched Frewer from afar, scooting furtively up and down the gray halls of their work place. In every instance, he had gone out of his way to avoid eye contact.

Perhaps it was different for a man? Being manhandled was unacceptable in any circumstance, but the Hungarian had made it clear that he wouldn't file trespass charges so long as they stayed the fuck away from his cat.

"I mean, Jack was never a 'hi, how are ya' kinda guy," she explained, trying to make sense of his coolness. "But getting a shift change to avoid me is a little over tha top, dontcha think?"

"Uh, huh."

"I can't even stare at him. The doors at work haven't got any windows."

"That sucks balls," her friend, an accomplished potty mouth, intoned. Bent over a massive pile of campaign signs to be used at a town hall meeting later that night, her forced sympathy was appreciated.

Banks leaned back on an overstuffed pleather banquette, one of several positioned with care inside The Skinny Pic on Main Street. A local hangout, it was conveniently situated just steps from the town hall, making it an ideal place for the Frettinger team to hatch strategies and devise black ops to undermine the opposition.

Errol Deutscher, Banks learned, now had tracking numbers that showed a worrisome spike in support for the Free Range.

"I'd care about this more if my personal life wasn't such a bore."

Banks' companion, a pretty thing that really didn't need chai lattes and probably never would, narrowed her eyes.

"I think your job is having a negative effect on you. You cared more when you were at City Works."

She grabbed another corrugated cardboard sign and exhaled before stapling it to one of the many wooden stakes that lay prone at her feet. These, once complete, would rise above the raucous heads of party faithful to capture the slavering attention of a press mob they could only hope would show up.

"I don't think it's the job," Banks said, rising quickly to spy something across the street. "I think it's Pictontown in general. Hasn't felt right in months." She eyed her friend. "Like this campaign. What are we doing here?"

"I thought it better to organize in a coffee shop. Kids like doughnuts. It's the kids we want."

Banks sniffed at the adjacent tables jammed with tweenies and mock millennials. Luring kids into politics with sugar and promises of a place in the New Order was bullshit.

"I don't like the optics—camped outside their meeting. We're telling the opposition we're coming."

Her friend shrugged. "It's got to be this way, darling. Look where being nice has got us?" She pointed to the poll results colorfully displayed on her tablet. It hadn't even occurred to her friend—not even once—that tubing a constitutionally sanctioned and wholly democratic public meeting was wrong.

Banks, still peering out the window, didn't respond. What her friend didn't know was that she'd run into Frewer earlier that day, but felt too lame to confide.

Her friend threw down her stapler. "What are you looking at?"

The unmistakable Dodge model utility van bearing the marks of her profession had come to an illegal rest next to a fire hydrant. For a moment, she wanted to hope. Instead, she almost fell over. In shifting her feet, Sils Banks had caught the pointed end of a wooden stake in the too big loops of her extra thick shoe laces.

Her friend snickered. "That wouldn't be your sweetie, would it?"

Why not dare to hope?

Banks had finally managed to corner Jack in the whole nuts section of the Bulk Barn where, rumor held, he could often be found purchasing trail mix and granola. From this intel, she inferred that her onetime colleague was a bit of a Lefty. But that was politics, and this was lust. Her political leanings leeched into the background the second his eyes locked onto hers in what was clearly a moment in the granola aisle. "Do you like granola?" he asked, waving a large aluminum scoop in her face. "Yes." She lied. She loved fucking granola. She loved *his* granola. She loved the idea of fucking him with granola if necessary.

The bruise on his face, a reminder of the Kárpáty slap down, had healed a bit, freeing her to take in for the millionth time, the strong, white, larger-than-average teeth evolved to gnash and tear flesh from bone. "I was hoping to get in a bike ride after work," she further lied, "but I have a town hall meeting tonight and I can't get out of it."

The less than casual reference to her private life had the desired effect. Jack Frewer asked her about her thoughts and feelings on the upcoming election, readily identifying with her disgust over the heady resistance to commercial development brought forth by the Free Range. Developing God's creation for the sake of the long view paid lip service to multiple interests, and that meant jobs and tax breaks— old and cherished concepts.

Banks' pulse had quickened then and there. Jack cared.

"I'm a conservative, Jack." She blushed.

She was conservative, 'yes,' but she wouldn't put herself above posting nudes on Snap Chat if it pleased him. She knew *she knew* Jack Frewer. All he had to do was let her prove it.

The charming screen door that let in way too much fall air swung open, swathing Skinny Pic patrons in a morass of melodrama and cheese. Banks' companion flinched as the "man" in the doorway hop skipped his way across the floor straight to their banquette. A gangly dude, he looked not quite twenty-two, freshly time warped out of the Seventies, bad hair cut and all.

Banks, stifling giggles, raised her eyebrow at her friend whose displeasure, unconcealed, growled itself out with an ignoble "What the fuck do you think you're doing?"

The kid choked on his spit.

"You're supposed to be undercover at all times!"

The kid, dripping wet with rainwater, shotgunned down a Dr. Pepper, then slammed the can hard against the table top. "There's a problem," he wheezed.

Her friend was annoyed. "What problem? What are you talking about?"

Campaign Bob looked nervously over his shoulder.

"I couldn't be sure. We went to her house the other day—by mistake."

"Who's house?" She rose to her feet to push him out the door. "You're supposed to be with the Free Range. What the fuck, Bob?"

It was Banks' turn to smirk. Clearly, her friend and her minion had been engaging in a little old-fashioned espionage.

He pointed to the big shiny campaign bus pulling into the square. "Bronagh Caley's house. That's 'who.' She met him. He got to her. She's gone over to the other side."

***

Across the street from The Skinny Pic, a group of concerned felines applied what knowledge they had of human relations to the scene unfolding in front of them. People gathering outside the town hall were jostling and pushing, as larger, helmeted Homo saps on horseback shooed them along with truncheons to make room for someone or something.

From his perch, a long-haired Persian of mixed breed *chirruped* a query to his companions. This was ignored. A fellow captive only lately gelded, he had taken freedom for granted, wasting days rubbing foot pads against chilly asphalt.

A large silver transport covered in effigies disgorged a phalanx of hangers-on of the kind not seen at the fetish club. Tall, immaculately groomed, and beautiful, they were straight out of a Güdderammerüng film.

The Siamese sniffed as the humans yawped their yawps of joy. They were known to do that—Homo saps—along with licking and caterwauling, though these were typically reserved for moments of estrus. Together and severally in this crowd, an exception had clearly been made.

The Beautiful Boy Politician raised his hands as he mounted a ponderously constructed platform geared to help him make his points over the yawl.

Siamese, looking askance, yowled at a chirping Burmese to submit. *This is the future, friend. Watch and learn.*

The beautiful boy opened his mouth, making species-appropriate sounds for the occasion:

> "The auditor's report, it's true, has been steam-rollered. Without the proper due diligence, Federal monies cannot be duly allocated, though my esteemed colleague will try to convince you otherwise."

The rain, gathering speed, sheeted down, drenching horses and humans alike. Only the Beautiful Boy Politician remained improbably untouched. Siamese, withdrawing further beneath a raised recycle bin, tried to quantify human skin:

*Frail, penetrable and elastic, lacking in utility and lasting beauty.*

*They make coats out of us,* Burmese chirred.

*I think you mean 'rugs,'* Persian corrected. *There are people who do that for money. Gustavo saw it on his T.V.*

Burmese's pupils dilated with the thought of it. He had been to Gus the Pilot's house, seen first-hand what the humans did, and never wanted to return.

The beautiful boy raised his voice:

> "Just look at what happened today? Over \$3.8 billion ear-marked for green energy initiatives brokered in the last session rescinded without an impact study, and, more telling, without an apology."

The crowd lost its collective mind.

He raised his hands.

"This will not stand. Coal-loving frackers everywhere may rejoice, but is your pipeline really coming? Really?"

He clasped his hands against the cold, tapping his right foot in unison with the sluicing H2O that continued to roll off his fragile hide.

"Isn't fracking to do with gas?" a stumpy-legged woman with thick ankles asked her neighbor, a bow-legged male with frayed pant cuffs.

"I believe it is," he replied, stamping his feet against the rain drops. "He seems to have an over-fondness for mixed metaphors."

"More like nouns, but who's counting?" She chuckled.

Siamese fixed her ears. Frayed pants kept talking. "There is a certain beauty to all of this. You know, in a perverse sort of way."

"How'd you mean?" thick ankles asked.

"Look how everyone worships him. He doesn't even need to make sense. He just stands there and looks good."

"You a pundit?"

"Naw. Just on the lookout for unusual things."

Siamese blanched. *Unusual things?*

Persian, licking a muddied paw, stopped what he was doing. *What do you mean, 'unusual things'?*

Siamese wasn't aware that she had thought out loud, the human's words having tricked her into an unguarded moment. This had happened only once before, the night on which she was taken—and on realizing this, she extended her claws.

Persian, eyeing the frayed pants, understood. *I know that mutt.*

Siamese hissed. *He's the dog that hurt us.*

Jack Frewer, leaving thick ankles behind to brazen the rain alone, moved closer to the Beautiful Boy Politician and the adoring throng. Digging into his trouser pockets, he fumbled, almost comically, for an unseen thing; a thing that Siamese intuitively guessed at. The fur on her back rose against the chill. The thick-ankled lady, also familiar to her, had been responsible for Carlos' incarceration and, quite possibly, many of theirs as well.

"This country, this community, this people, are ready for change, and not just for change's sake. The old ways are gone ways. The industrial revolution is dead. We must change the way we think. We must change, or be left behind. Ignoring what is in front of us doesn't solve the problems inherent in our fiber, in our core. Harnessing the good energy around us, giving back to those who need it most and—yes—showing the door to those who'd run the show through wallets and nimbyism is what being free is all about."

The audience, calmed, communed ultra-sonically, like elephants seeking water.

Siamese could not help but admire the beautiful boy, for not only had he asserted himself as the Alpha, but he'd done so without drawing a single drop of blood. She thought of Frewer and of the strange one with the YoYo. Sly and deliberate, they'd kill to assert dominance.

*Chirrrrrrrup!*

Siamese did not hear it at first, but the Persian had. From behind them, a mass of smartly appointed juveniles swirled out of the coffee shop on Main.

"Bloody storm troopers," thick ankles muttered, barreling for cover beneath a red and white beveled awning.

Could humans communicate as cats do over several miles, Siamese wondered? As the square filled with angrier species, big lights from even bigger satellite trucks boomed amperes on cue to light the rapid-growing tension. A mass of mostly younger people marching in arrowhead formation had succeeded in stopping traffic while others rushed the stage chanting:

"Carbon junkie! Carbon junkie! Cap 'n' trade my ass!"

"Carbon junkie! Carbon junkie! Cap 'n' trade my ass!"

Mayor Lagerqvist, appealing for higher understanding, had appeared from behind the beautiful boy with Errol Deutscher in tow. If anyone could parse a meeting of minds and turn it into a whole, it was her. But not today. A mounted policeman, caught in the fray, could not rein in his horse fast enough. The crowds pushed—passives versus aggressives—startling the beast. At a mighty 18 hands high, it was not reasonable to expect the horse to avoid the stage, and when animal met wood, and flesh met bone, Freja Lagerqvist fell. Stunned stupid, but not seriously injured, she took shelter in the arms of the beautiful boy and the Corduroy Man, who appeared out of nowhere to spirit her away with great finesse.

The papers would call it a high point in a low-rise campaign, with the messianic Free Range pulling ahead of the Frettinger's by six percentage points over night.

The cats couldn't have cared more. An esteemed feline linguist working out of Lapland had discerned that ninety percent of kitty meows were intended for human ears alone, while *chirps, chirrups,* and *chirrs*—all key puss 'words'—were reserved for cat-to-cat communication.

Communicate they did. They chirped and chirred and sometimes hissed all the way home, not out of a sense of awe or fear, but out of a realization that the humans who had abused them had revealed themselves, not as a separate group hiding under hoods, but as a single hollering mass in the rain, all, behaving badly.

Before quitting the scene, Siamese could not help but notice a slovenly dressed, heavy-set creature clunking over to bow-legged frayed-pants. With a sopping wet Frettinger campaign sign in tow, the human barely mewed out her words:

"You came!"

Frayed pants put a crummy blue YoYo back in his soggy pocket.

"I came for you, baby!"

Jack Frewer and Sils Banks, all slobbering tongues and roving paws working *in situ,* affirmed an understanding between them that might have been *really* animal in nature were it not for the fact that they were too far removed taxonomically to be authentic.

Siamese smiled as only a wise cat could. They weren't drawing blood, these fumbling humans—no. But they were pretending to, and that made them distracted, and that made them weak.

*What do we do now?* Persian asked on the road to home.

Siamese had the answer. *We meow, friend. We meow to these dogs.*

# Chapter Twenty-Two
## Adaptation

History is littered with solutions. The trick is finding them. It wasn't so much that Bronagh Caley had gone to the other side as much as she had experienced a kind of epiphany she couldn't ignore. For too long, she had been nice. She had played the good wife, the good mother and the good political operative. Heck, she had even tried her hand at playing the good lover.

Jaan the Plasterman, notwithstanding, had been a lousy lay, but she had learned from it. Altruism was gold when the altruist kept the bricks. Likewise, with self-determination. But on entering the back half of her life, something had changed. Overnight, the face she had so loved to look at gave in to hormones and gravity, each pulling it to ground with equal force. Surgeons' scalpels couldn't restore the larger thing lost. If she were to figure out where she belonged in the evolutionary chain, she would have to do something radical. She would have to change.

Pictontown on the Downs got its name when the rural community of Pic in the County of Down became a city. That residents claimed surprise should not have surprised anybody. The elites in the larger burgs had dithered for decades over transportation, hydro and sewage. No one expected Pic to become a city and even if it did, it would take competing municipal interests at least one hundred and fifty years to pull it off.

How wrong they were.

Then Reeve Freja Lagerqvist's dire warnings that Big Boxes would come and everyone would go to hell were ignored, as windmills and subsidized solar panel programs arrived en masse to keep overpriced and unreliable electric power company. Amalgamation, as it was called, meant joining with the neighboring communities of Blenkinskane, Boon, Port O' Rune, and Skent. Have nots all, the four burgs brought unique cultural markers along with them: plowing matches, bonspiels and color-coded washer tosses along with corn boils, huskers and a cool smash-up derby.

Most citizens were okay with this cross pollination of culture, especially those who called the old Pic their home. Rudolf Fischer was one of them. He, like Bronagh Caley, had no compunction about adaptation. But there were reservations. As the beneficiary of a tumultuous and unpopular history (The Third Reich), he believed, as many did, that one got a lot farther in a new community by either conforming or disappearing. Lying low, the latter of the two options, was his preferred course. Well into the rear end of his life, he saw no reason to tip the cart. If anything, he preferred to stay well back, observing, passing comment to Zoey's cat when it took the time to visit, and to few others.

His granddaughter held the opposite view, accusing him of burying his head in the sand ostrich-like whenever she failed to draw him into exchanges over current events. Of course, he never fell for it. Her most recent barrage after he foolishly reported to her that the cat had gone missing, set her off with the resultant intrusion on his privacy announced with a sharp rap at the door and an unwelcome and very unfriendly rebuke. "I am not the cat's master," he said to her in halting English. "In fact, I very much believe that he keeps me." Zoey, unconvinced, locked her freshly tattooed arms across her chest, huffing and heaving rage, such that her new bristle haircut grew a centimeter with the electricity coming off her.

That had been an unfortunate day.

Rudolf Fischer screwed his eyes tight to make the most out of the din. It had been years since he'd required the thing he was now looking for, and in a moment of dire frustration, he invoked his wife's name in a full-on curse.

"Irme! Damn woman." He, of course, did not say this in English, but in his native German which, he noticed, faltered from time to time when he tried to organize a sentence. Never first class in spelling and grammar in the English language, he now found himself incapable of spelling, and, sometimes, even thinking in German. He had never had to translate it from the English before. Why was he starting now?

"Irme! Goddamn you!"

This time he shouted it out loud and in English. There was no response.

The basement crawl space where he now found himself on popping knees was chock to the top with photo albums, pots and pans, linens and an assortment of other things schlepped over on the boat. These had not been looked at since their last move, and then only briefly in the time it took to repack memories that were about as useful as yesterday's newspapers. "Everything's stored digitally these days," Zoey kept saying, derisive of his hard copies. "You don't need all this crap."

Looking down at the mountains of musty photo albums, once lovingly curated by Irme, he could only surmise that his granddaughter was wrong...again. Stacked willy-nilly into the corners, the bound images, locked up like secrets, weren't rubbish at all. If anything, they were the only matter of record left of lives lived. Once spent, a human being could rely on a grave marker, but little else, and only if the family stepped up to purchase one when the time to lie down finally came.

A knock at the door above him, rather steely and determined, did not take his attention away from the thing he sought: Not photos—not today—but rather a thing more esoteric, and stubbornly so. He sniffed the air. It was beginning to turn, a stack of smelly newspapers kicked to the floor a most plausible cause for it. He winced. He knew that wasn't true. The bile building up in his gallbladder bubbled, heralding a multitude of stones on the move without report. The tube they were to pass through was too small and he blamed Irme for that too.

The banging above resumed after a pause, and this time he acknowledged it with a resigning huff. Where in hell had it got to that thing he sought? He couldn't split the vertebral column without it!

A key in the lock, followed by furtive little feet sissing across the linoleum above left little doubt as to the visitor. "Hello? Rudolf? I hear you. Where are you?"

He effected a croak, shoving fists into the pockets of his tattered bathrobe. The inevitable visit from the neighbor could not be avoided, and as the hall door cracked to reveal a young woman's silhouette, it dawned on him that he didn't mind.

"Are you down there?" She appeared smallish in the frame. Smaller than usual. "There is something I must tell you."

Rudolf flipped on the light above so better to study the fine creases battling for dominance on her charming brow; the same, appearing lattice-like at the corners of her eyes. Mounting the stairs, he held up his hand, hastening her to move out of the way. Poonam Khanzada Rajput obliged.

"Put the kettle on," he said, whispering through sandpaper vocal chords. "You can tell me over chai."

Again, she obliged, stepping over the refuse in the hall without comment, as was her custom. He loved her for that. He focused on her costume, gauzy and ethereal like gunpowder to flame, and his heart soared once again in her company.

Seated at the kitchen table, he broke into the short question and answer discourse that dominated their growing friendship. "What is it, dear one, that you have come to tell me?" He thought it had to do with the cat. Certainly, she had dwelled enough over the beast's welfare, transferring all her love to it, like so many lonely women do. But she surprised him, offering in place of the cat, a barrage of useless information that neither startled nor alarmed: a bleating neighbor, a faltering hero, a legal action aimed for a pint of blood.

He drifted off, trying to recall the last time he'd used the Husqvarna. Had he left it in the garage, or was it buried at the bottom of his friend Wilhelm's shed?

He looked into the eyes of his lovely companion, so earnest in their desire to protect him from the harridan with the red hair. Sweet child. If he couldn't find the chainsaw, he would use the hand-held instead.

# Chapter Twenty-Three
## Murder on Saffron Drive

Carlos, the remarkable feline who captured the hearts of all he met, was not the only one to see something untoward in Rudolf Fischer's garage. Bronagh Caley had noticed something too: The strange way the garage door hadn't quite closed; the multiple pairs of legs dashing this way and that behind it; the back end of the Fischer Pontiac Parisienne rocking and quaking as if bending under a great weight.

She stewed a lot over what she saw that day—broken foot day—the day that changed everything.

As always, she would blame Carlos for imposing himself on her, beseeching her with his otherworldly eyes to go against her own nature and intercede in the affairs of others. A strange thing to have happen to her given the events of her childhood—the little kitten found in the square and spirited home by her kind-hearted Da, who felt his daughter had grown too sullen even for a typical Irish. The kitty Blackjack had flourished in her care, ferreting out the mice that left their shite in the pantry, even earning an esteemed place with her Morai who, like most grannies, would have preferred to leave kitty outside.

Whatever happened to Blackjack was never determined. One day he was gone, and after three days of fits and sobs, she was dragged to the priest where she was reminded of the difference between man and beast. They weren't the same, humans and kitties. Kitties were beneath them, and hardly worth a tear, never mind such outrageous displays of grief, the likes of which were only shown by widows, and then, only briefly.

The damned cat broke her heart, and she swore never to love one again, at least not in the way she had loved Blackjack.

She had not thought about him for many years. Perhaps it was the trauma of the fall mixed in with seeing Jaan, and the recollection of the heat between Poonie Rajput and Zoltan Kárpáty that brought it all back for her.

Whatever the root causes, Bronagh Mairead Caley caught fire on Broken Foot Day, such that she would crawl—cast and all—out of her house under cover of night.

The air was cold, the sky, granite against a flattening moon. Her heart, slowed with thickening blood, pulsed to will off its torpor.

"It's 3 a.m. and the garage lights are on in that god forsaken house." She crossed herself three times, certain in the knowledge that Rudolf Fischer was up to no bloody good.

Bill would have dressed her down sternly had he known. But he slept hard, thanks to the ales he put back before bedtime. Would he condemn her for spying? Would he condemn her later for withholding what she saw?

A dirty window, a gnash of metal on wood. Wood? It didn't sound like wood.

*Screech-haw. Screech-haw.*

She strained to see through the window as men— more than two—with cutting tools in hand leaned over something supple and pearl-like.

*Screech-haw. Screech-haw.*

She was too delighted to scream out. Too delighted in knowing she had something unforgivable on the man who had done the unforgiveable to her. Rudolf Fischer brought her down to ground—quite literally—when he willed her off his porch. But the fall did more than break bones; it drove home a bad-arsed dose of truth:

She had osteoporosis, and that was why she broke her foot.

She had osteoporosis because she ignored what she had always known:

She was no longer young;

No longer vital;

No longer worth a tinker's damn.

She was just an old snoop looking through a dirty window at 3 o'clock in the morning.

*Screech-haw. Screech-haw.*

What had Mrs. Fischer ever done to deserve this?

# Chapter Twenty-Four
## Lawyering Up

The offices of Sapphire & Sapphire were gorgeously appointed, confirming everything Bronagh suspected about personal injury lawyers. Taking up two floors in a glassy high rise overlooking the lake, the rent alone had to be a cool $20,000 a month, if not more. Pain and suffering clearly had its advantages, showcasing its cumulative wealth in full view of the plaintiffs without apology or cognition.

"We have three offices," the operator on the end of the line offered helpfully when Bronagh made the call. "And the consult is free. We can come to you if you like."

No. Thank you. Shedding the soft cast in favor of a fixed one that guaranteed to leave her limping for months after it came off, she hoped to make an over the top impression with her lawyer of choice in person.

Jaan had advised against replacing the cast. Sure, it was a tad dirty, but she was healing just fine. So Bronagh, determined to fix that, took a long walk without it, landing her squarely back in Emergency by way of Poonie's Volvo, and a trunk full of Errol Deutscher campaign signs.

"I would prefer it if I could meet with one of the Sapphire's directly," Bronagh said, after taking her place in a fancy boardroom. She had seen places like this before. Recalling her time at the legislature several vintages ago, one of her many tasks was to deliver bottles to the bagman at Christmas time. Things were different back then, of course. Friday afternoon liquor parties were a norm among the elites, their offices playing host with wet bars to garrulous staff as a precursor to the pick ups in the meat markets that followed. That they capped off their evenings with a drunk drive home in the requisite German auto that defined the 'have's' and 'have not's' of the time, was a foregone conclusion rarely taken to task.

Ah. The good old days.

Decorated to impress, the Sapphire boardroom offered large screen snapshots of the staff doing cool things, like parasailing and rallye sport racing, all with keen smiles and fearlessness plastered across their toothy faces.

Interesting. It was like the images were trying to convey that Sapphires were invincible, and, by extension, their clients too after expert handling.

"Our success rate is tremendous," a young man in a fine suit said, entering the boardroom. Toting a large Sapphire coffee mug with a picture of the owner on it, the youngster radiated freshness and a desire to best everyone else around him.

Bronagh chuckled. That would be relatively easy given that the only other person in the room was an old lady with a hard cast. Scratch that. She was not old, merely changing…into a werewolf, or something of that ilk.

She flipped her tresses in homage to all the youth she'd encountered lately.

"I don't mean to be offensive," she said, waving the young man closer, "but I was hoping to see a Sapphire."

The young man smiled, projecting a confidence that seemed to confirm his place in the crown. Set behind him with geometric precision were the portraits of corporate jewels past. Beginning with mutton chops, the firm went from wing tip collars to button downs, to broad ties and, finally, three button horrors from the Nineties. The firm was old, but this was 2016. Bronagh wondered why the portraits hadn't been updated.

"Are you a Sapphire?" she said at last, waving away another offer of free coffee.

"Far from it," he said, extending his hand. "I'm not even a pearl."

Bronagh accepted this, noting that his hand was neither sweaty nor smooth. Sweetie used it when he wasn't using his brain.

"Lech Bobienski, at your service."

"How gallant," she said, feigning a guilty flirt, as Lech's youth melted away with proximity.

They took their places, opposite each other. "You marry one of them?" She gestured toward the fine portraits.

Lech grinned. He was used to this obviously. "As a matter of fact, yes."

He reached for a remote-control device at the center of the narrow, but incredibly long boardroom table. Thick and meaty, with idiosyncratic lion's feet legs and three heavy strut supports at the centre, the massive table hearkened back to Bavarian hunting lodges she had visited as a youngster. Out of place in its modern surroundings, the table appeared to say that it was here, that it lived, was a survivor, and, by right, could never be expunged, however much the crackpot designer the firm hired every two years or so might have insisted.

Bronagh liked that notion a lot.

The natural light dimmed as mechanized blinds covered the expansive bank of glass windows that commanded a panoramic view of the lake.

"Will I meet Mr. Sapphire after?" Bronagh asked, feeling stupid. Lech was impressive, but he wasn't asking her questions and she began to speculate as to why.

"The Sapphires," Lech said rather firmly, "do not practice."

"They merely show up on the backs of buses?" Bronagh couldn't help herself. Once, in the ladies' toilet at the stadium, she found herself staring straight into the face of one of them. Complete with decorative snappy banner art, the grinning rube screamed:

Hurt? Injured? Nowhere to turn?

Don't worry. Sapphire & Sapphire.

All things are equal now…

…*Even when a person takes a dump,* Bronagh thought at the time, re-reading the missive mid-wipe.

Lech cleared his throat. With the click of the clicker, a gorgeous slide presentation began, this time minus the happy daredevil faces of Sapphire & Sapphire.

*"Since 1919, Sapphire & Sapphire has been assisting injured persons in getting the help they need to get back to where they belong as viable contributing members of society."*

Images, some featuring prominent disabled persons from days gone by, whizzed past the screen to make the point.

Bronagh frowned.

*"You don't have to be alone,"* a fine looking middle-aged man who obviously worked out a lot, enthused. *"My great grandfather, his father, my father, and now I continue a tradition of excellence that puts the right back into the wrong. Equitable, fair, sensitive and sympathetic, we take nothing until we deliver. I'm Robert Sapphire of Sapphire & Sapphire. All things are equal now."*

"Impressive," Bronagh conceded.

A beautiful, thin woman on five inch stilettos tottered in with a jug and a pair of glasses.

"Cucumber water?"

"Sure."

Bronagh watched her leave.

"Yours?"

"No."

Lech's demeanor had grown serious. "Why don't you start at the beginning."

Bronagh had rehearsed her story several times, not wanting to appear awkward or half-baked. The old Fischer bastard hadn't necessarily pushed her off the porch, but he had willed it when he sent the cat.

Poonie cautioned at the time against looking false. "If you are too rehearsed, he'll smell a rat. He won't take your case."

As Bronagh gave him the broad strokes, she was less convinced about Poonie's assertions. This dude, with his sexy olive skin and arching eyebrows, didn't take his amber eyes off her the entire time. Looking behind his lenses, she could see his mind at work, constructing, deconstructing and then bending her tale into something that could turn into a nice payout for Robert Sapphire, who, more than likely, was the kind of jerk everyone hated.

*I bet,* Bronagh thought, as she related her pain and suffering at the hands of the uncaring neighbor, *that you, Lech Bobienski, hate Robert Sapphire's guts.*

"…and so, I came to in a pile of shite with only my closest neighbors to see to me. Fischer was nowhere in sight."

Lech Bobienski sipped on his glass of cucumber water. He had not taken a single note.

"And what became of the cat?"

"The cat?" Bronagh became uncharacteristically protective. "I believe he ran off."

"You know it's a he?"

Bronagh frowned. Lech was acting weird.

"I don't see what a damn cat has anything to do with my injury…"

"He has everything to do with this, Mrs. Caley. We are a slip and fall firm. Crosswalk knock downs, it is true, are our specialty, but so, too, are dog bites. In the cat, I see a unique cross over, a blending, if you will, of two disciplines."

Bronagh looked at him agog.

"If we can show that Mr. Fischer was harboring a runaway, possibly a dangerous one—did he bite you, by chance?"

Bronagh responded with a muted "no."

"Too bad. If he bit you and you had to undergo rounds of rabies vaccinations that would add to your claim. Shots, notwithstanding, I'm happy to say we do have something here. We'll, of course, take it on. But the emerging strategy is two-fold: we can go after Mr. Fischer *and* the City of Pictontown on the Downs: Fischer, for harboring a dangerous stray; Pictontown, for its dereliction of duty in not capturing and destroying the animal."

"Destroy?" Bronagh dribbled her cucumber water.

"Oh, yes. That's a given. We can't establish that he's dangerous without having him put down. Are you all right, Mrs. Caley?"

# Chapter Twenty-Five
## A Jerk in a Funny Hat

Barely a day passed after Bronagh's tête-à-tête with the lawyer when a sonofabitch in a van appeared with a tablet and a funny hat.

"Good morning, ladies. So lucky for me to find you outside on your stoops."

Bronagh, taking in the many bumps and inclusions dotting the man's lousy blue van, did not feel lucky. Identifying himself as Wompat from Animal Control, he was seeking a black cat accused of savaging wild bunnies and a child's pet.

Bronagh eyed Poonam who, backing cautiously against her open door, scarcely concealed the sleek ball of fur behind her skirts. "A cat that kills. Fancy that," she said, over jovially, as she eased Carlos into the house.

Wompat eyed Poonie. "The beast is very distinct, ma'am. The complainant described him as looking 'mangy,' 'drooly,' 'frothing' and quite obviously 'ill.'"

"Obviously," Bronagh chimed in, unimpressed. Wompat, like the building inspectors, was slight in stature and effected an absurd attitude by rocking on his Doc Martens.

Poonam, drawing her bathrobe close to keep out the cold, moved in, her intent to get into Wompat's face.

Bronagh chuckled.

"Your complainant, sir, is mighty observant. I'm glad I'm not a cat." She batted her eyes at him, a move that stopped him mid-rock on his fancy boots.

Wompat cleared his throat. "I obviously cannot comment on the victims, nor can I reveal the identity of the tipster. But we do know that wild cats can spread Lyme Disease if unchecked, and so, check him we must."

Smug bastard. Bronagh eyed the comely Lou, who, in a rare move, made her existence known by appearing on Zoltan's front lawn. Dressed only in a shift and a pair of wooden clogs, she appeared unfazed by the cold, causing Bronagh to wonder if silicon acted as an insulator in addition to its other bouncy utility.

"Well, I haven't seen anything like it," Poonie said, arms crossed. "And if it's wild, I'd give it weeks. Snow's coming."

"You'd be surprised, ma'am," Wompat said, his eyes now fixed on the incredible Lou, who raked the last of Zoltan's leaves. "Feral cats can live outdoors for years, especially when aided by human accomplices." He eyed silent Bronagh with last words: "And our information confirms that he isn't wild at all, but belongs to the couple at the top of the street."

Bronagh cringed with the thought of Rudolf Fischer, his stinky house, and busy, busy garage that burned lights into the wee hour's night after night.

Wompat adjusted his cap, a queer thing from another century, and completely at odds with the rest of his outfit. "Are you all right?"

Poonie, picking up on unspoken words, interjected before Bronagh could answer. "We haven't seen you around here before. Usually we get the other ones, that is, when the *other* other ones from City Works aren't harassing my friend here about her basement."

Bronagh smiled sweetly at Poonie. They'd grown close since the beautiful boy politician's visit to her home.

"Boundary changes, ma'am. I'm your dogcatcher now, so to speak. Please keep your eyes open. We can't have animals free ranging. The Lyme Disease, you know." He nodded meaningfully before tipping his hat and crossing the road on a direct course for the leaf raking Lou.

"You don't think he'll shake Herr Fischer down, do you?" Poonie asked.

Bronagh, for all she'd seen and heard of late, couldn't say for sure. What she did know was that she'd have to pony up the lawyer's fees sooner rather than later. If Fischer had in fact sawed up his wife in the garage, then she'd need to file a statement of claim before he got found out, and spent her settlement money on his own counsel.

# Chapter Twenty-Six
## Best Intentions

Rudolf Fischer didn't need a chainsaw to get the job done. He'd been dissecting animal protein for years. He ran his hand across the smooth back and over the full rump, now hairless, thanks to a straight razor, sharp as could be after a good strop on a rouged leather thong. He drew the large knife obliquely across the hind quarter, taking care to go with the grain. Ragged cuts he could not abide, and neither could Irme. It was she who had taught him how to butcher.

"Feel the bone," she'd say, guiding his clumsy hand with her own. "Sense it, as you work your way toward it."

And she was right! Like a magnet, the knife found its mark, separating the femur from the hip socket with a *flick*.

She would have been proud, more so than the lady Poonam, whose protestations left him cold. On her latest visit, she had been most emphatic in her examination of his memory. Was he taking his pills? Did he remember to clean out the fridge? Had the cat been 'round to visit?

Yes. Yes. And yes.

Was he sure that this was the best way to honor Irme? Oh, yes. He was sure of it.

The cauldron on the second stove began to heave its boil, this time a good deal faster than before. He made a note to thank his friend Wilhelm for the replacement fuses next time he saw him.

"How long do I boil the head for, Irme?" he called out. "Until it is done, my love," came the conjured response. He paused to wipe his nose with the backside of a bloody sleeve. Headcheese was a pain in the ass to make.

"It'll be worth it in the end. It's what you want. Isn't that right, my love?"

* * *

Love was the last thing on her mind, yet Sils Banks still found herself in the condom aisle.

"May I help you?"

Sils wasn't thinking about anything until Bull Dave, her pharmacist, blundered in. Tall, with penetrating yellow eyes, he was a good-looking dude, which probably contributed more to her reddening face than the aisle she was in.

"Ummmmmm."

"That was a really long 'um.'"

"No—" She tucked in her sloppy man shirt in an effort at self-improvement. "I was—"

"Just looking?" Bull Dave reached for a bright cherry-colored package with a honey-haired honey on the front sucking on a lollipop. "These are really great."

Sils Banks, unaware that she was holding her breath, let out a noisy gasp.

"I'm sorry," Bull Dave stammered through charming straight teeth. "I should never endorse. I just kill it."

"Condoms are no joke," she offered, steadying herself against his elbow, which came in at tit level. "But the twat on the package definitely is."

"You have an eye for detail, Ms. Banks."

Their repartee continued over coffee, followed by an extended lunch that would undoubtedly piss off her new partner, Wompat.

"A real jerk," she relayed to Bull Dave, who accepted her assessment of the new district dogcatcher with dimpled 'oh, yeah's' and 'uh huh's.'

She blinked sticky eyelashes his way. "You're way luckier than me. At least you run your own show."

"Yeah, I guess so. But I'm answerable to a board of governors, 'round the clock inspections, and there's always the threat of robbery."

Sils hadn't thought of that. "There was that case years ago of a freakshow that stole horse tranquilizer from the local Veterinary. Used it to drug people into embarrassing situations."

Bull Dave nodded over a sloppy joe, a curious choice for a man who drove an Audi. Sils dug deeper. "I mean, drugging people to get them to do stuff they normally wouldn't do. That's just greasy, right?"

He shrugged his broad, muscled shoulders. "About as greasy as what they're doing at City Hall."

Sils swallowed the gas bubble roiling up from the bottom of her alimentary canal. "I don't follow."

"They're in bed with the Frets. Wanna turn this place into Babylon."

Sils felt her eyebrows climbing. Bull Dave was a Free Range and an enemy. Strike One.

"You aren't for progress?"

Bull Dave dabbed his sweet kissy lips with a paper napkin. "I don't mind it. Just not in my own backyard." He looked over his shoulder before calling for the check.

Sils' heart fribbed. He'd ID'd her for a conservative. He was getting away.

"I read you loud and clear," she sputtered, placing a hand over his. "I wouldn't want an influx of prying eyes either, but change is good. Right?"

Bull Dave did not pull his hand away. Base Hit.

"Are you familiar with the work of Pilsen Güdderammerüng?"

\*\*\*

Before heading out to Gus the pilot's house, Bull Dave not only insisted that she remain in her Animal Control officer's uniform, but sealed his insistence with a pretty bauble. Never before had she, Sils Banks, been gifted so fast and so generously. Sitting next to him in his snazzy Audi, she wondered how she could have even considered Jack Frewer as datable material. She cringed at the thought of him, stuffing his face with crullers, padding accounts and breaking quotas. No wonder Wompat was called in. Jack was not only a dishonest asshole, but he was a rude one to boot. How dare he stand her up after the Town Hall meeting. How dare he fake interest in her. How dare he ignore her after she gave him a taste.

And he smelled bad!

Bull Dave ran a free hand through his flaxen wavy hair which made an amazing backdrop to the genuine rose gold Rolex on his big, strong yummy man wrist. She shifted in the ultra-luxe butter soft leather bucket seat.

*And he's a pharmacist!*

"So how do you know this Gus?" Sils asked, having never met a pilot she didn't like.

"At the airport, in the small planes hangar, when I went for my private pilot's license."

*Gawd. He flies too!*

"Was it intense?"

"Meeting Gus? Naw. He's a good guy."

Sils flashed him a look. He was doing it again, making crummy jokes. Strike Two.

"I'm kidding," he said, whizzing past a cyclist who'd veered dangerously outside of the designated bike lane. "Yeah. Flying was pretty intense, at first. They made us look at crash photos to make a point. Screwing around at thirteen thousand feet—bad idea."

She went silent, taking in the countryside opening up outside her window. Her conservative view began to give a little.

"I guess you really do have a point, you know, about hasty development. Pic was a jewel before the girders came in, but we can't live in the past either."

"You know it," he winked, pulling the Audi up to the curb. "We're here."

Sils fingered the pretty pendant around her neck. She liked it a lot. She liked the giver a whole lot more.

"I know this neighborhood," she said, looking around. "I've been here before."

"Oh, I doubt that," Bull Dave purred, taking the cat pendant into his hand. "I would have remembered you."

Sometime later, they got out of the car, Sils adjusting her clothing hastily. Flushed with their furtive tumble magically finessed over Dave's retro gear shift, she made a half-assed effort at smoothing her hair.

Bull Dave, the randy pharmacist, chuckled with the Home Run. "You don't have to worry about that." He pointed to her mussed hair. "This is a special kind of party. It's in you to like."

Sils sucked in the cool evening air. She was drunk with the sport of him. "What does that mean, 'in me to like'?"

"You'll see," he said, grabbing her hand. "I just tested you, and you passed."

Sils Banks, Animal Control Officer for the city of Pictontown on the Downs, grabbed hold of the pretty kitty cat fob she'd accepted in kind, and from a Free Ranger no less.

*Tested me? I tested you.*

Strike Three.

"Change is good. You said so, remember?"

Using her words against her. The nerve! Strike Three for Bull Dave, the flying pharmacist.

*You're out, mate.*

# Chapter Twenty-Seven
## Taken

Zoltan Kárpáty, swinger and all around good guy, was not thinking of Poonam Khanzada Rajput when he reconnected with Sils Banks. Heavy set with thick ankles, she wasn't exactly his type, but her messy hair, smudged lipstick and ill-fitting uniform struck a chord that vibrated right down to the nether. The hardness working across her features like quick dry cement reminded him of the border guards back in Hungary.

Lou, holding up an over moist furry, seemed unimpressed, as she appraised the other woman with shrewd eyes. Sils Banks, in her roughness, represented everything she despised.

The lugubrious mascot, a yellow bird commonly associated with a local pizza chain, overheard her cruel comments, and cut in with a sodden squawk.

Lou would have none of it. "Back off you sonofabitch! Why in hell did Gustavo invite these freaks?"

Zoltan backed away. It was common policy that no one be judged aloud or in private at a Gustavo party. And that included furries, a tight little micro community that prided itself on playing out cartoon fantasies in a controlled and loving environment. Clearly, Gustavo was branching out: the same people having the same sex week after week had become a bit of a bore. But the bird, in this instance, was coming on rather hard, and Lou, clearly not of that species, was right to expect the animal to keep to itself.

Birdie, extending fluffy wings in a dramatic mea culpa, scooched away to an adjoining room scarcely visible from behind thick hookah vapors.

"Bong?"

Zoltan, eyes across the room on the ever-growing anxious woman in uniform, blew Lou off with a curt "Later," leaving her to sandwich between a couple of Gus' flight attendant pals. Stepping over a growing pile of mostly post-coitals, he helped himself to a couple of Jell-O shots that, he had on good authority, would loosen up the tightest ass. The hard woman with the cat pendant looked prettier and much younger tonight, and for a moment, he reconsidered the hunt. Youth and beauty wasn't always pretty, especially in the time and place he found himself in. Goddess Moonbow had written extensively on this in carefully worded articles in the conservative *Downsview* periodical. Citing an infamous White House intern as a classic example, Moonbow cautioned against the fallacy that people with something to lose will always keep quiet. Loud and lurid was the ruling ordering principle, Moonbow insisted, with book deals and a guest spot on a reality television show not far behind.

But Zoltan prided himself on being a pretty good judge of character as did every Güdderammerite present. Trying things on was sanctioned, and consent was everything. There were no locks on Gustavo's door and she wasn't leaving.

"You're drooling."

Sils Banks slapped her mouth shut.

"It's okay. Everyone does that in the beginning."

"It's you."

He held up his big hands, the same ones that forced her to the ground in the woods. "No cats here. I come in peace."

She eyed the Jell-O shots. "I should have you arrested."

"You'd be right to do that. But you're here."

"So?"

"Means we have more in common than you know."

Her eyebrows arched like pretty little caterpillars avoiding pesticide. "How many of you are there?"

"Ideally, only a few, and only on proscribed nights," he said, taking care to keep a hospitable distance. "But lately, there have been more." He passed her a Jell-O shot. "Your friend is unconscionable in his indiscretion."

Bull Dave, engrossed in conversation with a large bunny rabbit, took no notice of his date or the man so keen to bed her. Like Jack Frewer, he was a flash flame—catching fast, then burning out with a *crack*, leaving on-lookers temporarily bereft of sight.

"He's my pharmacist," she said absently, grabbing hold of the second Jell-O shot. "He thought I'd be into this. He was wrong."

It was Zoltan's turn to make caterpillar eyebrows, only his ran to the threat, knitting tightly together into a single ape brow, he knew, incited more curiosity than disgust. Then too, he also knew that his own eyes—a disconcerting basalt that cooled as they neared the surface of things—got to the core of human matters faster than mere animal trickery.

Sils Banks took a step closer.

He eyed her, bemused. "Your uniform is curious. Very East Bloc. I know what you do, but may I ask what you are really doing here?"

Sils fingered her pretty cat pendant. "I am with Animal Control. I came here with Dave after work. No mystery in that."

Behind her and adjacent to Gustavo's pleasing zebra striped divan, Goddess Moonbow appeared on the arm of Pilsen Güdderammerüng. It had been rumored that he stayed on after the art fête. This was confirmation.

Zoltan took the plunge. "So, you put animals down?"

He said it over-loudly, possibly on purpose. He could not say so for sure after the fact, but what happened next gave him pause as to whether he'd attend another Gustavo party ever again.

Goddess Moonbow raised a hand, bringing the room to an immediate silence. Then long, silvered nails dug deep into Pilsen's wavy hair, drawing blood at the roots. The assembly held its breath as she issued her edict:

"No animal shall ever be put down in our presence, nor shall one ever be put away, but mark me—you, over there—" she lobbed a tankard full of mead at the head of Sils Banks—"you will not see the light of day until you taste what you mete."

And then two largish creatures—one a fox, the other, a vole—stepped forward, and seized the animal control officer by the elbows.

"There's no point in fighting this, baby," the Vole warned her. "You're not the only one who keeps cages in Pictontown on the Downs."

Zoltan Kárpáty cringed. He had warned the Goddess against letting Jack Frewer back in.

# Chapter Twenty-Eight
## The Corduroy Man

Bronagh Caley felt incredibly uneasy in Campaign Bob's presence, and this, on its own, confirmed her changing ways.

"The team can't stop talking about the way you finessed Deutscher and her dog," Bob began. "It's like you really believed every bullshit word he said."

Bronagh shifted on her banquette at The Skinny Pic. She *had* believed every word.

Bob took a long pull on his soft drink. "And I can't thank you enough for trusting me with this mission."

And there it was: the crux of her conflict. It was bad enough that she had to endure Bob's presence in her home the day the beautiful boy came to visit; but being the token behind his hire was simply intolerable.

"It's like I'm a spy, or something."

Bronagh screwed her eyes tight. "You *are* a spy, kiddo. Don't be such a rube."

She cringed on recollecting her conversation with the central organizer at Frettinger H.Q. An old friend and co-conspirator back in the day when she needed cover to tryst with Jaan the Plasterman, he had been instrumental much later in removing her from her job and then bringing her back for 'special tasks.' "There's no one out there like you Bronagh," the smug bastard schmoozed. "No one shallow enough like you." He'd grinned at her when he said it, as people do when paying a compliment. But it wasn't. Nor was she shallow. Just hollow.

She thought of Blackjack the cat, trying to make a connection between his loss and her loss of conscience. She couldn't find it.

Bob pushed a gluten-free muffin into his mouth, then talked as the residual, reduced to mush, disappeared down the back of his throat.

"I can't link him directly to anything unsavory. But his people—as you well know—are another story."

She took a hit off her low-fat, no-fun chai pumpkin latte. Perhaps it was redemption she was seeking? Why else would she sacrifice a lamb in place of a goat?

"Our interests, son, are rooted less in the prurient. What we want are greased palms, not greased cocks. Get it?"

*"Do this for me,"* the organizer promised, *"and you can have it all back."*

She swallowed her regret. She wished she'd never met him. The campaign needed a mole; someone smart and naive enough to not draw a lot of attention, but have the potential to get close. "Like an earthworm," she volunteered, catching his drift. "Cut his head off. Remove his ass. He just keeps coming."

Precisely.

She looked across the table at her earthworm, whom she'd only known at arms-length as he cartwheeled through the lowest rungs of Pic society.

"Why do you wear corduroy?" she demanded, not placing any great weight on the answer. She herself had been fond of the material in her student days and derived a strange feeling of déjà vu every time she saw him.

"It makes a statement."

"A statement?"

"Yeah. That I don't care…about fashion, you know?"

Corduroy had been extremely fashionable in her time— that's what drew her to Bob in the first place.

Sucking back her no-fat no-fun chai pumpkin latte, she noted strange parallels between the drink and her companion. Sensible and strange at the same time, they had a season: the pumpkin, for Hallowe'en and harvests; Bob, for random acts of treachery, which—now that she thought about it—had never really gone out of style.

She studied the front page of *The Downsview* and the lesser-valued *Pic*. Both featured large cover photos of the beautiful boy with pages of pictorials inside. Bronagh, feeling her eyebrows cross, forced them back into position. "You may not care about fashion, but *he* does."

Bob took another hit off his Dr. Pepper. "His handlers know that. It's a drawback, but a good one. Makes for a healthy subterfuge. Deflects his shallowness, all of which endears him."

"You learn fast."

"So do you," he said, pointing to her Franken boot.

"A miscalculation…" she conceded, suddenly thinking of Bill. "But a useful one."

Bob flicked a rubber band across the room, reminding her that he was still a kid in kid's clothes playing a grown-up's game.

He leaned in to get closer. "Your injury culls sympathy. I told them you'd switched sides by the way. Told 'em right here on Town Hall night. Just like you wanted me too."

"That's good. The best operatives are the ones not known to be so…especially among their own." She was referring to herself.

"So, you are still a Frettinger?" Bob asked, a little too soberly, revealing a weakness, casting doubts.

"Of course. We get as close as we can. That's politics. That's what we do." She thought of Bill again, packing his bags, gearing up to move out. "The next thing I'll do is go work for them."

Bob, inclining his head in what appeared to be an all-knowing cognition, didn't have a goddamned clue what she was on about, and she knew it. She'd get close all right, but not to gather intel on the enemy, and not to salve a growing curiosity as to the beautiful boy's source of incredible power. What she really needed to know—what she'd really been after from the get go—was how much Poonam knew about her relationship with Sikander.

# Chapter Twenty-Nine
## The Affair

In another time, Bronagh Caley fashioned Sikander Rajput out of whole cloth. Mystical, forged in the furnace of the Raj, he emerged, liquid eyes rimmed in kohl, to sweep her off her feet like a Brahmin, far removed, and above everyone else. At least, that's what crossed her mind the first time he asked her if she'd seen his recycle bin.

"No," she had stammered, her features reddening in the face of the man's raw animal power. She remembered him grinning, his cheeks dimpling up to frame the corners of his full mouth. Lord, it had been years since she'd felt that way.

Floating above the tops of trees to the rhythm of her beating heart, she reminded herself again of her pledge to quit the field. Nothin' good came of playin' around. The priest had told her so. And she'd done her level best to keep her promise. But Sikander Rajput was a true thing of beauty; a leopard with many spots, possessed of a worshipful countenance to be explored. Oh! If only she hadn't re-watched Poldark on the public television. Oh! If only she wasn't a romantic at heart. Oh! If only his wife wasn't so incredibly stupid.

Poonam Rajput, aside from possessing a ridiculous sounding name, appeared too vacuous to be deserving of such a man. But she did have youth on her side, her husband clearly appearing to be much older. Bronagh could not resist drawing the unsuspecting woman into a conversation, whereby endearing parallels were drawn between Sikander and William Caley. Over time, Bronagh learned that their marriage had been arranged; that he was a friend of her father's; that he was forty-four years old to Poonam's twenty-eight.

That was ten years ago. It hadn't taken long for the affair to start. Hadn't taken long for him to show her things she had never seen before. The cat pendant he gifted her with on their first anniversary matched his own, which he carried around discreetly on a fob with a single key. "What does it unlock," she asked playfully, after one of their sessions at the Motel 6. She had expected him to answer with a dreamy 'your heart,' or some other such bollocks. But instead, he answered her with a cocked brow and some pretty extreme candor. "It unlocks a door to a place where people go to be more than just people."

She had never figured him for a cat person, let alone one who gallivanted with others of that mind. At forty-two, she had prided herself on being open-minded in private. But the cat people had caught her off guard. Her reluctance to don masks and shed clothes was not her cup of tea, nor was it appealing to use living creatures in concert with sexual gratification. It was too weird.

He never asked her to go back. Never spoke of it again, as if ignoring it somehow sequestered it, making it unreal. But she remembered, every time he couldn't meet her. Every time he dismissed her. It was bad enough that Bill made her feel like a wife, but Sikander made her feel that way, too, not only when he was alive, but even more so after he passed.

*** 

Bronagh found Poonie on the boulevard nailing up big arterial Errol Deutscher campaign signs. Armed with metre and a half stakes and a sledge, she was incredibly impressive. Poonie wasn't alone, accompanied by a campaign flunky of the first degree. Passive aggressive with flinty eyes that said: 'I'll kill you if you don't vote for my guy,' Poonie's companion wasn't the first of his ilk that

Bronagh met. Still, she held caution close to her chest. Her political leanings, now known to the neighbor, meant that an association with the Free Range would appear heretical from all sides. If she was to get in for real, she would have to make it convincing.

"That looks like fun."

Poonam wound up with the mighty sledge.

"You shouldn't be driving with a fixed cast. I don't care what your lawyer says."

The sledge came down hard, hard enough to send the stake deep into the ground with a single blow. Clearly, she had been practicing.

Bronagh swallowed hard. She hadn't told Poonie the whole story. Hadn't told her that the cat would have to be put down.

"Lawyer, huh?!" the kid volunteer yelped as he reached for her hand to help her out of her parked car. "You here to help?"

Bronagh grinned. Infiltrating was going to be easier than she thought. "I'm a fiscal conservative," she mock-faltered. "And I'm having a bit of trouble with the marijuana aspect of your campaign."

A distinct chill overtook the air. It smelled like snow.

"We're not about putting drugs into the hands of kids," the kid said. "All we want to do is eliminate frivolous prosecutions."

Well put.

"We could really use some canvassers."

Poonie Rajput raised her hand like a crossing guard stopping traffic. "My friend is not a hundred percent, physically or philosophically. Unless, of course, our leader had a healing effect on you?"

The kid broke into a grin. "You've met the leader?"

Bronagh chose her words carefully. There was nothing to be gained from being too easy. "Yes, I have. And he almost had me convinced. But peace, order and good government aside, I've been out of the game for far too long, and wouldn't know how to edge myself back in."

"That's easy," the kid said, reloading Poonie's power stapler from a bag of tricks that included an unopened Dr. Pepper. "You've met the leader. All you do is follow."

"You gave him muffins," Poonie admitted. "And he was very good to the cat."

Bronagh clasped her hands together.

"You see?" the kid said, stapling another sign to a vampire-sized wooden stake. "He has that effect on everyone. All he does is look at you and you turn to goo."

"It's his youth," Bronagh agreed, sizing up the beautiful boy's image featured front and center on the Errol Deutscher campaign sign. "And his message. He's a dove in a sea of hysterics and he rocks it. Few dare to oppose the Frets around here...except you lot. You know better, I guess."

They nodded in unison.

Bronagh turned to Poonie. "I didn't pull up to politic, anyway. What I wanted to know is if you'd back me up with witness testimony when the suit against Fischer goes ahead."

Poonam's face visibly darkened.

"If it wouldn't be too much trouble."

Her neighbor's features softened, but her voiced arched. "We *do* need canvassers. Telephone canvassers. No one would see your face."

Bronagh had packed on a few pounds and had changed her hair color too. Anyone outside the Fret circle not already aware of her treachery would not be the wiser. She was scarcely recognizable anymore.

"And you shouldn't be walking around anyway with that foot of yours. Mummy worries constantly over your health. I feel duty bound to keep an eye on you."

*Exactly.* "So, you'll testify if called?"

Poonie exhaled heavily. "If I really must, then, 'yes.' But only under duress. I agree with Mummy that ratting out a neighbor is not good for the soul."

Bronagh drew out her words for maximum effect. "Well—seeing that you're willing to compromise your principles for me, I suppose I can do the same for you."

Poonie embraced her, something she had never done in their ten-year acquaintance. "Just a few calls B, to get the vote out. Election's in ten days."

Bronagh Caley smiled. Convinced more than ever that her neighbor hadn't a clue about the affair, she now focused on a new mission: sending Free Range voters to the wrong polling stations on election day.

# Chapter Thirty
## Into the Drawer

On the same day Sils Banks was confined to a cage, Sanjay the actor died of a pulmonary embolism. Mummy Ji nearly lost her mind. "So young! So young!" and so forth had been the governing mantra in their house for almost three days.

Poonam, tired from her work on sign crew, summoned all her resources over the kitchen sink. Sanjay was just an actor. It wasn't like he was Sikander.

"Sikander was an okay husband, I don't deny it," Mummy said, "But as a man, he had his short-comings."

Poonie, bent over a large cast iron skillet, stopped washing. It was unlike Mummy to be disingenuous. She was up to something.

"Aren't you going to ask what I'm driving at?" A hint of a grin took shape around the old woman's mouth.

"No. You and Daddy picked him. I had no say. Remember?"

Mummy Ji remembered. "I remember giving you the option between marriage and a dissolute life as an old maid."

Poonie shut off the stove fan to make sure she heard correctly. "Old maid?"

"You heard me."

For as much as Mummy had made great advances in the modernist thinker's department, there were times when she fell back on old ways. Was it the shock of Sanjay's death, or was she beginning to lose it?

"If this is about me finding someone else, you have nothing at all to worry about." She thought of Zoltan, her Hungarian love god.

"The man across the street? He lives with a harem. That's not living."

Poonam could not deny this. The dancer Lou's comings and goings were a favorite talking point for Mummy.

"Sex. Sex. Sex. That's all you young people think about," Mummy said, waggling her favorite cane. "Which is not a bad thing as long as the marriage contract is solid and there is no stepping out."

Poonam had done her best in the last six months to remain strong if only to please her mother. Mummy valued strength above just about everything else. If she made a pretense of moving forward, she could at least be spared another story about some other widow back home who honored her household better and faster than she ever could.

She smoothed her hair before taking a seat opposite the old lady. "Mummy Ji, you know how much I have valued your counsel over these last difficult months. I even took your advice and put myself out there…" She paused to push back thoughts of Zoltan and his rocking little trailer stashed away in the magic wood. "But I think—maybe—I have done too well, and this is why you carry on so about Sanjay."

Mummy Ji set her cane down on the floor in what appeared to be heavy preparation in advance of a Herculean soliloquy. It wasn't. Just a statement of facts she had refused to face.

"I make a great play of Sanjay's passing to make a point, my love. You have done well. You have 'moved on,' as you young people are so fond of saying. But since I've come to live with you, what I have not seen in you is anger. And you cannot be whole without it."

Poonie reached for a sugar cube. Popping it into her mouth, she made no comment other than to break it under her molars. Grateful that it wasn't ice—the cool material cracking against the acid welling up in the back of her throat would have put her brain into a spin—she considered the words. In the months preceding Sikander's death, she had felt many things: regret, resolve, and remission, coupled with a very strong desire to 'redo.' What she had not felt was anger. At this juncture, she began to wonder why.

"Why do I need to be angry, Mummy? The murtis have given no indication that anything like that is required. I pray to Ganesha daily, searching for a road that's clear. It's working."

Mummy nodded. "Yes. Yes. The elephant sent you a cat; the cat led you to a man."

Poonam stifled an inappropriate giggle. Not only was Mummy talking in riddles, but she was beginning to sound a lot like Dr. Seuss. She cleared her throat. "And the cat will make me angry?"

"The cat will show you the truth."

Poonam, exasperated, pushed away from the table. There was much work to do before election day. "So, I'll just wait for cat to come over, shall I?"

"No. He is with that woman—that neighbor who so occupies your time. This is not so odd—your desire to make nice with her—but to understand why, you must follow the cat. You must find him upstairs in the drawer."

Poonie had no idea what she was talking about and made her thoughts clear, mouthing a silent "Whaaaaa?????"

"The drawer," her mother repeated. "You know the one. Get on with it."

The staircase leading up to what had once been their bedroom was still lined with wedding photos: the red Ghagra Choli, annoying nose chain, and gorgeous ropes of gold that she wished she hadn't loved so much featured prominently. "I feel like I'm selling out for gold," she confided to a friend weeks before the big week. "I'm drowning in the shit." Her friend, a blonde-haired shield maiden straight out of Odin's den, saw nothing wrong with getting a week-long party and a shitload of gold.

"And look at him," she reassured, referencing Sikander. "He's not ugly."

Sikander's face on the wall beamed back at her on the second to last rung at the top of the stairs. No, he wasn't ugly. And that was the problem. Madhya Pradesh, where her father came from, was the heart of India, and Sikander Rajput was to be her new heart.

She tried.

Their bedroom, their sanctuary, was where the magic was supposed to happen. Decorated head to foot in European swag drapery of a type not seen since the Seventies, it was supposed to be elegant, refined and a place of dignified repose. He had designed it himself based upon tastes picked up in England and France where he'd been sent to study after his first university degree. He was her father's friend, and while he never made a point of reminding her that he'd done her a great favor by marrying her, it was always there.

The four-poster bed with pineapples had been her idea and he, unremarkably, consented to the purchase on condition that she allow the heavily carved Italianate side tables with the cumbersome sheet marble tops. She had never liked them, the heavy pieces reminding her of the sarcophagi found in 11th century English church basements.

She walked over to the right side of the bed that had been his side. Since his death, she had not deigned to move over into it, her irrational side counseling against the violation of this most personal space. The same went for Sikander's nightstand. Though it was never locked, it was understood that she was not to go into it under any circumstances.

"Until we part, my dear." She reached down, her hand pausing meaningfully on the scrolled brass hardware. If she looked inside, she would not be able to go back.

A gentle tug and the ornament gave way to innocuous things like loose change, cigarette lighters, his passport, and brochures on northern fishing camps. She exhaled, almost disappointed at not finding anything. But then something pulled, a force unseen, but very real, willing her to dig deeper. She extracted the innocuous documents, placing them on the bed.

A cat in a hat. A cat in a drawer. What the hell was Mummy on about? Deeper, she found stale cigarettes and a pack of unopened breath mints. A tattered jewellery box with a battered old ring inside was of nominal interest. It probably belonged to his mother. Needless to say, he hadn't cared to pass it on to her. Their union had been fruitless, childless. Maybe she wasn't worth receiving heirlooms?

And then she saw the thing she sought, tossed aside casually—it was not boxed—an odd, even garish bauble that she wouldn't wear in a million years, wedged into the far right corner of the deep drawer. Mounted in silver and dressed in a sickly pink enamel, the cat was strange jewellery for a man to keep, even if it was on a key chain.

She had seen it before, swaying casually around the neck of another. Poonam took a seat on Sikander's side of the bed, wondering if he'd ever brought the neighbor here.

How could she have not seen it when it was so clear to Mummy; the 'obsession' with the neighbor having less to do with an inconvenient renovation, than with actions over several years that she'd failed to give voice to because she was a coward, a chicken shit, a lover of ease.

Poonam, clutching the pink kitty, thinned her lips. Bronagh was somewhere out there beyond the window pane. Sikander had been reduced to ash. This made the young woman very glad.

Finally, she was mad.

END OF ACT 2

# Chapter Thirty-One
## Revelation

The creep in the hood eyed her queerly as he pushed an all-grain bagel at her through the bars of her prison. Sils Banks, half-pissed and half-terrified, wanted to tear the zits off the asshole's face. Skinny, sloppy—even apologetic— he was not her idea of a jailer, his lack of finesse in all things sinister, alerting her to the idea that she might be in the middle of a huge prank. They had met before.

"Am I being punked?"

"I'm not really sure," he said. "I can't believe the Goddess would do this to you. But she has her methods, and in there somewhere, some of this makes sense."

Sils Banks doubted that very much. Being shut up in a basement could not be in anyone's best interest. Not even the furries with their preference for heap sex would find anything worthy about solitary. And who the fuck was Goddess Moonbow? The skinny witch in the flea market hippy clothes was not even close to rocking the ethereal, never mind attaining goddess status. What a bunch of bullshit.

"How old are you?"

The lad screwed up his face, tight, like she had insulted him. "What difference does it make how old I am? You can't ask me that anyway—not in interviews or apartment renting."

Apartment renting? He's a kid.

"So, kid, you gonna unlock this ridiculous cage, or you gonna leave me to wet myself?"

He looked at the red pail next to her, filled to the top. "I hadn't thought of that. I'm Bob, by the way."

Bob. Of course, your name is Bob. Sils imagined all kinds of scenarios where she'd overpower Bob, beat his brains out, and then find Bull Dave and drive his Audi into the lake.

"You know Dave, the pharmacist, Bob?"

He didn't.

"I'll pay you a lot of money to fuck with his shit. That is, if you let me out of this cage first."

Her gut growled and the bagel, still on offer, along with a bottle of warm spring water, started to look good. She accepted them under duress. Baiting him was risky, even foolish, yet she'd seen enough crime T.V. to know a killer from a rank amateur.

She gestured with a greasy hand at her captor's cape. "That's a funny rig you got on there, Bob. You some kind of superhero?"

Bob picked his nose before reacting to a sound above their heads. Like a feral cat afraid of its shadow, he leapt to his feet, tearing the hem of the garment.

"Who the fuck is that, Bob?" Her voice took on an edge.

He rose to his full height, anchored by a pair of basketball shoes that made her think of the Tenth Doctor.

Bob's eyes took on a peculiar shine, the kind that lovers display after an amazing workout.

"The Controller," he said, checking the lock on her cage, before departing in great haste.

She studied the flimsy lock that kept her in place. A Mastercraft No. 3, it could easily be dispatched with a couple of blows from a rubber mallet. Yet, no matter how many times she surveyed the near-empty basement, there was no such item.

How long had she been here and what did these freaks hope to accomplish? Had Bull Dave set her up? Was Jack Frewer a keeper after all?

She strained to listen, trying to believe that Bull Dave was upstairs securing her release. He had left the room with a couple of furries before Moonbow lowered the boom. Maybe he didn't know? Maybe he was just finding out because he missed her? This hope, both childish and pathetic, evaporated as the voices above her gave way to muffled shouts.

If shrillness could be sanguine, the kid Bob was pleading her case. He didn't appear to be doing that well. The other voice, sexless and deep, countered the kid's words, now punctuated by emphatic taps that knocked out an obscure message against the tile floor.

Tap, tap, tap.

What in hell was that?

The tapping continued amidst shouts and appeals until, at last, it came to rest above her head, which was spinning like a top. Subconsciously or not, Banks felt herself reaching into her pants pocket, just as Jack Frewer always did when they passed time in the van. What was he reaching for all the time, and why had she tied the noise above her head to a single, not very noteworthy action?

The bagel forgotten, she now focused on two things: getting the hell out of there, and taking a pee. She strained against the confines of her space, trying to will the lock and door it held shut open. Her circumstances, too ridiculous to process, took a sharp turn when two sets of eyes appeared out of the darkness. Almond and ovoid, green and blue, the eyes came into sharp relief with the thinnest fiber of silken sunlight, forcing its way through a smallish window. Left open to clear the stench of mold from stale basement air, it provided the perfect entry way for the black cat and his Siamese companion.

She reached for them both, beckoning, not finding one more unusual over the other. They were house cats, plain and simple. But the keen intelligent look of the black resonated deep in the roots of her dorsal ganglia; a place, she recalled from school, where humans divined things human, well beyond the comprehension of brute animals.

How could this be? she wondered, reaching for him, as if he understood her problem.

It drew closer, rubbing its forehead against the bars, in what had to be tacit cognition. Could a damned cat appreciate her predicament?

Banks drew her knees up to her chin, releasing a flow of urine that could no longer be held in. The cat, smelling her mark, responded in kind with a long *chirrup*.

"Who are you?" she demanded, broken in her own wet. "Can you help me?"

The black and the Siamese exchanged glances, like an old married couple accustomed to making decisions together.

"These people are crazy. They put humans in cages."

She cried—cried into nightfall—unaware that the black and his mate had left her alone in silence. The voices above her had stilled, along with the sinister tap, tap, tap against the tile floor. The owner of the house—the pilot, and Bull Dave's friend,—could not be discerned in the heaviness, he likely having flown the nest with his attentive flight attendants.

She leaned against her cage, placing dirty hands against the cool metal. "Help me. Help me," she cried to no one, straining for a sound—any sound—to announce itself from outside.

Outside! The window is open!

"HELP ME!" she yelled. "SOMEONE! HELP ME! I'M DOWN HERE!" She reached for one of the water bottles left for her by the pimply asshole named Bob. "BOB! WHERE ARE YOU? I KNOW YOU'RE THERE."

Scratching, snarly slobber was her only answer, as the dark shape blocking out the moonlight filled the tiny window above her. Banks thought about Fogler and the bear.

"Am I going to die tonight?"

She pushed on the bars and the door gave way, the Mastercraft lock having somehow fallen away. She didn't take time to ask herself why; didn't give a thought as to who might be at the top of the stairs when she got there. She would kill anyone who got in her way; such was the by-product of captivity.

Clawing on all fours, she took the wooden steps from the unfinished basement by five's, head butting open the unlocked hall door that separated purgatory from the swingers' den. Down the hall, still on all fours, she passed the zebra divan heading straight and sure out of the open screen door into the waiting thrall of a gigantic fucking Rottweiler.

The mutt, licenced and collared, undoubtedly was up to date with all its shots, but this was her least concern. The beast, staring her down at eye level, pulled its lips back to reveal uneven yellow teeth in a fetid hell mouth that spelled D-E-A-T-H.

"I will not die tonight, you motherfucker. I'm not Fogler."

The dog, bracing, withdrew at the sound of a silent whistle, announcing itself with a glint of metal in the moonlight.

A mellow, masculine voice, broke the tension. "It's all right. You're safe."

"Call off your mutt if you're the owner," she cried, aware of a wash of emotions that betrayed her rage.

The man, dressed in a big fuzzy hunting jacket, walked slowly into her peripheral view, offering his hand in the same way she did when approaching an unfamiliar animal. She sniffed him. The man said nothing.

"Do you know what I've been through? Do you know what goes on in that hell house?"

Zoltan Kárpáty answered her, but only indirectly. "There are a lot of things that go on here in the Downs. Weird things. Greedy things. You got caught in the crossfire."

Banks, on her feet, followed him, fully aware that the man was leading her away to the woods. "Are you going to kill me?"

"You're in shock. You need warmth and a safe place. Did they harm you?"

"They humiliated me."

"Do you need medical attention?"

"I need a lawyer."

"You need time."

\*\*\*

She didn't connect him with the assault, her short-term memory clearly locked after the second Jell-O shot. But she would eventually. All *he* needed was time.

On reaching the clearing, Zoltan Kárpáty ushered her to a vacant trailer. Small, but beautifully appointed with many fluffy pillows, the surroundings withered her suspicions, and she let her guard down, accepting a change of clothes and a hot cup of cocoa.

"No, friend," she said at last. "I need a lawyer."

Zoltan reached for a pack of smokes, but decided not to offer her one. "You need to leave and never come back. It's not wholesome here."

"You're telling me. I should have this whole fucking town locked up. I should have that fucking pharmacist locked up for fooling me."

Zoltan paused to weigh a great decision. He folded his hands. "Dave is a bystander, a mere witness concerned more with entertainment than advancing the position."

The woman he had eyed appreciatively at the party prior to her incarceration returned as confusion took over her features. The dog, Pálinka, sensing her fear, came to rest at her feet to reassure her. She drew away.

"I remember, now. You didn't do anything to stop them."

Zoltan held up his hands in supplication.

"I couldn't. I wouldn't. At least, not until I had the right guarantees that they weren't going to harm you."

Banks' eyes widened. "That was you upstairs then? The one yelling at the pimply faced geek?"

Zoltan didn't know what she was talking about and said so. "Gus is long gone on a lay over in Europe. He's heading farther east. Whoever you heard is someone I don't know." He removed the cocoa mug, now empty, from her clutching, cooling hands.

"What I tell you stays between us. Do you understand?"

She nodded, mutely.

"I'm going to tell you a sad, sordid tale about an incredibly wicked creature, whose ends truly 'justify the means,' if you can stomach that."

Sils Banks visibly clenched, her reaction, he deduced, coming from an untapped certainty that her lover Bull Dave was involved in something salacious. He put those fears back in the box where they belonged with careful reassurances that hit the mark.

He looked out the trailer window, noting the number of lights coming on in the adjacent caravans. The occupants—all friends—had fired up their lanterns in abject disregard for the grid that had screwed them so roundly.

"I'm going to tell you about the Goddess Moonbow of Yarker and her true program."

Banks, lowering herself to the floor, bounced back and forth on her haunches in heightened expectation, her moves not unlike Pálinka, the Rottweiler, who followed suit.

"She is a great woman when you look at the whole picture," Zoltan began. "But you have to understand her roots to understand her motivations."

A simple farm girl from Yarker, she fell under the spell of Pilsen Güdderammerüng after just one viewing of *Blod av Däggdjur*. Ambitious and obsessive, she made it her business to seek him out, endearing him through missives so sweet that he hopped a plane from Oslo and never went back.

"Never went back?" Sils Banks didn't understand. "Güdderammerüng is internationally renowned. He's seen everywhere and continues to win awards year after year. How can he do that if he stays in Pictontown?"

"That's easy," Zoltan explained. "Satellites and Skype, and agents acting on his behalf. The lady, herself, has accepted several awards, although always in disguise."

Below middle income and unaccomplished, Goddess Moonbow did what every heroine in every novel she ever read did: she adapted, and she wooed, well above the abilities of those around her.

The Güdderammerite's, like the great man himself, were an easy target. Horny, delusional, and staring down the gun barrel of endless evermore, they embraced her feverish pleas to journey from anywhere in the world to serve him and advance his beliefs.

His system was not so very shocking where he came from—the recently repealed German bestiality laws being a case in point. But selling his lifestyle to an increasingly intolerant Western civilization would be tougher, and she was well-able to meet the challenge. At least, that's what she told him when he finally agreed to embrace her.

It was better than she had anticipated. Güdderammerüng's dislocation from reality was completely and thoroughly augmented by a steady diet of boutique barbiturates that soon had *her* hooked. Nights spent wandering semi-nude through the woods in the company of large wolves that did not bite, convinced her that a fine future could be had, not just for her, but for the residents of her new home. The good people of Pictontown on the Downs were in for something wonderful if they'd only see it her way.

They didn't, at first. They thought she was a kook. But Pils had lots of money and enough cachet to exploit.

"She bought them," Banks said.

"She did. With a casino and a hotel."

Though not yet realized, the empire the simple goddess from Yarker sought, was well under way when the shovels broke ground and the McMansions started going up. Lamborghini's followed, and so did the equine center. All good things unless you didn't conform.

"Look around you," Zoltan said, pointing at the lights. "These people you see in the trailers could not be bought, could not be persuaded. They are true Pics."

"And you? You were at that weird party—"

"More than a few. But I draw the line at the blood letting."

"Blood letting?"

"Yes. That's how she draws you in and keeps you there. You're so ashamed after a letting that you can't escape."

"She blackmails?"

"No. There's not a lot that shocks anyone anymore. What she does is bring you around to the idea that everything is normal. Once you know this, you're stuck."

He paused to look at her, taking in her facial features and body posture as they heaved and changed, leaving the old Sils Banks behind.

"I get it now," she said, resuming a relaxed position upright and human-like on the upholstered bench.

"And do you still need a lawyer?"

"No," she whispered. "I don't think I do."

Zoltan hung his head, an unlit cigarette dangling from lips freed of their heavy burden. To share is to be free, he mused. But in this case, it was to resign.

"You'll be staying then?"

Banks touched his arm, smiling. "Of course, I'll stay. There's nowhere else to go."

# Chapter Thirty-Two
## A Tale of Two Bitches

Bronagh Caley walked into Errol Deutscher campaign H.Q. firm in her conviction that she could not be held responsible. Poonam had asked for her help, hadn't she? And with Bill committed to a six-month contract away from her, what better way to spend time than campaign for the beautiful boy politician who had so captivated her?

Errol Deutscher thumped into the room on thick-soled sensible shoes. "What are *you* doing here?"

The politician's snarl—over loud—clearly hinted at reservations, something Bob assured her would not happen. Everything would be on the level.

It wasn't.

Deutscher's demeanor, hovering somewhere between screech owl and tweetie bird, could easily frighten off the less sanguine. But never Bronagh Caley. She was in a war now, not just for her political beliefs, but for her soul as well.

Bronagh hobbled over to the candidate, the emphasis on the 'hobble' being a little more than was actually true. On reaching for the candidate's hand, she deliberately flashed the cat pendant, which dangled conspicuously from her dimpled throat. "So good to see you again."

Deutscher pulled back, appalled. Among the numerous conditions imposed upon top tier Güdderammerite's was that they never engage publicly. Bronagh had broken this with as much ease as she took up a position by the nearest phone.

"Odd how we still do this, eh Deutscher? You'd think that campaigning in the modern age would be as simple as beaming the message in telepathically and then reaping the harvest without leaving the room."

"That day will come," Bob said, busting in with a microwaved cup of instant coffee made specially for her.

"One day soon, we can all vote posthumously. Won't that be fantastic?"

Deutscher sniffed, as Bronagh accepted the cup.

"That's been going on for years. You can confirm that with our friend, the Fret."

The room went quiet as Bronagh ignored the assault. Zealots were easily taken down; one need only cease to listen, to wag the tail until it fell off.

She dialed up the first call of the day.

"Hello? Mrs. Ehlers? This is—"

Bronagh put down her coffee. She hadn't thought of an assumed campaign name. "This is Endra Awkers calling from Errol Deutscher campaign headquarters. Is this a good time?"

"You know it isn't," the voice on the other end replied. "You're calling a nursing home and you know I'm too polite to hang up. What tha hell d'ya want?"

"Mrs. Ehlers, we're holding a campaign rally in the run up to election day, and as part of the charge to boost involvement, and keep momentum rolling right up to the last ballot, we are offering rides—"

"Hold on a second," the old lady interrupted. "Where are you calling from?"

"Errol Deutscher campaign headquarters. You remember Errol? She was instrumental in getting Mayor Lagerqvist re-elected—"

The woman huffed. "Oh, yeah, the mayor."

"Yes."

"She's the one who let all those free loaders in."

Free loaders could have meant just about anyone, and as much as Bronagh wanted to keep the call going in a forward direction, she couldn't resist asking the question.

"What free loaders are you specifically referring to Mrs. Ehlers?"

"The ones with those goddamned Eye-talian cars. They roar around here all hours of the day and night, keeping me up when I ought to be down."

Bronagh knew what she was referring to. The gentrified class annoyed her also, but in her role as devoted Free Ranger, she was duty-bound to defend the entitled.

"I understand that noise can be a bother," Bronagh said, "but surely you agree that development is the best way to grow our tax base to, you know, pay for things."

"Things like me?" The old lady's voice grew tarter.

Bronagh cleared her throat. "Well, I wouldn't put it that way. It's a way to cover health care, housing. Things like that."

"And the casino? And the hotel complex? What about those?"

Mrs. Ehlers was not only informed, but she had a broad appreciation for the irony of their situation.

"And the toll roads? And the whorehouses?"

Pictontown was changing, not just in terms of its infrastructure, but culturally as well. She thumbed her kitty fob. "The leader has promised to look into those things once elected. He has, for example, committed to me personally, to revisit the airport scheme as well as the proposed waste disposal site."

"The shit from Blenkinskane."

"Yes. The shit from Blenkinskane."

Ehlers, audibly exhaling into the phone, sounded swayed. Now all Bronagh had to do was get the old people on a bus and drive them to the wrong polling station on election day.

"So, can we count on your support on election day?"

"You can."

"And can we offer you and your friends a ride to the rally—we're having a big rally—and then again on voting day?"

"I'll take a bus ride to the rally, for sure, honey. But I don't need any ride to the poll."

Bronagh sensed her mistake even as she lobbed out a feeble question: "You still drive?"

"No honey, of course I don't drive. I can't take a pee without assistance. You called a nursing home, remember? Our polling station's in the cafeteria."

Bronagh hung up the receiver, her plans for contriving voting irregularities scotched, because she was rusty.

"Struck out?" Deutscher asked, looming over her shoulder with a moon face and blue cheese scent to go with her attitude.

"Not quite."

Bronagh was about to dial the second name on her list when Poonam Rajput stormed into the committee room, all business and purpose. Weighted down by shopping bags and a handful of Skinny Pic lattes wedged into a cardboard tray, she swept past her neighbor without so much as a 'hello' or 'still alive, I see?'

Deutscher seemed to approve the snub, nodding her head in appreciation.

"Poonam Rajput is one of our most dedicated supporters. She's here day and night."

*Day and night?* Bronagh doubted that, doubted that very much, though her friend had been spending a great deal of time out—at night—in the woods.

# Chapter Thirty-Three
## The Next Day

Poonie found it incredibly easy to rid herself of Zoltan, for as much as she loved the sex and attention, sharing him with a broad pool of people just wasn't her cup of tea. She felt the first pangs of jealousy mere hours after their first sojourn in the caravan, but blamed it on a lack of sophistication. Then Mummy, glued to the window one evening, called the plays like a pro at a hockey game, describing one girl after another cycling through her lover's home. This wasn't new, but it nagged. Poonie had been aware of his proclivities going in—had even tried to embrace the Güdderammerite ethos—but no amount of prayer or self-affirmation took away the reality that she lacked a swinger's appetite.

When Mummy informed her that Zoltan's assemblage of 'freaks and hermaphrodites' were using cats on their skins, including a black that looked very much like their own, she decided to confront Zoltan head on, but found, instead, his affable Lou, decked out in a cat suit and tail.

"Oh, hey. It's you. He's not here. I'm carving pumpkins."

Poonie had never seen the inside of Zoltan's house, and with a pause in the conversation, took the plunge and invited herself in.

"Is that a Finn Juhl chesterfield? I haven't seen one of those in years." She moved past Lou, who did nothing to stop her.

"Chester what?"

"Chesterfield. It's what we used to call large sofas. At least, that's what the old people called them. This one is a four-seater. It's remarkable."

Lou closed the door, her lack of interest in the antique apparent by her audible *huff* and blinking eyes.

"We can talk in the kitchen if you like. I have to get these pumpkins done, you know, for the party."

Poonie followed her love rival into a large modern kitchen that extended well past the original building frame to allow a high ceiling and roof finished almost entirely in glass. Though she had no prior knowledge of any party, and wanted to ask about it, her interest switched to Lou and her amazing surroundings.

"Did you do all of this?"

Lou shrugged over her pumpkins, a white and an orange, their faces in various states of completion.

"No. I'm just the pumpkin carver in this house." She paused. "And a tenant. Really. Nothing more."

She swept her blue eyes over Poonam, conveying a depth of understanding that moved them both. Despite every effort to dislike the tall, willowy woman, Poonam could not help but give her points for her efforts. Lou was trying to tell her that she wasn't as important to Zoltan as Poonie clearly was.

"You don't live in the woods?"

Lou laugh-snorted. "No. That's for the weirdo's— the back-to-earthers. That's what I call them. I like heat, you know? And fur. I wear fur. Real fur. So, I'm not really for them."

Poonam looked around the kitchen, scanning for the cat. The thought that her vahana had somehow become involved in a Güdderammerite ritual made her sick.

"I was wondering if you'd seen my cat?"

The question went over Lou's head. "I thought with winter coming on, the little trailer park would disperse. But, no. The little community our Zoltan's built seems to thrive."

"He always has tenants," Poonam agreed. "Real colorful, interesting ones."

"Like the Goddess Moonbow."

Poonam studied her face. "You don't like her."

Lou hacked out a jagged tooth with her big knife, making the orange pumpkin more sinister than she might have intended.

"He told you about *her?*"

Poonie didn't know how to answer. Zoltan had been emphatic about Moonbow's importance in bringing Pictontown out from under the rocks.

"Not really. My guess is she seems like the type who'd live in a glade."

A nerve had been struck. Lou drove the large knife into the head of the white pumpkin with a little too much force.

"That one is anything but extraordinary. She's as ordinary as—my mom—" She smiled. "—or *yours.*"

"My mom is not ordinary," Poonam said, stifling a chuckle. "She's been calling the plays for months since my husband died. She's been pretty accurate."

"About your life?"

"Mine and everybody else's."

Lou sliced the knife, now retrieved from the hapless pumpkin, through the natural light coming in from Zoltan's super skylight. "You were looking for your cat? The black one, right?"

"Yes," Poonie said, her voice trailing off with thoughts of Zoltan and Moonbow. Suddenly she didn't like either of them very much. "Mummy says she saw him the other night in this house. I don't want him in here if he's going to be used for some dark purpose."

Lou squared her toned shoulders. "You don't have to worry about him. Panzer's a good boy—more human than cat—and neither Zoltan nor I buy into that crap Moonbow and the German spin about humans and animals getting down to business. It's just a lot of shit for a lot of rich people on drugs to play around with."

"My cat is safe?"

"Of course. They all are. The weirdo's that actually believe in this crap were shut down weeks ago when Moonbow called a halt to the blood letting."

"I beg your pardon?"

"Blood letting. Moonbow liked to get the fat cats liquored up at the warehouse and then convince them that dragging kitties across their backs qualified them to invest in the hotel/casino project. Really contrived shit to separate 'us' from 'them.' I never bought into it. I'm a dancer. I can't be scratched all to rat shit."

Poonam smoothed her skirt which fit a whole lot better since she started losing weight. The mourning weight she piled on was understandable, but with her new knowledge, there was no reason left to destroy her looks, especially on Sikander's account. On no one's account.

"Is everybody mad?"

"Pretty much."

Poonam pushed away thoughts of the Free Range Party and its beautiful boy leader who meant so much to her. It was impossible to believe that he would endorse such behavior. Or was she just being naïve again? She looked at Lou who returned to her pumpkin carving.

"I was looking for Zoltan."

"Out buying stuff for the party. You're coming, right?"

Her question appeared sincere.

Poonam rose to her feet. "No. I don't think I'm cut out for it. I'm not cut out for any of it. You'll tell Zoltan?"

Lou put her knife down. "I'll tell him you're not coming to the party. As for your doubts about our guy that's up to you."

Poonam looked at her new friend.

"Everyone's involved?"

"Everyone with a cat pendant, sweetie. Investors with a ton to gain. We're just waiting for Phase II."

As Poonam trudged to her sensible Volvo, she wondered how much Sikander invested, and where the money had got to, now that he was dead.

# Chapter Thirty-Four
## Healed

While it was common for people on both sides of the ocean to embrace the 'nine lives' myth as it related to cats, the felines themselves knew better, and always had. Always one step ahead of the bipeds, Carlos knew when it was time to leave, survival depending more upon changing addresses, than a physical shedding of one life for another.

Perhaps it was the accrued knowledge from all the places he'd been that added up to the fairy tale nine lives, in which case he had more lives than any elf could guess at.

The street he had called home for several years, now blossomed with campaign signs to compliment pumpkins of differing hues, carved to elicit fear and delight.

Though film was more his spécialité, the election campaign that saw the humans bustle and bray like the mules he'd seen in the barns in Cavan, had done more to steel his resolve. The wound from the dart still hurt as did the realization that the rot from the creepy humans was greater than first thought. Something had to be done.

He should have heeded Pálinka's warning about his master's parties. How alike they were with the hooded ones. But curiosity—the penultimate cat killer—overtook him, directing his eyes not just in the direction of Zoltan Kárpáty, but Bronagh Caley as well. For as much as she tried not to know Bob, the Corduroy Man, she could not evade the cats' eye on the street. Either one or both had a hand in his initial incarceration—he was now sure—and he could not go until that was fixed.

*I don't know why you care so much,* Persian hummed from his vantage in Zoltan's rafters. *They don't keep us in cages and we are well-fed.*

*I was brought here for a purpose,* Carlos replied, watching Poonam Rajput keenly, as she dragged her weary frame across the street. *A purpose that is now clearer.*

*Whatever do you mean? What are the humans to us?*

*Nothing much in the grand scheme, dear friend. But they are our raison d'être. Without them, there'd be nothing to complain about.*

*Maybe it's vanity,* Siamese offered, joining them. Like Carlos, she had been excused from participation in the human drama that was Zoltan's castle, having paid her dues through her attentiveness to the black cat, whilst injured.

*The freaks in the hoods fed us garbage and did not give us our proper due.*

Carlos looked at her, taken aback by her arrogance.

*We are cat, and so by history and by tradition, we do not need anybody. But in our collective wisdom, we have developed an ability to care. The bipeds don't, and it is that which I need to address. You can come along, or not.*

\*\*\*

Rudolf Fischer, resigned to the fact that his wife would never come back, pushed the ground up seasoned pork into sausage casings. Still glistening from a lengthy bath in salty brine, the intestines could have been coated by the old man's tears. What difference did it make to him that people were bickering about nonsense like politics? His wife was dead and her spirit was muted. Without word, without a sign, what was left for a half-blind old man?

He considered the street he lived on. Hallowe'en was supposed to be fun, yet strict rules had been imposed to limit as much of that as possible. He had read about it in

*The Pic,* which celebrated the moratorium on nuts and chocolate as a bold step towards greater understanding.

"Understanding what?" he asked his beloved Carlos/Panzer, who had snuck over after a prolonged visit with the neighbors. "I doubt they could understand anything past their own assholes."

Carlos meowed his assent.

"She loved you," he said, adjusting the crank on the manual sausage maker. He wiped his nose on his sleeve. "I suppose now, I love you too."

From their basement lair, both creatures worked side by side in studied silence, the momentum broken once in a while by wispy coughs and the occasional sneeze. The man, dedicated to his peculiar culinary craft, and the cat, whose function it was to watch intently and provide comfort, made a perfect picture of how to cope in miserable times.

"I loved her. I really did. A pity no else saw it."

Carlos' ears pricked.

"A pity no one noticed after she was gone."

The front door blew open with tinkly chimes, a bit of magic facilitated by a pen light battery stuffed into a cheap plastic device purchased at the dollar store.

"Opa! Are you here? Your car's in the garage."

Rudolf, wiping his hands on an apron dotted with day's old blood, took a seat on an old wine barrel still rich with scents from the previous season's yield. "Down here, Zoe. We both are."

Zoey hadn't seen Carlos in several weeks, the last visit devolving from a controlled discussion to a hideous argument on how to avoid Animal Control. She had been very cross with her grandfather over Carlos' injury, her rage at him exacerbated by inflammation from a new tattoo on her right forearm.

Ugly to him at first, Rudolf, on a second look, decided that the shield and dragon selected by his granddaughter was quite grand.

The cat, trotting over to see her, wiped away any residual animosity. "Hello, Carlos. How's my boy?"

Rudolf, judging, shook his head. "Where do you get a silly name like that from? He's called Panzer now, and you know it."

"I know a lot of things, Opa, including a Carlos when I see one."

She reached down and scooped up the nuzzling kitty, who, more affectionate than she'd ever recalled, seemed to be telling her something important. Zoey looked down at the writhing sausage and wrinkled her nose.

"Opa. Must we—"

"*We* have nothing to do with it. It's for your grandmother."

"She was no fan of it either."

Rudolf held up his hand in a universal gesture to 'shut the hell up.'

"You are a German and so was she. Vegetarianism is out of the question."

He recalled the first time he asked his granddaughter to help with the headcheese, and how happy she was to get the first of two pigs eyes, boiled through and laden with frothy goodness. She was seven.

"Oma would have begged to differ if she were still here."

"Ah, the animals. She did love them so. Sometimes she put them before me. But in the old country, we had to live. After the war, especially. There wasn't a dog or cat to be found."

"You miss her, don't you?"

"Of course, I do. We all do."

He smiled at Carlos/Panzer. "He's coming around more, like he knows I need him." He wiped his nose on his sleeve again. "That pushy witch from up the street was spooking around again, trying to get the goods on me."

"The one that fell on her fat ass?"

"The very one. Poonam thinks she thinks I killed your grandmother." Rudolf nodded at the sausage.

"She's ridiculous!"

"He doesn't think so." Rudolf nodded to Carlos/Panzer.

"*He* told you?" Zoey rolled her eyes.

"Yes. And Poonam too. Our neighbor has a grudge." His voice trailed off.

"How is the lady Poonam?" Zoey asked, a big grin crossing her face. "She visits you a lot."

"You can stop right there. She has a boyfriend now. She is doing fine."

Zoey, still holding the cat, took a seat on an adjacent wine barrel. "I'm all ears."

"I don't gossip *mein kind*. That was your grandmother's department."

"But you know who she's seeing…"

"Of course."

Zoey put the cat down and crossed her arms in her customary Zoey fashion. "Well?"

"Oh, very well. The gardener from across the street."

Zoey's eyes widened. "The swinger?"

Rudolf snorted. He was old, but he wasn't out of it. "I don't know anything about that. I know he's Hungarian. That's all I know."

Zoey rubbed her hands together. "So, your little doll has outgrown the bonds of widowhood. Good for her."

"Why do you say that?"

"Everyone knows Sikander was no prize. He was stepping out on her with more than a few, so I understand."

"You hide out with your binoculars at night like that crazy woman?"

"The Caley woman? No. But I can read. Read Goddess Moonbow and then read between the lines. It's all there."

Zoey's triumphal grin guaranteed everything she said as a hundred percent accurate.

They continued to talk for several minutes: the old man, about his wife and of how the pancreatic cancer took her quickly and with mercy; the girl, of silly things, like road tolls and the importance of everyone paying their fair share, even after they've paid for it a million times over.

The old man smiled. His granddaughter was such a socialist. Maybe she should run for office?

"And Animal Control? Are they still after our boy?"

"Not so much, I think. The Hungarian does his part to keep him sheltered as does the lady Poonam. I think he is through the worst of it."

He smiled at the cat, curled up in a tattered old hockey blanket.

"There are more important matters to attend to."

Zoey seemed to agree, the muscles in her face contorting and relaxing. "I almost forgot. There's a whole helluvalot of commotion two streets over. Police and fire and an ambulance too."

END OF ACT 3

# Chapter Thirty-Five
## Revenge

Reaction was swift. In the time it took to liberate Sils Banks from her metal prison, dress her wounds, and feed her fresh, clean water, Pic residents had moved in to assign blame and make it stick. But before any of this could happen, she had to be found, and it had been up to Zoltan to make it so.

The idea to put her back in the cage had been entirely her own. He had protested at first, citing the odiousness of confinement as a sidebar. The real issue was an ethical one. Zoltan was passive when it came to resistance. Setting up the Goddess for a fall, in his mind, went beyond the laws of nature and he told the animal control officer so.

"Best to let things unfold."

"The hell I will!" Banks shouted, tearing off the loaned flannels that had put a little pink back into her skin.

"If what you say is true, and all this weird fucking pervy shit with cats and the assholes in costumes is nothing more than an elaborate scheme to raise funds for more hotels and casinos and shit nobody wants, then I'm far from fucking out. I'm fucking in. Ya hear?"

She wrinkled her nose at the dank uniform that had, days ago, been a party outfit. The stink off the cloth, lingering somewhere between an outhouse and a good sweat at the gym, made her mad, forcing back to mind thoughts of Bull Dave and that dick Jack Frewer. She wriggled into the garments.

"Someone's gotta take a stand, my friend. What are you? A Boomer? An Xer? No matter. Only need you a little bit. Got some motherfuckers an' I'm gonna make 'em pay real good. Ya know what I'm sayin'?"

Her flesh, radiant to her own touch, fired the synapses in her brain. *Nowhere else to go? My ass. I have everywhere to go.*

At the sight of her nakedness, Zoltan Kárpáty had averted his eyes. This amused her.

"It's one thing to play at being cool," she asserted. "It's another to *be* it."

She thought of the tranquilizer darts in the gym bag in the trunk of her car, then touched her companion's cheek, now sallow under the weight of his own guilt.

"You'll be fine. Watch me."

\*\*\*

Banks' companion, Bull Dave, was known to Zoltan, as were so many others. Jack Frewer, like his idiot friend Bob from City Hall, had been tasked to find the cats; Moonbow, the cash. But it was the mysterious 'Controller' who managed it all, and it was this person that Zoltan Kárpáty had so mightily feared.

The caravan park on the vacant lot existed by the grace of this omnipotent being, so often referred to, but only in whispers. Güdderammerüng, in more lucid moments, suggested that the Controller wasn't real, but merely a device to move the story along. He said this often, usually over canapés, but more often after the group sex, at which point Moonbeam would either stare him silent, or bring her retractable leather *Whip It*™ down on some hapless furry.

Sils Banks' stare had taken on a power not unlike the Goddess,' and in the wounded woman's presence, Zoltan felt a shame of the kind he first felt when kitty wrangling was held up as something noble.

"The symbiosis between feline and the feline feminine is awakened on touch," the Goddess would opine over opioids, incense and a bottle or two of Shiraz. "But it's the god in us all that transcends the normal, the base and the boring. We are the deciders now."

*Deciders?* he thought at the time. *That wasn't even a word in Hungarian or English.*

A decider or not, he had been party to a 'group think' convinced that it was doing right in growing the neighborhood, when in fact all it did was invite the sports cars in, along with some really lousy architecture.

MockThatMansion.com warned of the negative side effects of gentrification when it reported on a west coast uprising involving enough Molotov cocktails to keep the fire adjusters in luxury for years.

"Don't you want to be rich, pet?" the Goddess had cooed into his ear when he tried to hold back his initial deposit.

Zoltan looked at Sils Banks, now dressed in her soiled, smelly clothes. "Don't you want to see this community grow?"

Sils looked at her broken finger nails. "I'd rather die."

"I think that is a very extreme statement."

Banks shrugged. "Yeah. It is. I have no intention of dying. But this life we live in The Downs—it's not living; it's plastic."

She handed him her phone, which had died one hour before her captivity began.

"I relied on this piece of shit for everything until I really needed it. I don't need the fucking thing anymore."

Zoltan understood. She had suffered an enormous disappointment. No. That was a rude and insensitive over-simplification. She had been *animalized*, made to behave like prey. She was pushing back now, back to her rightful place in the food chain.

They were halfway to Gus' house when he realized this, and now, deferring to her asked: "What will you have me do?"

She smiled as she pushed the unlocked door open. "You're going to make sure all doors are locked before you break one of them down. You will play this as before. You will 'see me' through the basement window, and you will 'save me.'" She looked around the darkened living room. In the light of the moon, it was clear that someone had been through to sweep the place after the party. Her purse, no doubt, had been taken up with the trash.

Finding a pen and a notepad on the kitchen table, she scratched out a hasty note.

"After you call 9-1-1, and after I'm safely set up in hospital, you will call this number. Tell the person on the other end to go to my place and get my car. I want her to pick me up in that car when I'm released from hospital. Be mysterious. Don't tell her your name."

Zoltan nodded, impressed. She was thinking it through.

She touched his arm. "We have never met, my friend. And I don't know how I got into this cage."

They were in the basement now.

"I'm shocked. I'm traumatized. I'm a victim. I remember nothing."

She got into the cage. Zoltan, mindful that she had ingested cocoa in the caravan, brought this to her attention.

She smirked. "Not the kind of food a captive normally gets. Yer catching fire, my friend."

She stuck a finger into her mouth, pressing hard on the epiglottis. "This'll get rid of the evidence."

\*\*\*

The fat little detective called Grech made himself at home on the edge of her hospital bed. He'd been there for hours.

"And you're quite sure you have no prior recollection of how you got there?"

Banks, stacking and unstacking used styrofoam cups like a psyched-out character she once saw in a movie, nodded dumbly. The less said, the better.

Jack Frewer, inserting his body between hers and the cop's, made like the protective jerk he always painted himself to be. Like the cop, he had no indication from her that she remembered anything, and that included the party and his being there too.

Zoning in and out, she made out that she had flashes of people that weren't exactly people, dancing around a Seventies-era disco ball in a place she didn't recognize.

"What about the doctor?" Jack prompted helpfully. "The guy you went to lunch with?"

Typical Jack. He'd got the story of Bull Dave, the flying pharmacist, bass ackward. She reached for a cruller.

"He's my pharmacist, Jack. I don't know where you get 'doctor' from. Jeez."

"Okay," Det. Grech interjected. "You had lunch with your friend the pharmacist and then?"

"I went home. I thought I did." She shrugged. "What day is it?"

"Hallowe'en," Jack piped in.

"Election day." She furrowed her brow. "I forgot to vote."

The younger, way more attractive detective who had accompanied Grech into her semi-private room chuckled, as if her civic-mindedness gave legs to some biased impression he had about her.

"Yeah, buddy," she yelled out, inflamed. "I'm a Fret. What tha fuck of it?"

"Yeah, what the fuck of it?" the older lady in the bed next to her repeated.

Their nurse protector entered the room. "Let's wrap it up, gentlemen. The patients need rest."

"You bet your ass we need rest, honey," the old bag hollered. "I was supposed to vote today. I made a promise at the rally. I got a bus ride there too."

Jack Frewer glanced, not unkindly, at Francie Ehlers, late of the Water's Edge Retirement Home.

"I got a phone call from Deutscher campaign headquarters," she wheezed, "And they took me for a ride." She burst out laughing.

Jack leaned in a little too closely. "Are you sure you don't want a private room, baby? This old bat is whacked."

Sils Banks smiled coyly at her very disappointing ex-lover. "I'm sure. I need the company."

Jack eyed the extra-large floral bouquet from her partner Wompat, who also moonlighted at the local funeral parlor. A dedicated Free Ranger and pot head, he believed it a civic duty to recycle every bouquet left behind after mourners paid their respects. This one smelled like formaldehyde.

"You seeing Wompat now?"

The dogcatcher with the stovepipe hat was not her type and she said so.

"Besides, I only have eyes for you."

The barfy cliché, straight out of the American Song Book, had the desired effect on her mark. He was there to find out what she knew, what she remembered, so that he could report back to the skinny, five-foot tall Moonbow elf-freak from the bumblefuck borough of Yarker.

Fucking vole. He would exit the room with nothing.

She clasped her head, the length of her run-on thoughts too much to bear. That, or she was playing the part too well.

After he left, Francie Ehlers mumbled at length about *her* injuries:

"I was at the Errol Deutscher campaign rally. Real cheesy stuff, but I figured I could get free grub and maybe a close-up look at that cutie from Channel 4. Anyway, everything was going well. The jerks in the hats sucking up to us old people like their future livelihoods depended on our every vote—which they probably do—had me in my safe place. Then, all of a sudden, the guy with the hair comes into the room and everybody goes insane, like he's Perry Como or something. And then, something strange happened. This creature—like no creature I ever seen—comes out of the woodwork with a stumpy hand and a YoYo."

Sils Banks cocked an eyebrow at the old biddy.

"I know," Francie Ehlers, affirmed. "It was like something out of a Darvon™ drunk. You ever take Darvon, sweetie? No, I guess that was before your time. You know, we had the best drugs back in my day. Yellow jackets, poppers, dolls and some of the finest barbiturates known to mankind. That's when being stoned had an elegant quality to it. Anyway, I digress. The young man next to me honking on a big glass bong sez to me, 'Yer wondering who the hell that is, cuz the look is so imposing, but you have nothing to worry about. You've seen that look before.' Yeah, I thought, after a minute or two. I had seen that look before. On top of a stage, on the back side of buses, on late night T.V., promising me everything and not. What was it doing here? It didn't belong here. That look. The Hair takes center stage now. We don't need that creature anymore."

Banks had never taken Darvon. Had never even heard of it before Francie Ehlers. Now she wished she had some. Depressing the call button next to her bed, she conjured up some dialogue to fool the nurse into giving Francie something stronger to shut her the fuck up.

"So, then I start to feel woozy, like The Hair was singing me to sleep. That YoYo, ya know, I told you about the YoYo, right?—it's like a pendulum, scooching back and forth, and then the stink of the pot—smelled like skunk and cat piss—reaches down into my stomach, and I start puking on the bong boy. That's when I blacked out and hit my head on the concrete."

She pointed to her bandaged head.

Banks reached for her crumpled copy of *The Pic*, which detailed, in all its glory, the daring rescue of a local woman by a man known for conservancy and clean living. She looked at Francie, waiting for a break in the monologue. When it at last arrived, she offered some insights of her own.

"Do you know how I got here? I'll tell you. There's some nasty people out there who think they can tell us how to think and feel. They put me in a cage."

Francie Ehlers, grasping for her own wrinkled copy of *The Downsview,* couldn't have cared less. Here yellow eyes, shining under the florescent tube lights that absolutely tortured, were looking for poll numbers.

"Do you think he'll win? The Hair, I mean?"

# Chapter Thirty-Six
## Election Day

In anticipation of a great rush, polling stations beefed up security to herd the throngs. They didn't come. In fact, they did not come in such numbers that election night pundits, baffled by their complete misread of the situation, began to accuse each other of election fraud.

Bronagh Caley, hunched over her kitchen table, wondered if she should go to the committee room to watch the returns, but then her muddy alliances took over.

"What do you think?" she asked, reaching for the black cat that had wrapped itself around her cast. "Do I stick with my people, or sell out completely and hang with the Hair Cut?"

Polling numbers in the last twenty-four hours proved that no one really knew who'd win until the people had had their say. And with six hours to go before the polls closed on the west coast, she wasn't sure if she could sustain her curiosity.

The cat, now settled in her lap, eyed her with an intensity that freaked her out, his eyes glowing greener against the pale gray outside her French doors.

"It's All Hallows Eve," she said, "and Goddess recommends keeping you indoors."

All manner of crazies came out with the pumpkins and the politicians alike, she sniffed, prodding a crooked finger at the column on Page Four. Not only had Moonbow weighed in on Trick or Treating safety, but she'd also suggested that elections had no place among one of the pagan's highest holidays. "Whatever a person's beliefs," she intoned, "it is up to us as a community to pay the appropriate lip service at minimum, if we cannot honor, with a straight face, ancient beliefs at a maximum."

Bronagh frowned. It was an odd sidebar to the main story about a local woman taken by force and confined for a period of days right here in their own backyard.

"Jesus!"

The woman, who could not be named, was identified as a city official hi-jacked while discharging her duties. Whether it had anything to do with the election was 'immaterial,' Moonbow stressed. The important thing was that the woman had been found 'relatively unharmed.'

"You hear that?" Bronagh asked the cat, who seemed to be following the story with his own eyes. "A woman 'relatively' unharmed, as opposed to 'completely and utterly.' That's buggered. I don't see the difference. Do you?"

The cat, pinning its ears back, seemed to concur.

"There, there." She stroked his fur, and her companion, now uncomfortable, wriggled away, allowing her to read further. 'Local woman injured at political rally.' 'Three-day forecast calling for snow.' 'Ban on Hallowe'en nuts and chocolate to be strictly enforced'—that one made her laugh—'Yarker talc mine to remain closed pending investigation.'

This last item did not make her laugh. The Yarker mine was Bill's mine. She kept reading. Easement rights ceded by the council of chiefs of the local First Nations had been extracted, it was charged, under duress, and had come to light only after a money for influence peddling scheme had been uncovered at the highest level.

The mine had been closed for almost nine days, and in that time, there had been no phone call, no email, no text message, no nothing from her Bill.

She looked at the clock and then she looked at the cat as if each held the answer. Preposterously, they did. At the five o'clock chime, the cat bolted for the front door where unremitting mewls announced his desire to leave. Bronagh, convinced that the Goddess was right, and that the cat should not leave the house, walked haltingly in his direction. Then she stopped. The cat arched his back and then hissed in what seemed to be a profound act of ingratitude. Had she not worked overtime to keep him from the clutches of Animal Control? And had she not made peace with her neighbor Poonam to the great benefit of the now snarling, bitching beast?

She moved toward him, not sure if she'd kick him or caress him. The animal, dropping the histrionics, brushed against her cast.

"What is it? What is it?"

He moved to the window box in the living room, jumping up on the lush upholstery. There, he dug his claws in, tearing and ripping at something she had made herself, and loved enormously because of it.

She wanted to tell the little demon to get the hell off her summer project, but couldn't. Her eyes were drawn out and to the left. There, at the bend in the road coming out of the woods, a man and woman, hands joined, engaged in harmonious conversation, punctuated by toothy grins and giddy laughter.

Bronagh gasped. "Bill?"

***

Bill Caley woke on election day to the fragrant smell of hot cocoa presented to him by the attentive Ludmila. A native of Ukraine, Ludmila's English was not great, but her heart was huge, giving off a warmth that filled the tiny caravan on a frosty October morn.

"You drink this, Bill," she commanded, from behind a fringe of thick gray hair. "I made it on the Sterno."

He blinked once, and then several times more, as was his custom since returning from Yarker. Ludmila, studying him intently, smiled, her gold teeth betraying a depth of wealth very few in The Downs could ever appreciate. He checked himself. He had gone to bed the previous night in the same fashion he was born: unprepared, unwilling, and completely exposed. Self-conscious, he drew his flannels closer.

Ludmila smirked. "You were late, and you were loud last night." She thrust the cup into his free hand. "Why you wear those silly things?"

He shrugged. He had put on his Ray Bans.

"You hiding?"

He chuckled under his blankets. That's exactly what he was doing. He put the dark glasses back on the battered bed stand.

"Mister Zoltan told me to tell you that he found heat. We will have it soon."

Bill combed the crumbs from last night's dinner out of his beard. "Heat? As in hydro?"

"No hydro. We don't do the grid."

"Well then, what kind of heat?"

Ludmila still had a point to make. "Grid is for slaves. We're free."

Bill understood. Ludmila, like all the other residents, believed strongly in her civic right to mind her own business.

She gestured out the dirty little window just above his feet. "Zoltan found stoves in the junk houses before they got knocked down. He says 'retrofit.'"

Bill thought about all manner of stoves available that could fit into a tiny Air Stream. "Pot Bellie?"

"Bellie?" She shrugged. She didn't know what he was talking about. "Your lady left early."

"Yes, she did," he replied, referring to Lou and her random act of kindness without further detail. Ludmila was nosey, and he had no intention of feeding her primary character trait. Reading his mind, she seemed to conclude that too, and left him with a wave of her magic cocoa-making hand.

Alone, he searched for his one and only pair of clean pants. These, he found buried under a multitude of spent takeout chicken boxes and crumpled cans of Dr. Pepper. Dressed, he moved outside, and on sighting the blue-green evergreens, marveled at his newfound freedom, taking in the sharp smoky air warmed by Ludmila's fire. The frosted grass crackling songs under his heavy boots seemed to call out to all the things that were important to him now. Zoltan might have asserted that they were animals, but Bill privately differed. As a thinking, feeling being, he was duty-bound to exercise his right to perform decent acts with kindness and generosity. He rejected baser instincts. Zoltan assured him that he'd come 'round.

Bill's eyes, uncovered and opened, scanned the flattened ground for his lady, who'd minxed away before the dawn. Perhaps she was shy, or perhaps she'd taken what she'd wanted. He couldn't divine it.

Curtains in the surrounding caravans rustled, revealing faces unconcerned, unapologetic and whole. He waved a hand to all of them. And then she appeared: the sweetest of images on a fresh day. He greeted her with arms wide, welcoming something warm and familiar and good. She rushed to him, leapt at him, and took shelter in the warmth of his thick, leathery neck.

"Hello, my darling. I've missed you."

Siamese purred her dear music, reminding him of his first day in this most serendipitous of places. "Where is your mate?"

Bill hadn't seen her or Carlos since the day the cat's injury closed. "No more darts, I hope."

*Chirrup*, said Siamese, who seemed to think he needed reassurance. He didn't.

"Don't worry, my pet. No one's going to hurt you ever again."

\*\*\*

When Poonam married Sikander Rajput, she had done so with the best of intentions. She had, it was true, been alone for a long time, and after a string of unsatisfying affairs with men her parents would never approve of, she decided to put her faith in God and them.

Sikander didn't seem to mind that she had 'experience' in matters of the heart. He, in fact, commended her for having such. "You are a modern girl. I would have been very surprised and disappointed if you hadn't been around the track a few times."

He said this before they cemented their social contract in the weird bedroom he'd designed. She knew what he was getting at, regardless of how unfortunate the phrasing. She had been around the track, but when he said it, was he thinking of dogs or horses? She brushed it off. He was so much older than she, and people of his generation had odd little clichés that they hung on to.

"You have to get over it. You have to get on with it." This was what Sikander repeated to her over and over in her dreams. He was dead. What was she waiting for? Perhaps she was never meant to be happy?

She pondered these questions when she returned to the woods to break up with Zoltan. Instead, she found Bill Caley.

\*\*\*

Watching them, Bronagh knew she had every right to be infuriated with the happy couple. They had done an end run around her, getting back a little of their own for the things she had done. She should kill them—she knew—chop 'em up like Rudolf Fischer did to his poor old sick wife. Maybe she could borrow his meat grinder, and they could dine out on Oktoberfest sausage until they felt better?

She shoved the cat off the window box, sending him careening against the nearest wall. The animal landed on all fours with a howl and a hiss. A privileged creature, he did not take kindly to rough handling. Well, she didn't either.

Life was a cruel fucking state of affairs, putting the right people in the wrong place at the right time, just long enough to screw it all up and suffer for it until they rotted in their graves.

She grabbed at the kitty fob around her neck with a mind to strangle the hissing, mewling, midget shite of a thing that bled scandalously from a reopened scab on its side.

She looked out the window again, wondering if the foul betrayers were coming her way to smudge dirt in her face. No! That already happened when she fell on her ass and broke her foot.

The kitty, still cross in the corner, looked a lot less pretty than the first day she saw him. She reached into the pocket of her chenille bathrobe, which she hated, but couldn't seem to part with, as it had been a gift from one of her children.

"The smarter one," she said aloud.

The crumpled parchment, still there, opened up in her hands. The notice from the jerks at city hall offended her as much now as it had then.

"Keep what's yours indoors, or face the consequences," she mouthed bitterly to the black cat, who, much calmed, leered back at her.

"I loved him, you know. I loved him more than I loved my life." She winced. That sounded way too dramatic. "I loved him more than the life I was leading. I would have burned the whole thing down if only he'd had me."

Sikander Rajput was gone, and so, now, was her Bill too.

Bloody hell.

The cat inched toward her, communicating with liquid movements, a peculiar kind of understanding.

"I'll say to you what I said the first day we met. We are misunderstood, and it's not right."

Bill and Poonam, no longer in sight range, had wandered off to places unknown. She looked at the cat who maintained a careful distance.

"Our lady has taken a position against me. And now I have to take a position against her."

It wasn't enough that Bronagh had fucked Poonam's husband. The poor, dim, stupid, pretty thing had no idea. She had to be made aware. She had to *feel*. The only way to do that, was to strike back—hard.

"I'm sorry," she whispered to the cat. "This is not your fault. You're just in the wrong place at the wrong time."

# Chapter Thirty-Seven
## The Best Decision Ever

When Poonam Rajput left Catsuit Lou's kitchen, she did so, determined to shake things up. She crossed the street to her idling Volvo and shut the car off. There were more important things to do today than go to the committee room. Sure, there was an important election just hours away, but not even her civic responsibility could dissuade her.

Something had to change.

The black cat, her vahana, had appeared out of nowhere to wait at her heels like he always did before her next great leap. She looked at the gray woods with its naked, inter-lacing branches that seemed to single her out. They beckoned *her*, daring her to journey to where few others would go.

*Chirrup,* the cat said, sensing—correctly—her need for encouragement.

"You sent me out there before," she said, smiling, "and look where it got me."

She hadn't spoken to Bull Dave since the interactive art expo, her carryings-on with Zoltan in full view, too embarrassing to be held up to Dave's scrutiny over the drug counter. She ignored his calls instead.

She picked up the cat, which purred very loudly, so much so, that she turned her back to Bronagh's window in case she was there spying from behind her curtains. She had shared her husband with her neighbor. She would not share her cat too.

"Go," she whispered in his ear. "Go, before the witch grabs you."

He shifted in her arms, as if he understood every word, but made no effort to leave. The wound on his side, less angry, was still apparent, and she queried him with her eyes.

*Go to the woods.*

She hesitated. The cat, stubborn and steadfast, said nothing more.

"Go to the woods, eh? All right. All right," she laughed, no longer self-conscious at carrying out a conversation with an animal. "You know me better than I know myself."

It wasn't until she reached the clearing and saw Ludmila's fire smoking that she realized something was different about the place. Very often, the residents did not venture out until after dark, and only then to make a quick rush to the grocer or wine kiosk before Downs law enforcement vehicles came out to prowl. This afternoon, they were all about, chatting animatedly amongst themselves. Something good had happened.

"Welcome, my beautiful," Ludmila called, her braceleted hands clinking among the cups and clay pots. "We have a guest." She beamed in the direction of the much larger caravan normally reserved for Zoltan.

"Is he here?"

"Ahhh," the old lady cracked, slyly. "So, you knew he was coming!" She rose from her crockery, closing the distance between them in three girlish strides. "I'll take you to him."

Poonam shrugged her off. "I don't think he'll like what I have to say. I'm breaking things off."

Ludmila shot her a queer look. "You work it out. Okay?"

With everything that had happened to her, she had thought herself capable of a bloodless break-up, yet as she approached the little hovel she had come to see as her dearest salvation, she found herself faltering. 'What if I'm making a mistake?'

*"You are not,"* her angel answered. Silent since her foray into politics, she had wondered if her guide had abandoned her in favor of her much more colorful demon.

She paused at the door, reaching with childish hands to spin the knob that would open it. Somewhere, in the back of her mind, she hoped the angel on her shoulder would intercede to talk her out of it. He didn't. Instead, the devil turned the knob.

"Hello."

Bill Caley, her neighbor for more than ten years, looked very different standing in Zoltan's doorway. Her surprise at seeing him—clearly evident by the heat taking over her cheeks—made him laugh out loud.

"I don't think you were expecting me."

Poonie looked down at her feet like an idiot. "Actually, no."

"He's off buying stuff for—"

"The party. Yes, I know."

Things would have got awkward pretty fast were it not for the dependable Ludmila and her cocoa, which she pushed into her hands.

"With a little chili. Spice things up," she winked through her golden teeth.

Poonam rolled her eyes.

"I can get my coat, if you like," Bill offered. "It's a nice day. Unless you'd rather come in here. I've made an awful mess of it, I'm afraid."

Poonam tugged at her earring. "No worries, my friend. We are hardly strangers."

Bill Caley wasn't kidding when he said the place was a sty, but as with Rudolf Fischer, she found she could not hold it against him. Mess, she found, was a clue, often to things of great weight. Bill Caley had come home and not. It wasn't her business to know why.

"Thanks," he said, brushing wrappers, beer bottles and spent paper towels off the little side bench she routinely used after a roll with Zoltan. "You're probably dying to ask."

She wasn't, actually. She'd come to know enough about his wife to allow her to draw some pretty fine conclusions. But how much did this man know? Not much older than her late husband, he displayed a kind of vitality missing from practically everyone she came into contact with. Sturdy and assured, in rough-hewn cable knit, with shoulder length wavy steel hair and a beard to match, he reminded her more of a sailor than a miner. But then, maybe that was what was so sexy about him. The rover tied to the earth tricks Fate by staying put and never stalling.

"You know why I'm here?" she asked, feeling shy.

He smiled broadly, making her feel self-conscious. She averted her eyes.

"Poonie, darlin.' I have no idea why you're here. It wasn't the question I was expecting."

She buried her nose in her cup, pondering ways to get out of the hole she'd just dug. After a lengthy silence, she decided to go for it, hoping that she was speaking to a broader mind.

"I was looking for Zoltan. He and I—you know—became something of an item—you know—while you were gone...um. It's all buggered up. I mean, I buggered it up. I was pretending to be something I'm not, and I—"

Bill took the cup out of her hand and stole a sip, something quite unexpected, but ground-breaking.

"You don't have to explain anything to me, my dear. I should probably explain a thing or two to you."

Poonam held her breath. Did Bill Caley know about his wife and her husband?

He took a deep breath, let it out, and took a seat opposite her. Then he took her hand. "It was wrong of me to do to you what I did. But Bronagh was so bloody insistent. She's a good woman. She *was* a good woman. And then she kinda lost her way."

"Bill!" It was the only thing she could think to say.

"Let me finish. The renovation I could easily blame on her. Say it was all her idea. But the truth is, I wanted it too. I thought it would bring us closer. I never thought about what all the dust and noise would do to you, especially after you'd lost Sikander."

She hung her head.

"I'm sorry. 'Lost' is such a stupid word, but I'm not good at these things. Neither of us is, which is why we dodged the funeral and you."

"It's okay. It's okay. I'm managing."

"It's not okay, my darlin.' It's not. Your mummy gave me right and proper shit for not seeing what was going on in front of me. I'm so sorry."

He was clueless. Now it was Poonie's turn to not know what to say and say something anyway. "Bill, what are you doing in Zoltan's trailer?"

"Ah, there's the rub," he said. "The rub. You know it? Shakespeare used it all the time." He pulled his hair back into a pony tail with a multi-colored scrunchie—one of Lou's, she guessed—but in Zoltan's world, one couldn't be sure. "I'm here because I'm apart."

She reached for the shared cocoa cup. "A part? You've joined the collective?"

"No, no. You misunderstand. I've grown apart— from my wife."

Poonie nodded. "The rub."

"Yes! No! She's rubbed me the wrong way—yes. But this time, something else has happened. I've grown apart. I've grown apart from my life."

Poonie thought of Sikander's pre-deceased wanderlust. "It seems to be epidemic around here."

They talked for several minutes: the man, uttering the usual platitudes about it 'never being too late;' she, about her own kind of homespun wisdom designed to get to a point.

"The renovation has stopped?"

"Yes," he said. "Bronie's Irish pension had its limits, I guess."

Poonie nodded, coming out of a thought. "I never had a foreign pension. I was born overseas, but I left when I was young."

"I don't have one either," he chuckled. "And neither did Bronagh. Came out of the blue." He cracked his large knuckles. "I gotta hand it to her for going after it. I don't have that kind of patience."

"Neither do I," Poonie said, lying.

Nothing comes out of the blue, least of all, a pile of money.

# Chapter Thirty-Eight
## Hidden Treasure

Carlos, hog-tied and weighed down by one of Bill Caley's work boots, canvassed the lock box at the back of his brain. Sniffing out the rot in the nest of humans had proved more difficult than first thought. Perhaps the Persian had a point once upon a time. They were eating well, and they weren't confined. But the game had changed now, hadn't it?

The biped in the piggy colored robe paced angrily across the kitchen floor, her smallish eyes disappearing beneath a mighty snarl. Few humans, Carlos noted, possessed natural canines in the mouth, and even those came under suspicion when paraded oh-too-prominently across a flat screen vampire fiction on the T.V.

Bronagh Caley, in the round, in the twilight of this day, had neither artifice, nor attractive non-mercury filled lighting on her side. The pits in her face, the thinning spots in her hair, and the jagged, tartar-filled teeth were all hers. She was, he thought, an incredibly ugly beast, worthy of everything nature intended. All he had to do was wait.

The phone on the wall rang in unison with the one in her hand, and for a moment, the cat wondered which one of so many suspects might be calling to debate his future.

"Hello," she said, grabbing the thing off the wall, "I'll put you on speaker."

The buzzy device in her hand, abandoned to the animal-shaped ottoman dragged in from the larger room, flashed persistently, the figures rolling across it forming an imperceptible: J-A-C-K.

"Can you hear me?"

The sound, loud and unfamiliar, was that of another biped.

"Yes, I can Mr. Bobienski. Where are you calling from? There's a lot of noise in the background."

She took a seat on the ottoman.

"I apologize Mrs. Caley for calling so late in the day. I'm at a party. Thought you'd want to know, I've heard back from the Respondent."

She turned to eye the cat on the floor. "I'm listening."

"Mr. Fischer's counsel has indicated that he desires no further quarrel and is open to a mediation."

"What does that mean?"

"It means that you can sit down with an independent third party and have a conversation. Just two level-headed adults working out an agreement without a judge."

Bronagh sucked in her breath, the tightening of her abdominals revealing a much thinner frame beneath the folds of her bathrobe.

"That's money out of your pocket, isn't it?"

Carlos licked a free paw. The female who'd visited him weeks before in the basement was about the same size, but heavier set. Had he been wrong about Bronagh Caley being one of the hooded freaks? But if so why was she confining him now?

Bobienski laughed. "It is, if you decide to pursue this route. But I would encourage careful and sober thought. You are neighbors."

She reached for a wooden box on the table. Decorated with painted flowers, it appeared to hold food, but when she clamped its contents between her lips and set it alight with a barbecue wand, he knew he was wrong. After a fulsome inhale, she coughed out clouds of cat piss and skunk.

"Mrs. Caley?"

The noise coming out of the other end of the speaker increased markedly, such that she winced.

"Where did you say you were?"

"The Polish Sailor's Ball. It's an annual event."

She coughed again. "Sounds like a hoot."

Lech Bobienski laughed for the second time. "Admission is contingent on a lot of vodka shots dispensed from tall silver samovars. It takes a lot of practice, but if you're willing—" He paused. "I beg your pardon, we're off topic here."

Carlos didn't know a thing about Polish sailors, what they looked like, or how many shots were enough shots to make them acceptable in collegial company, but he knew a crossroads when he saw one.

Bronagh Caley took a huge hit off her spliff, then paused like a statue in a frieze. Bobienski, waiting silently against a backdrop of violin music and horns, was as powerless as the cat. Something outside the window had captured the woman's attention, and her feline prisoner, looking for clues, followed her sightline. A light next door in Poonam Khanzada Rajput's kitchen went on, just as the doorbell rang to announce the first Trick or Treater.

"Mrs. Caley?"

"Get lost you little bastards. I don't got any candy."

"I'm sorry?"

"Kids at the door," she recovered. "Hallowe'en." She choked back her vices, butting out the heater with tremendous force. "I have to think about this, Mr. Bobienski. Please enjoy your vodka." She disengaged the line.

Poonam's kitchen light went off; in its place, a flicker of fire from a candle to dress the shadows of two figures locked in embrace. Leaving the ottoman and the cell phone she had been sitting on, she moved closer to the window to get a better look.

Carlos, understanding at once, mewed his mea culpa, communicating his lack of knowledge behind the events taking place in front of them. But she did not hear. The cell phone on the ottoman sounded again, and again she ignored it. The buzzing persisted. J-A-C-K would not be ignored.

"What the hell do you want?" she snapped into the device.

J-A-C-K, louder than Bobienski, thundered expletives punctuated with raspy throat clears and what sounded like some very determined spits. This went on for several minutes.

Bronagh slid to the floor. Hurting the cat to get back at Poonam for banging Bill was a mental move, not just because she had snuck around with Sikander in happier days—and that made them even steven's—but because it would go against everything Sikander had loved about *her*. Her flawed skin, hair and attitudes never bothered him, never warranted a mention. It was her heart that turned him on. In her stark imperfection, she was more human, more real, than any thought, word, or idea communicated by sage, pundit or wonk. And if she had any doubt about her lover's gratitude, the little blue passbook bearing a six-figure balance swept all of that away.

The next morning, Bronagh Caley dialed up Animal Control. "You still looking for that mangy cat? I know where you can find him."

Carlos, sheltered in her arms, gave her face an appreciative lick. She smiled. "You're not out of the woods yet, m'darlin'."

The animal control officer on the other end of the cell phone, misinterpreting her whispers, asked for clarification.

"In a minute," she replied.

*"For you,"* Sikander whispered across the divide. *"For us."*

She buried her face in the cat's back. What had she been thinking—putting a portion of their money into this stupid house—as if taking Sikander out of the equation fixed everything wrong with her and Bill?

Woman and cat, now at the front door, exchanged a final nuzzle. She flipped the lock and the door, now opened, let in a freshening gust along with the day's newspapers, their headlines screaming election results at her feet. "These" she muttered, "can wait."

She put the cat down.

"Go."

## Chapter Thirty-Nine
## Baiting the Trap

*Two days later…*

At home, in her bed, Sils Banks prepared to receive visitors. Buried somewhere between election news and sports, her story was gaining currency.

"Are you sure you want to talk to these assholes?" her friend, the political operative with the dirty mouth, asked.

"I do," she said, adjusting her posture against the bank of fluffy pillows arranged to dwarf her. "Be sure to hide the gun before they get here."

Her friend had recovered the hockey bag from the trunk of her car after a ton of requests that even Banks felt bordered on harassment.

"I will, I will," came the reply. Her pretty blonde friend, infatuated with her X-Calibur $CO_2$-Powered Cervid Dart Gun, struggled against putting the thing down.

Banks chuckled. "I can only guess at what you'd do with the loop."

"I have a few ideas," her friend winked, replacing the gun in its snappy carrying case. "Are you gonna tell me what you're gonna do with the harpoon?"

"It's a portable delivery system, sweetie, designed to drop critters."

"So, you're going hunting?"

"I am…after I plant an idea or two." She sipped on her bottle of sparkling water.

"I hear cars," her friend said, making a great show of dashing over to the window. "I'll go let them in."

When the coterie of concerned citizens entered the bedroom, they found Sils Banks pale with her head thrown back, eyes closed, and mouth agape.

"She looks terrible."

"Is she awake?"

Banks fluttered her lids in response.

"Are you there, my dear?" The voice, velvety and otherworldly, was all-too familiar.

"Mistress?" Banks mouthed, barely making a sound.

"What's she saying?"

"What she call you?"

The little group drew closer, ringing her bed like figures out of a 17<sup>th</sup> century Flemish painting.

Goddess Moonbow took her hand.

"It's Goddess Moonbow from *The Downsview*. Your representative texted me."

Banks opened her eyes. Even in daylight, free of technical arts, Goddess was beautiful.

Her friend stepped forward with great authority. "That is correct. With so much misinformation flying around, and all the chatter coming off the election, we felt it important that Sils' story be told accurately, if that's even possible."

Goddess nodded, her concern for Sils' well-being self-evident in the way she squeezed down on her hand. Banks flinched in an effort to add some drama.

"Ms. Banks has no real recollection of what happened to her the night she was taken, but there is one thing we are certain about: Taken, she was."

The hack from city hall gasped.

"Yes!" her friend said, elevating her pitch. "There is something wrong in Pictontown on the Downs, and it mustn't be reduced to an inch and a half of print."

"I agree," Goddess said. "An inch and a half is an essay if we're talking digital. What we need here is a book."

Banks turned her head toward a large woman with a tablet. "Who are you?"

"I'm sorry," Goddess jumped in. "Let me introduce everyone. From Community Development and Recreation, Arch Blomfield—"

"Hello."

"From Community Watch, Northern District, Isabelle Vötter—"

"How are you feeling now?"

"From City Hall, Community Outreach, Ilmur Sigurðsson—

"Halló."

"And, finally, special assistant to Pilsen Güdderammerüng, Hinrika Þorsteinn Filippusdóttir."

"That's a mouthful," Banks said, pulling herself up to a sitting position.

The large woman with the tablet— Þorsteinn Filippusdóttir—snapped her head forward and back, acknowledging the obvious.

"We're here," Goddess said, taking the only chair in the little bedroom for herself, "to hear your story, damp down hysteria, and maybe even find the person, or persons, who did this to you."

"It is to motive that we are most interested," Þorsteinn Filippusdóttir interjected.

Goddess raised a delicate hand for silence. "In time, Hinrika. In time."

Banks cleared her throat before unloading a pile of bullshit that focused exclusively on her lunch with Bull Dave.

"He has been questioned and released," Blomfield offered.

"Yes," Goddess said, glaring at the man from Develop 'n' Rec to be silent as well. "I was there when he was brought in."

Banks dabbed her eyes with a tissue. Goddess, understanding, shared with the group, Bull Dave's concern for his good friend from Animal Control, whom he held in "the highest regard" and looked forward to visiting "as soon as practicable."

"I appreciate that," Banks said, blowing her nose. "He's a good guy. Anyway, somehow, some way, I was drugged, and when I woke up, I was in the crate."

The man from city hall gasped a second time.

"I knew it quite well—" she continued. "—the crate. Same kind we use at Animal Control for large dogs."

"Leading us to suspect," her friend jumped in on cue, "that the person, or persons, who took her had a beef with her job."

"Yes," Banks nodded. "Someone with access to our equipment, or at least, the same equipment city staff have, possibly through the same distributor." She looked at Moonbow meaningfully.

Goddess, raising her eyebrows, made no effort to take notes. "That would be quite a story: City employee taken by city staff or people who knew city staff."

"It is to motive that we are most interested," Þorsteinn Filippusdóttir repeated.

Goddess shifted in her seat. "Is there anything else you can add?"

"Tell them about the hypnotherapy," her friend said, again on cue.

"You were hypnotized?" Goddess asked, leaning forward.

"I was."

"And you won't believe what she said."

Her friend, muscling in with eyes wide, served it up beautifully.

"Some really crazy shit, if you'll pardon my French."

***

Animal Control Officer Sils Banks had, indeed, been hypnotized at the attending psychiatrist's insistence. Emotional trauma, it seemed, was a tough sell in enlightened Pictontown, and so in keeping with all the other strange things going on, she had no problem surrendering to the professionals. Whatever she said, she decided, would do the trick.

After the required police swabs and a clean bill of health was issued by Dr. Fingle, she was turned over to a man named Jaan, who applied a soft cast to her left hand, which she had injured after her 'first' escape. Good looking and chatty, the hairnet-wearing Jaan was more than willing to share his theories about what might have happened to her.

"You can't be too careful around here."

"You can't be too careful anywhere," she agreed.

"No. I mean you can't be too careful *here*." He squeezed her hand through the semi-hard fiberglass cast. "If you get it wet, you'll come straight back to me, and you don't want that!"

"No, I don't," she shivered. His familiarity was unnerving.

"Do you know who did this to you?"

"You know my story?"

"Everyone does. It's all over the halls."

What the fuck ever happened to confidentiality, she fumed. "I have recollections. Strange ones."

Jaan was all ears.

"It involved furry mascots and groups of happy drinking people doing stuff under a disco ball. I don't know if it was real or not. A lot of it seemed to come from a movie."

Maybe it was in his eyes—that undefinable thing that poets always ramble on about—that made her 'trust' him. Or did she see Moonbow all over him and sense an opportunity to draw her attention?

Two days after disclosing to Jaan the Plasterman her strange, manic visions, the animal control officer would find herself at the center of a media feeding frenzy that almost capsized her plan for revenge. Goddess Moonbow, taking the bait, not only made a feminist hero out of the hapless civil servant, but she also "mistakenly" hinted at Banks' home address, for which she immediately apologized on-line, expressing not once, but twice, her deep regret for any unwanted attention her error might have caused. That wasn't all. Moonbow, continuing her journey of deep regret, expressed her disappointment at the public's failure to elect the Beautiful Boy Politician.

"First you cry, then you get mad" she opined on All Soul's Day. Was the silver-haired beauty issuing a call to arms, or was she merely being sour grapes?

Sils Banks didn't have time to root out all the hidden meanings. If Moonbow was gunning for her, she would have to get to her first. She loaded a syringe into her X-Calibur $CO_2$ unit, taking careful aim from the privacy of her service vehicle. Her friends at Fret Party H.Q. would provide the alibi. All she had to do now was hit her target.

# Chapter Forty
## A Meeting of Melted Minds

*In an old warehouse backing on to the wharf lands, a group of men and women gather. Well dressed and influential, they wait for a central figure to decide their fate. Shrouded, their leader is well-known to them; the elegant cover up, mere artifice.*

*To Persian cat watching them from above, the central figure is the one and only YoYo Man, the same evil creature that contrived to consign him and his compatriots to a life of a loofa. To the people gathered, She is their savior.*

*"The permits are stalled pending the recounts, but we, ultimately, will decide. What it was all about at the end of the day, was getting the financing to get the city hall built. The rest was icing on the cake."*

*"Are we disbanding?" one of the suited men asks, the treble in his voice betraying a dependency best treated in a nice place with prescription meds and many trees.*

*"We are, Arch. We're much too old for this shit."*

*Arch Blomfield looks like he is going to cry.*

*Mayor Lagerqvist, adjusting the sleeve on her short arm, eyes her colleague. "We'll rise again."*

# Chapter Forty-One
## Putting it Right

Days later, after the ballot boxes were counted, and then counted again, Bronagh Caley had a surreal discussion with Campaign Bob, The Corduroy Man.

"How did this happen?"

Bob, fighting consciousness on a banquette inside The Skinny Pic, concealed dark circles under heavy makeup.

"I thought the Hair Cut had it."

"We did too," Bob said, switching his attention to an extra-large cup of Rolling Gold, a conflict-free super fuel offered for free to distressed electors. "He was supposed to win. The Controller said so."

Bronagh didn't buy it. "The Controller isn't real."

"Oh, *she* is," Bob winked, "You just didn't know her when you saw her."

Bronagh spat into a tissue. She was getting a cold, thanks to all the little bastards that rang her doorbell, and then bitched about the quality of her Hallowe'en goodies. Neither safe nor nut free, they had threatened to report her after she slammed the door in their little faces.

Bob picked up a thumbed copy of *The Downsview*, his eyes now open enough to take in an article that had the shop buzzing:

### SHUT UP AND CARE
### By Goddess Moonbow

*It appears that voters are having a hard time coming to grips with the result and who wouldn't? For who are we to refuse the gift of a private life when it is offered? And yet, we have.*

*Hacks and stalwarts assure us that we are headed for the edge, and maybe we are. But maybe there's a parachute in there somewhere too.*

*The beautiful boy with the fantastic hair and shimmery suits has been pummelled into the ground by the old guard in what many see as a gigantic 'fuck you' to anything resembling change, and they are right. Change needs a mighty 'fuck you' every now and then to determine if it's 'good' or mere 'twaddle.'*

"What in the hell is she doing?" Bronagh coughed, amazed.

"She's talking about the twats at City Hall, I think," a nice, artfully kept young man with flip flops seated behind them chimed in.

The shop keeper turned up the flat screen T.V.:

*"I think it is this obsession with keeping everything the same,"* a woman identified as Bhagyashree Raghuwanshi, offered under questioning, live and on-the-street, at the local Take It And Go convenience store.

Bronagh recognized Poonam Rajput's mother immediately.

*"It is why I voted for Mayor Lagerqvist last year. It's people like her that keep the next great idea far away from us."*

Bob kept on reading Moonbow, aloud:

*Many agree that change has come too quickly to our quiet burg, often, at the expense of our neighbors, the case of the captured public servant, an obvious proof.*

"She's mixing her metaphors, I think," flip flop said.

"Shut up."

*Clearly, a message has been sent, and we, the people of Pictontown on the Downs, read it loud and clear. We have a duty to care as quietly as possible.*

As much as Bronagh had liked the kid with the fantastic hair, there was no way in hell she would ever vote for him, even if she had flirted with the idea of it, and then, only briefly. For accountability, she learned a long time ago, was the shits in the seat of power. From her place in the deep, dark, shadows, she—and so many others like her—had got a hell of a lot farther undermining the schmucks who'd walked in the light.

"We're so fucked," Bob fumed, throwing down the paper. "We're gonna have to run this mess."

"Yes, we are," she grinned.

Her idiot companion continued to babble, but Bronagh had stopped listening. She thought of Bill and Poonam getting it on in Sikander's house instead.

"So that's why she's doing this, mixed metaphors and all?"

Bronagh looked at Bob with her best stink eye. "Goddess is courting damage control, obviously. I don't really give a shit anymore."

Bob hung his head. "I could O.D. on edibles, but I guess the dispensaries are gonna close too."

"That and more," she nodded.

Since the election results were announced, a maelstrom of press releases out of the office of the Fret leader made good on the promise to 'slay the windmills,' 'stay shoddy construction,' and recycle 'every glass bong that ever passed for recreation.'

Bob reached for one of her antacids. "We're going backwards."

"Can't go there."

"But we are."

He fidgeted with the child-proof cap, before passing it to Bronagh to open for him.

Goddess Moonbow's op-ed called for cooler heads in the face of progress' death.

"No good idea ever goes unpunished, as the saying goes."

Bronagh thumbed her pretty kitty fob. "She doesn't know what side she's on anymore."

Bob, eyeing her trinket, agreed. "But if anyone can land on all fours, it's her."

\*\*\*

Goddess Moonbow, pulling her tresses into a multi-colored scrunchie, made a face outside her snappy Range Rover. Anyone familiar with entitled persons would know that she expected her driver in the driver's seat with the plush wagon idling gently in the frosty November air.

The driver was nowhere in sight. He was in the back of Sils Banks' van.

"You got the loop?" she asked.

From behind her, Zoltan nodded silently. He didn't have much to say. Didn't have anything to say, really. And that suited her fine. His purpose today was to load the dreaded cargo into size-appropriate accommodations.

She wiggled the fingers of her broken left hand, hoping that, in the moment, it would not let her down. Zoltan had offered to fire the weapon for her, but she declined, seeing his offer as a lame-assed attempt at salvation.

Salvation had nothing to do with this. Taking back what belonged to her—to everyone—was the thing. "Come on, dummy," she muttered. "Look this way."

A frigid drizzle, fresh out of nowhere, caught Moonbow's attention.

"Not a sound," Sils ordered to her captive and her accomplice, Zoltan Kárpáty. "She's headed this way—"

"Mistress!"

The smallish figure, less ethereal in her scrunchie, dark roots, and name brand sweats, responded with a wolfish smile that belied her size.

Banks hit the button on her driver side door, rolling the window down with a cyborg whir. "Are you locked out?"

The Goddess, in the middle of the street, advanced, unaware that the lady with the broken wing didn't give a shit about her.

"Yeah! I'm locked out of the goddamned building too."

The animal control officer beamed. Pretensions fizzle under a few drops of water. With no one else around, it was as easy to mobilize Pictontown's muse and social mover, as it had been a hapless civil servant at a booze-fuelled sex party.

# Chapter Forty-Two
## Intemperate Congress


Revenge is a funny thing: It almost always backfires. Rudolf Fischer, going through the morning papers, marveled at the commotion over a local scribe's disappearance, as if Goddess Moonbow's exit from local culture marked the beginning of the apocalypse.

No such luck. In addition to several biographical footnotes celebrating the woman's contribution to the community, there were others drumming a very different beat, calling for calm in the face of alleged voter fraud, gerrymandering and extortion that all tied back to "ill-considered sexual congress."

The old man sniffed. He liked sex as much as anyone else, but like so many, had become a mere spectator. Nothing was lost on him—not the parties, not the partner swapping, not the costume-wearing—all of it happening six doors away, and, now, beyond. Never bothered him, never interested him. But his wife was gone, and this gave him a new focus.

He stroked the pretty Siamese, now busy kneading the morning headlines papering the tops of his wrinkly knees. He chuckled. His lawyer had called earlier to tell him that the Caley woman was not backing off, her clubbed foot clearly representing something larger than what it was.

"She has an axe to grind," his lawyer explained. "Not unusual in cases like this."

Another knobby old bitch looking to get a pound because she hadn't lost a thing in her life.

"Look at us," Rudolf whispered to the pretty kitty, which now accepted from him, regular morsels of the fine bratwurst sausage fabricated with his own two hands. "No one would believe that I could love something like you, and, yet, here we are."

He glanced again, this time at a new headline smudging under the butt end of the cat.

## TWO MORE MISSING

Not all sausage-makers were serial killers, as his neighbor liked to think. Then, too, no one could really be sure about their neighbors.

Rudolf Fischer smiled.

*** 

Jack Frewer wasn't fucking around when he put the screws to Bronagh Caley over the cell phone. Ever volatile since the constructive dismissal that cut off his access to lucrative street-ready animal tranquilizer, he was feeling the effects of his dependency in abundance.

"Where is she?" he demanded, as if Bronagh would know about Goddess Moonbow.

"I don't know, Jack, and I don't care." She had seen the headlines, too, and cringed with every turd that hit the bowl:

## BELOVED CULTURAL ICON MISSING

## FOREIGN FILMMAKER ON LAM

## 90,000 HOUSING UNITS CANNED

Neither political party, it seemed, had a lot to say when asked about the abuse of trust, mishandling of funds, tax fraud, and exercise of really poor taste. They were too busy challenging each other in court.

## GODDESS CULT UNCOVERED

## AUTEUR HELD AGAINST WILL

## THREE MORE MISSING

And then, the bon mot:

## ANIMAL ABUSE RAMPANT, CHARGES PENDING

Mayor Lagerqvist weighed in:

### "WE LET THIS HAPPEN"

"You're getting cold feet," Jack accused.

She knew what the smell in the Fischer house was, and after turning it over in her head a million and one times, she had made the mistake of sharing her suspicions with the one person she didn't trust.

"I know what I saw," she began, a smile building under the bile in her gall bladder.

"You mean you think you know."

"You can't be sure unless you see for yourself."

Jack Frewer paused long enough to turn her inside out. "I can't do that."

She gripped the cell phone claw-like: Jack, clearly, had to go. "You only think you can't. I think *you're* getting cold feet."

Jack's voice, reeking of the buff stink of withdrawal, reminded her that weakness was a friend to hold on to. "Four people have disappeared, or do I have to remind you of that?"

She thought of Fischer and his saws. No, she didn't need reminding: "So, you believe me then? About the old man?"

Jack Frewer sneezed into the phone. "I believe you'd rather blackmail a serial killer than open your wallet."

She thought of Sikander, the money he had gifted her, and of how Jack put her 'inheritance' together, when her lover's deposit failed to show up in Moonbow's condo development account. How it was that he felt entitled to a piece of it spoke more to his shallow delusions than her fear of exposure. Still, she was reluctant to give up the truth about her clandestine relationship, especially when Bill was so happy. She owed him that, even if she was going to pick his pocket in the divorce.

"You have no trouble extorting funds from me."

Frewer laughed the kind of laugh that always made her melt. She hated that about herself—liking things that turned her life to shit.

"Of course. I know you. I've known you forever."

Again, she thought of Fischer and his saws. In a few short weeks, she had learned more about her neighbors than ever before, and she owed that to the Fischer cat. She didn't want to upset the balance, particularly when she had all the money she would ever need and was now deliciously close to being free of all encumbrances. If everything went according to Hoyle with Poonam and her Bill, the divorce could net a super lump sum from his pension, so much so, that if it was really super, she'd happily give him away at the next wedding.

"I don't really care where you get my money from, Bronie dear, s'long as I get enough to blow this shit show."

"I'll need time," she lied.

"You need to stop covering up for a wife murderer."

Bronagh grinned. She'd dug herself a deep hole, but still had the wherewithal to get out of it, and rid herself of a couple of pests too.

***

It didn't take a lesson in civics to know that something was going wrong at the top. Shortly after her disappearance, Goddess Moonbow was joined by Arch Blomfield, Ilmur Sigurðsson, and, in the absence of Pilsen Güdderammerüng—who'd gone on the lam—his assistant, Hinrika Þorsteinn Filippusdóttir.

"I can't believe Pils abandoned me," the Goddess intoned through viscous nasal discharge signifying regret. Many times, she apologized; many times, she was ignored. Vanity and crassness had overtaken her, she explained, along with the alpha female's drive to eliminate rivals. "That's why I had you caged. That's why I sent you to the basement."

Sils Banks, unmoved, tossed her a bagel. "And all along I thought it was because I was with Animal Control."

"I don't give a shit about Animal Control," Goddess insisted, stuffing half the bagel into her mouth. "You got a job to do and so do I." She paused to chew some more, "So *did* I, once upon a time."

"You did make a folk hero out of me," Banks conceded. "I can thank you for that."

Banks had never been perceived as a strong person, yet Moonbow had done a bang-up job of painting her heroic escape from captivity in both *The Downsview* and *The Pic* with incredible verve. "I knocked the Hair Cut off the front page."

"We had great hopes for him. He was all for growing the community, nay, the nation. And Lagerqvist had him in her back pocket."

Banks sighed. "I knew he was too good to be true."

"Don't bullshit a bullshitter. You're a Fret. I saw you skulking around with the wedge."

Banks shrugged. "And Bull Dave? How did he fit in?"

"A good friend. He told me how committed you were to your cause. I admire that. I really do. I wanted to see how committed you were in a cage."

"Really?"

"No. I just didn't like you. You didn't fit with our vision."

"All things are equal. That's *your* vision."

Moonbow shook her tatty locks. "No. We're animals now. *That's* what it's about."

"You're insane."

The goddess nodded. "Probably. One thing I know for sure—you're no killer. Neither am I."

That was true, and Banks had no problem confirming the Goddess' assessment.

"So, what are you going to do with all of us?"

Banks had been pretty clear about it in her mind from day one.

"I'm gonna dump you lot on the front lawn of City Hall."

"Really?"

"Yup. I figure you can parlay the adventure into something really good."

"I have a talent for that."

"That's what I thought."

"And Zoltan? You seem pretty close."

Banks had to think about that—again. She'd been mulling it since the project began. Did she really want to live in a caravan with a bunch of refusniks?

She held her hands up in response.

"I could style the whole cage thing around you," the Goddess said. "Maybe tie it back to a stunt to raise awareness."

"Why would you do that?"

"Because I admire you—now. And because I'll need a folk hero in my corner when the shit hits the fan."

"Plausible deniability?"

"Oh, yeah, sister. There are no minors involved. The sex 'n' cats thing was a gag to draw in investors. Pilsen locked the funds with his reputation and all."

"And now he's gone."

"Yeah. But he's demented. I doubt he'll miss a few million or two or ten."

They chuckled.

Arch Blomfield, hiccupping from somewhere down below, reminded them that not everyone was privy to their new plan.

"You gotta lot of nerve bringing us here. It's still a crime scene, isn't it?" Moonbow said.

Gus the Pilot had expressed deep concern over the going's on in his home when contacted by Homeland Security mid-way on a red-eye.

Banks smiled. "What crime? It's all a joke, remember?"

"And Zoltan?"

Banks shrugged, thinking about her new deal with her new devil.

"He loves to suffer. Let's leave him to it."

# Chapter Forty-Three
## Consequences

Bronagh Caley counted down the minutes that became hours while she waited for Jack Frewer. In the interim, there was a telephone, and when it rang, her daughter—the smart one—chimed back at her with a smarmy assertion that she had voted Free Range.

"That's nice, dear."

"Nice? Are you all right?"

"Of course, dear. Everything is going to be fine."

"Where's dad?"

"At the mine. I told you that."

"Um, yeah. But the mine's been closed, like, for days."

"Oh, yes. The work stoppage. I forgot about that."

"So, he did come home—right?"

She thought of Poonam and Bill, canoodling in that ridiculous trailer in the woods. "Yes—sort of. I'm very glad you voted for the Free Range, honey. It's every child's duty to rebel. Shows spine."

"Mom?"

She didn't answer. Rudolf Fischer was spooking around outside her window.

\*\*\*

Broke, unemployed and bitter, Jack Frewer drove to his destiny in a beat up vintage Datsun. For the paltry sum of $10,000, he could begin life anew in a rented side split in Yarker. All he had to do was ring the dough out of the old bitch before she grew a pair and realized that no one cared about who she screwed now, then or later.

\*\*\*

Bronagh Caley, glued to her window, eye-balled Rudolf Fischer like a demented chicken. What was that old bastard up to now? Trussed up in blood-spattered overalls, he rooted around the yew hedge looking for something lost.

\*\*\*

Carlos the Wonder Cat took it in with interest.

*I think their story is ending,* Persian offered, his paws, folded neatly beneath his girth to form a perfect loaf.

*That and some.*

*The woman misses her man.*

*Yes, but which one?*

\*\*\*

Bronagh Caley opened her window and shouted at Rudolf Fischer. He was trespassing. He was freaking her out. If he ever wanted to settle, he would have to do the decent thing and apologize.

\*\*\*

Rudolf Fischer, spying his missing kitty, beamed, just as Animal Control Officer Wompat's white utility vehicle rounded the corner on to Saffron Drive.

*I believe the old man is calling for you,* Persian chirped.

But Carlos was already on his way.

"That moron from Animal Control is back," Rudolf said to Bronagh Caley, "and I suspect it has everything to do with you." He clapped his hands together.

Bronagh, now on her front stoop, looked past her nemesis with horrified eyes. Beyond the hedgerow on the west side of Zoltan's property, three figures huddled like lovers. "Sikander," she whispered. "Sikander."

Rudolf Fischer grinned, knowing what she knew and more. He scooped the cat into his arms and after the briefest of nuzzles, released him with a gentle "go."

Carlos obliged, picking up speed as he ran into the path of the on-coming Datsun.

# Chapter Forty-Four
## Opinion

Local media were chock full of stories. Never in the history of Pictontown had there been so much bloody business to report:

### WOMAN DIES SAVING CAT

*A woman, known to side with the city's oft criticized animal control policy, was killed when an early model compact slammed into her on Saffron Drive. The woman, who could not be identified pending notification of next of kin, was killed instantly when the vehicle, driven by a former city employee, who also cannot be identified, collided with her after swerving to avoid a stray cat. The cat, believed to be unharmed, has not been seen since.*

*The driver of the vehicle, in critical condition, was thrown several feet after colliding a second time with an Animal Control utility van and a spruce tree.*

*The driver of the second vehicle was not hurt.*

*"A terrible thing to see," local resident Bhagyashree Raghuwanshi said. "Very tragic. Another case of people being where they ought not be and Fate catching them out."*

*An enthusiastic animal lover, Mrs. Raghuwanshi indicated that the tragedy happened because of a colossal misunderstanding. "They minded their own business in all the wrong places. They had a duty to care, just not so much."*

## CAGED PUBLIC SERVANTS CALL A HALT

*In a startling move, city officials took to cages on the front lawn of City Hall as part of a consciousness-raising exercise to shine a light on community misgivings linked to too-rapid, and very shoddy building plans for our new city.*

*"I agree it's unorthodox," Community Development and Recreation Board Chair Arch Blomfield relayed, emerging from his cage somewhat dirty and 'a little hungry,' "but we had an election to compete with, and a relative few who gave a damn about zoning."*

*Not surprisingly, this paper's own special correspondent Goddess Moonbow was in on it. "We box ourselves in from time-to-time," she said, without irony. "Many of us here wanted to grow the community. We just tried to grow it too fast."*

*The group, found early yesterday locked in large crates normally used for canines, had nothing but praise for Pictontown's own Sils Banks, whose recent turn in a cage bordered on the extreme. "I'd like to think that I was a part of this from the beginning," the self-effacing Banks explained. "But the truth is, I wasn't. Goddess stepped in when I had too much to drink. We were almost too late."*

*The discovery that international film auteur Pilsen Güdderammerüng's interest in our burgeoning community stalled at the prurient cannot be excused, even on an artistic level.*

*"No matter how many times we looked at it, he was building cardboard houses that were way too big. We needed to go smaller. We needed to go back to bricks and mortar," Moonbow said.*

*Güdderammerüng, pictured above with Pic resident Louise du Pommier, did not reply to our requests for comment, nor did his government in Sweden, when asked about the whereabouts of investments intended for 90,000 residential units. Born in Norway, Güdderammerüng divides his time between Sweden and Panama.*

## MAYOR SAYS "NO MORE YOYO'ING"

*Mayor Lagerqvist, after consultation with the ombudsman, police, and a closed session of city council, revealed that charges will not be laid in the fake disappearance of local celebrities.*

*"While the resources expended in police and amber alerts cannot be recouped, the money saved by exposing hustlers, malcontents and nincompoops cannot be counted."*

*The Mayor, seen for the first time in public with what will likely become her signature blue YoYo, promised greater transparency in future.*

\*\*\*

In front of the murtis, Poonam Khanzada Rajput clasped her hands.

"I hope you aren't praying to Shiva," Mummy Ji interjected, intruding on her solace in her usual timely fashion.

"No Mummy, I'm praying to Vishnu."

The old lady frowned. "And why would you do that? Do you have a guilty conscience?"

"I was thinking about Sikander."

"Oh."

Poonam, gathering a mohair shrug around air-chilled shoulders, stopped what she was doing to glare at her mother. "Oh?"

Mummy Ji smiled. "You are a daughter reacting to perceived judgments, real and imagined. I haven't said a word above 'oh,' and you find in it something sinister."

"I am feeling guilty."

"About what?"

"Many things. Sikander. That woman—" She faltered. "My cat."

"Ah. That part is unfortunate. I did not foresee a despicable death under the wheels of a car. Can I make you some chai?"

Poonam made a conscious effort to crease her features. "Mummy. A person is dead and another may follow."

"Yes. And two people are living."

"Bill Caley."

"And you. Don't forget about *you*, daughter."

She hadn't, though she couldn't rationalize Bronagh's death as tidily as her mother could, and she said so.

"It's easy," Mummy said, over her favorite pan and the hot milk and fennel she was cooking in it. "You say you are guilty and that is silly. What have you really done? A woman you don't like runs into the street to save Shashthi's vahana and splatters all over the sidewalk. She did a good thing, and God will take note."

Poonam fingered the kitty fob, the same one taken from her late husband's bedside table. "I took something that didn't belong to me, and now I will pay for it. God will see to that too."

"You mean the beard?"

"He has a name."

"I know," the old lady said. "I even used it before you got mixed up with him."

Being with Bill had been her choice. But in light of recent events, Poonam could not be sure if it was love that guided her, or revenge, pure and simple.

# Chapter Forty-Five
## Aftermath

Bronagh's funeral, beautiful to watch, grew in poignancy with the tremendous outpouring of love and support from every quarter. Even the hooded ones were represented. Bob, the bitchy campaign coordinator from Deutscher headquarters, got up to say a few words:

"To say that Bronagh was a handful is to not do her justice. She had principles, and she stuck to them, even when she bent them…"

Chuckles.

"It was difficult for her, at first, to cross the lines and join the Deutscher campaign. She did this clandestinely, not out of shame, but out of respect for the people and party she had dedicated most of her adult life to.

"I first met Bronagh campaigning with the leader. Like every person who answers a door he knocks on, she was blown away by his message…

"All things are equal now.

"I don't know if Bronagh can hear me—politicians stay away from religion…"

Chuckles.

"But I know she knows her death was not in vain, for she died in the service of helping another…"

Bob gestured to the closed casket behind him.

"For Bronagh Caley, that was the only way to go."

"She was one of them, you know" Sils Banks, seated in a back pew, muttered to Wompat, whose chronic eye dabbing clearly indicated a soft heart under his enforcer exterior. The black cat, in his sights—as all wandering creatures were—had eluded his grasp. This touched him deeply as did the spectacular florals he hoped to recycle after the service.

"Frewer still won't say why he was cruising that neighborhood, but if he thinks his behavior is beyond scrutiny because of his injuries, he's got another thing coming."

Banks nodded dumbly. Jack would be in a body cast for months. After that, with his feline raison d'être removed from the equation, his next steps were anyone's guess.

"They say," Banks whispered under the next speaker—a Fret who'd worked with Bronagh at the Legislature— "that ol' Jack got himself mixed up in some spurious stuff and that even more higher ups will be implicated."

"I heard that too," Wompat said, looking into her eyes. "And if you stay close—I mean, really look for it—you'll find that everyone has a part to play."

Sils Banks was not surprised when he offered her his hand, and then pressed into hers, a very pretty pendant similar to the one she'd received from Bull Dave.

She shrugged. At the end of the day, they were all beasts, burdened under the weight of their own illusions.

* * *

In the front pew, Poonam Rajput took Bill Caley's hand. Surrounded by his family, she found her task incredibly awkward. There was something very important that she had to say to him, something that couldn't wait until the reception.

"Bill—"

He looked down at the scuffed chapel floor. It needed refinishing. "It was kind of Rudolf to offer up the sausage for the reception. Don't you think?"

Poonam nodded, agreeing that the old man's recipe went beyond anything the commercial manufacturers could offer. "It was. You know he intended it for Irme's memorial."

"I should thank him."

She spun the gold wedding band on his hand between her thumb and forefinger, not knowing how much her new lover knew about his late wife and her Sikander.

"Bill—"

He withdrew his hand, pulling off the band and placing it in his breast pocket. "Don't. I know."

"I couldn't be sure, but it had to be said—out loud—to make it real."

She fought a near-overpowering desire to kiss his hand.

Bill sighed. "I didn't want it to turn out this way. I didn't want Bronagh to get hurt."

She understood. She knew where his mind was. She also knew where her husband's money had got to. But her care and concern for the man sitting next to her had grown exponentially with the secrets they kept. Now, thanks to beautiful death, the heart's secrets would stay with the hearts that held them.

Bill Caley kissed Poonam Rajput's hand.

"Bronagh and Sikander will be together, as shall we."

Was it love, or something else?

She would have to find out on her own.

There was no vahana left to take her there.

THE END

# Epilogue

The cat's passing was mourned deeply by those lucky enough to have known him. In time, the salacious gossip focusing on Lou and her new life in Oslo faded, along with speculation about Rudolf Fischer's other-worldly deli-quality craft meats. Government's would come and go along with the next big idea. So, too, would the ambitious plans of men and women who sought to build up in their own lifetimes, legacies better left to gods and time.

Those who contend that free range beings get what they deserve can write their rules in memos on fine parchment paper. Others, like Zoey Fischer, will tell you that the spirit and the intent behind a rebel always wins.

Somewhere, on a quiet road, the black cat walks home to Cavan.

*A. B. Funkhauser's next novel,*
*THE HEUER EFFECT,*
*Releases Fall 2018*

# *Coming 2018*

## The Heuer Effect

*The year 1979*

Mike Engler looked down at his vomit-soaked feet wondering if he should call for help. His socks and running shoes had been missing for several hours, along with his car keys and watch, and this gave him pause to wonder if he'd been robbed after all.

Heuer—pale and unresponsive—lay face down on the rug. He had been drinking for several days. Cal Homewood, their host and sponsor, stood poised in the galley kitchen cooking up something questionable.

"How did we get here?" Engler yelled, lighting up an old roach from the night before. Homewood, carrying a tray of grey-coated saltines, emerged spectre-like from his kitchen cave. Tall, Casper-skinned and ginger-topped, he floated surreally across the shag rug on a crest of cannabis and Valium.

"Got kicked out of the Brunswick House. He went head first."

Heuer, silent and glassy-eyed behind half closed lids, was nonplussed. Making speeches well into the night about struggle and disappointment and the mind-numbing monotony of not knowing what was coming next, had sucked the life force out of him. Clearly, he had a burr up his ass, but in the diatribe, lacked the decency to say what it actually was. Then he groped the big-assed waitress with the gargantuan-sized knockers and all hell broke loose.

Engler wiggled his toes, which had purpled over from lack of circulation. He, too, had consumed copious amounts of alcohol, losing all feeling in his lower extremities, and their failure to respond to any external stimulation caused him tremendous concern. His vascular circulation, like his thoughts, was scattered willy-nilly, like dots on a child's place mat that had yet to be joined by pencil or crayon.

He jabbed his errant digits into Heuer's side, hoping, at least, that either one or the other would revive.

Nothing.

Homewood cracked open his Pez dispenser.

"Valium?"

Engler laughed out a Hail Mary and a Holy Fuck.

"I'll pass. Thanks." He took a deep draw on the old joint, holding in its healing smoke. Homewood's saltine and grey creations, geometrically arranged on what appeared to be a silver tray, looked almost appealing despite the perplexing striations that interfered with the tray's elaborate scroll work. Gifted to Cal on the occasion of his marriage to Katarin, a Russian émigré whom he'd embraced out of sentiment, it was now stained, vericosed by oxidation.

Engler gestured in the direction of the curious crackers. "I'm more than a little intrigued by those things."

"The hors d'œuvres?" Homewood beamed, pleased at the invitation to elaborate. "My own creation. Have one."

Engler shrank back. Stories about Homewood and his penchant for experimentation had been circulating for years. It was said that, in the face of an empty cupboard, he had no compunction about substituting grocer's ingredients with things that—well—didn't come from a grocery store.

"No thanks. I don't eat what I don't know."

Cal insisted. "It's tuna. It's good."

Engler hesitated. He'd never seen tuna like this.

Trying one, he winced. "It tastes like shit."

Heuer stirred, waves of sticky drool confirming vital signs.

"Do you think he's brain damaged?" Cal asked, betraying nothing of what his mind was working at. At thirty-five, he was the oldest of Engler's circle of intimates and, without doubt, the strangest. Thick lenses fixed by austere wire frames damped down pale eyes that saw through everything. That was Homewood's gift, and while it was enviable, it was also intimidating.

"Naw," Engler said, lifting himself up to his full height. "Too many ales." He and Heuer had written their last exam the previous Wednesday and wasted little time in getting as soused as possible. With a new year just weeks away and their entire lives ahead of them, there was a lot of drinking to do.

Heuer stirred a second time. His limbs, stiff with disuse, pinked up sluggishly with the exertion.

"Come on *Arschloch*," Engler said, kicking him in the ribs for the second time. "You're embarrassing yourself."

Homewood, back in his kitchen cavern, took care to rinse out the Puss 'n' Boots tins before dropping them in the waste basket.

"Make sure he has some hors d'œuvres," he said, eyeing the rows of cat food neatly arranged in the kitchen cupboard. "They'll straighten him out."

## About A.B. Funkhauser

Toronto born author A.B. Funkhauser is a funeral director, classic car nut and wildlife enthusiast living in Ontario, Canada. Like most funeral directors, she is governed by a strong sense of altruism fueled by the belief that life chooses us, not we it.

Her debut novel Heuer Lost and Found, released in April 2015, examines the day to day workings of a funeral home and the people who staff it. Winner of the Preditors & Editors Reader's Poll for Best Horror 2015, and the New Apple EBook Award 2016 for Horror, Heuer Lost and Found is the first installment in Funkhauser's Unapologetic Lives series. Her sophomore effort, Scooter Nation, released March 11, 2016 through Solstice Publishing. Winner of the New Apple Ebook Award 2016 for Humor, and Winner Best Humor Summer Indie Book Awards 2016, Scooter picks up where Heuer left off, this time with the lens on the funeral home as it falls into the hands of a woeful sybarite.

A devotee of the gonzo style pioneered by the late Hunter S. Thompson, Funkhauser attempts to shine a light on difficult subjects by aid of humorous storytelling. "In gonzo, characters operate without filters, which means they say and do the kinds of things we cannot in an ordered society. Results are often comic, but, hopefully, instructive."

SHELL GAME, tapped as a psycho-social cat dramedy with death and laughs, is the third book in the series, and takes aim at a pastoral community with a lot to hide. "With so much of the world currently up for debate, I thought it would be useful to question—again—the motives and machinations championed by the morally flexible, and then let the cat decide what it all means."

Funkhauser is working on *The Heuer Effect*, the prequel to *Heuer Lost and Found*.

**Other Solstice Books by A.B. Funkhauser**:

**Heuer Lost and Found**

Unrepentant cooze hound lawyer Jürgen Heuer dies suddenly and unexpectedly in his litter-strewn home. Undiscovered, he rages against God, Nazis, deep fryers and analogous women who disappoint him.

At last found, he is delivered to Weibigand Brothers Funeral Home, a ramshackle establishment peopled with above average eccentrics, including boozy Enid, a former girlfriend with serious denial issues. With her help and the help of a wise-cracking spirit guide, Heuer will try to move on to the next plane. But before he can do this, he must endure an inept embalming, feral whispers, and Enid's flawed recollections of their murky past.

http://myBook.to/heuerlostandfound

## Scooter Nation

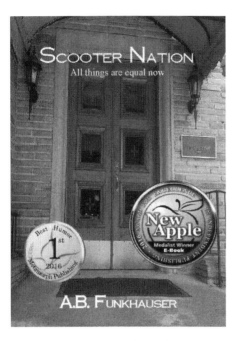

Aging managing director Charlie Forsythe begins his work day with a phone call to Jocasta Binns, the unacknowledged illegitimate daughter of Weibigand Funeral Home founder Karl Heinz Sr. Alma Wurtz, a scooter-bound sextenarian, community activist, and neighborhood pain in the ass is emptying her urine into the flower beds, killing the petunias. Jocasta cuts him off, reminding him that a staff meeting has been called. Charlie, silenced, is taken aback: he has had no prior input into the meeting and that, on its own, makes it sinister.

The second novel in the *Unapologetic Lives* series, *Scooter Nation* takes place two years after *Heuer Lost and Found*. This time, funeral directors Scooter Creighton and Carla Moretto Salinger Blue take center stage as they battle conflicting values, draconian city by-laws, a mendacious neighborhood gang bent on havoc, and a self-absorbed fitness guru whose presence shines an unwanted light on their quiet Michigan neighborhood.

http://myBook.to/ScooterNation

## Praise

"Funny, quirky, and sooooo different."

—Jo Michaels, Jo Michaels Blog

"…writes with a take-no-prisoners style of prose."

—Steve Cronin, American Funeral Director Magazine

"Eccentric and Funny. You have never read anything like this book. It demands respect for the outrageous capacity of its author to describe in detail human behavior around death."

—Charlene Jones, author *The Stain*

"The macabre black comedy Heuer Lost and Found, written by A.B. Funkhauser, is definitely a different sort of book! You will enjoy this book with its mixture of horror and humour."

—Diana Harrison, Author *Always and Forever*

"This beautifully written, quirky, sad, but also often humorous story of Heuer and Enid gives us a glimpse into the fascinating, closed world of the funeral director."

—Yvonne Hess, Charter Member, The Brooklin 7

"The book runs the gamut of emotions. One minute you want to cry for the characters, the next you are uncontrollably laughing out loud, and your husband is looking at you like you lost your mind, at least mine did."
—Teresa Noel, Teresa Noel Blogspot

"The writing style is racy with no words wasted."

—David K. Bryant, Author *Tread Carefully on the Sea*

"For a story centered around death, it is full of life."

—Rocky Rochford, Author *Rise of the Elohim Chronicles*

"Like Breaking Bad's Walter White, Heuer is not a likeable man, but I somehow found myself rooting for him. A strange, complicated character."

—Kasey Balko, Pickering, Ontario

Raw, clever, organic, intriguing and morbid at the same time … breathing life and laughter into a world of death.

—Josie Montano, Author *Veiled Secrets*

**Social Media Links**

Publisher: http://solsticepublishing.com/

Website: www.abfunkhauser.com

Email: a.b.funkhauser@rogers.com

Amazon Author Page:

https://www.amazon.com/A.B.-Funkhauser

Twitter: https://twitter.com/iamfunkhauser

Facebook: www.facebook.com/heuerlostandfound

Branded: https://branded.me/abfunkhauser

Google Plus:

https://plus.google.com/u/0/118051627869017397678

Goodreads: http://bit.ly/1FPJXcO

Tumblr: https://www.tumblr.com/blog/unapologeticadult

Geo Buy Link: http://myBook.to/ScooterNation

Geo Buy Link: http://myBook.to/heuerlostandfound

Walmart: http://www.walmart.com/ip/Scooter-Nation/53281677

FAQ's: http://abfunkhauser.com/faqs/

**Awards**

New Apple E-Book Award 2016 "Humor" *Scooter Nation*
New Apple E-Book Award 2016 "Horror" *Heuer Lost and Found*

http://www.newappleliterary.com/awards

Winner Summer Indie Book Award (SIBA) 2016 "Humor" *Scooter Nation*

https://metamorphpublishing.com/summer-indie-book-awards/

Winner Preditors & Editors Readers' Poll 2015 "Horror"
*Heuer Lost and Found*

http://critters.org/predpoll/

# Acknowledgements

*Shell Game* is one of those rare gifts. It comes unexpectedly, and then lingers, offering something new with the passage of time. I did not set out to write a cat tale. Indeed, I had planned on going into the prequel for *Heuer Lost and Found*. But something calamitous happened back in the fall of 2015 that forced my hand. A letter from Animal Control, hand delivered to the doorsteps on my street—and only my street—cited numerous kitty offences that included, but were not limited to, wanton wandering. Failure to confine kitties, it warned, would result in a most punitive fine, and maybe even a loss of feline freedom courtesy of well-intentioned folks with cat safety in mind. Fearing for my own dear Kobe, I took steps to correct the situation: I wrote *Shell Game*.

*Shell Game* is more than just a cat and mouse story. It's really an examination of community—who we are, and how we relate to one another in a questioning world. Written with tongue firmly in cheek, it asks us to open our eyes, see better, and have a little more patience.
This is my third novel, and so I happily find myself thanking the usual suspects for their love, patience, belief and support:

To my family: John, Melina, and Adam; the moms, Eleanor and Despina; and the darling extended's: Eric, Mark, Tory, Sam and Maggie: TYSM. You never doubt me, and I love you for that!

To my sister in writing: Cryssa Bazos and her dear Angelo, thank you for all those hours spent drinking wine and hashing out plot wrinkles. You really put the fun into the process.

To Bri Volinz and the Gubernat Clan: What a gift you are! Not only are you stellar neighbors, but you deigned to share your beloved Kobe with me. And look how that turned out! And finally, to my beloved Kobe cat: Some say you are just a common tabby cat with a recessive gene, but you and I know better. You came to me at just the right time, and you stayed with me when things went wrong. You stood by me when I missed you, offered comfort to those who needed you, and saw through the dark when others could not. A mere cat? Nay. You are far from that, my love.

Most honorable mentions to:

My publisher! Solstice Publishing, featuring Melissa Miller, Kathi Sprayberry, and the unflappable KateMarie Collins. Thank you so much for having me back! You make the publishing journey a wonder to behold.

My editor: Rachael Stapleton. TYSM for getting the voice and the gonzo!

My cheerleaders: Sisters in Crime-Toronto Chapter, the Mesdames of Mayhem, the good people who put on Noir at the Bar, the Writer's Community of Durham Region, the Rousseau Family – Gilda, Luke, Rachel & François, and, especially, **my amazing writer's group, The B7: Marissa Campbell, Susan Croft, Connie Di Pietro-Sparacino, Ann Dulhanty, Rachael Stapleton, and Yvonne Zach.**

And finally,
My chiropractor, Dr. Michelle Frazier, and my naturopath, Dr. Cecilia Ho, for keeping me glued together.

A. B. Funkhauser
September 1, 2017
Toronto, Canada

Made in the USA
Middletown, DE
13 July 2018